The Last Hero

The Last Hero

Craig Gaydas

Other Books by Craig Gaydas

There are two days of importance in a person's life. The day we are born and the day we discover why.
-Mark Twain

Freedom is never freely given by the oppressor; it must be demanded by the oppressed.
-Martin Luther King Jr.

They say a man never really knows himself until everything he ever loved has been taken away.
-Bryan Whittaker, AKA Soulfire

Contents

May 1ˢᵗ, 2015

The dimly lit pub reeked of cigarette smoke and stale sweat. At one end of the bar an old man engaged in a heated debate with the bartender, something which had been going on for the better part of an hour. One minute he ranted about the city's undisciplined youth and the next he argued about the corporate elite repressing the working poor. It was enough to drive a sane person mad, but the bartender seemed to possess an iron constitution.

Opposite the bar, stuffed away in a dark corner of the room, a middle-aged couple sat in a booth with their heads bowed, more interested in their drinks than each other. She sipped a light beer while he stirred his martini with his finger. With the exception of these folks, there was just one other person in the bar. The secluded stranger sitting at the opposite end of the bar cradled his drink as if he were prepared to make love to it. He bowed his head and, with both hands, cupped the glass in a lover's embrace. The hood of his sweatshirt hung loosely around his face like a cowl. No one in the bar, except the bartender, paid any attention to him. The man preferred it that way. He embraced privacy and wrapped it around him like a shawl. The quiet solitude was the prime reason he frequented the place. It sure wasn't for the overpriced, watered-down piss they called liquor or the squealing crap they called music. The garbage coming from the jukebox was like nails on a chalkboard and enough to drive a person into an uncontrollable rage. The man heard better music coming from a dentist's chair.

The old man at the other end of the bar paused his arguing just long enough to run to the bathroom. The bartender used this welcomed break to wander over and check on the stranger.

"How ya doing, buddy?" He smiled and tapped the side of the glass with his index finger. "Do you need me to fill her up? The high octane stuff?"

The stranger nodded, swallowed the rest of his drink and slid it toward the bartender. Before the bartender could lift the glass, the man's hand shot out and grabbed his wrist.

"Don't bother putting any ice in it," he growled. "I think you have watered down this piss enough."

The barkeep's smile wavered, and he measured the stranger, studying him to see if the man would pose a threat. The bartender normally kept an aluminum baseball bat underneath the bar. Enough blood stained its surface to prove to people what happens to uncooperative assholes. The last thing he needed was a violent drunk tearing up his place, and he would not hesitate to let the metal fly.

The man let go of the bartender's wrist and gave him a thumb's up. "High octane is always good," he muttered.

After studying him a little longer, he finally concluded the stranger would not cause a ruckus, at least for the moment, and departed to fill up his glass. When he returned, he slid the glass gingerly across the bar. The stranger looked up and pulled his hood back, revealing dark brown hair, greasy and matted from old sweat. The hair fell lifelessly across his forehead. He flicked it away from his dark, hollow eyes like someone would swat a fly. The man's look was one of someone who had just crawled from a ten year bender in a wine cellar, buried deep within the earth. Salt and pepper beard stubble landscaped the lower half of his face where crusted remains of his last meal could be observed.

Junkie. That was the bartender's first reaction. When the stranger lifted the glass to his lips, he narrowed his eyes as a sense of familiarity washed over him. It wasn't until the stranger put the glass down, wiped his mouth with the back of his hand and smiled that the bartender recognized him.

"Holy cow, it can't be!" he exclaimed with eyes as wide as saucers. "It's you!"

The stranger's smile faded and his eyes closed. He drew in a deep breath and let it out slowly. The man reached into his pocket and produced a pack of cigarettes along with a plastic lighter molded in the shape of a firetruck. He shoved the cigarette in his mouth and pushed the button on top of the cab causing an orange flame, tinted with just a hint of blue, to erupt from the rear of the truck. The man lifted it to the end of the cigarette and lit it. After breathing in a couple long drags, he shoved both the pack and lighter into his pocket.

"And who might I be?" the man inquired.

The bartender nervously cleared his throat. "Hey listen, buddy, I meant no trouble by my outburst. I just thought...I mean...people thought you were dead."

"Perhaps I am," the stranger responded dryly. "You shouldn't believe everything you hear on the streets. The road leading from this city is paved with fallacy."

The bartender relaxed slightly and chuckled. "Yeah sure, whatever." He removed a rag from his back pocket and polished the countertop in a vain attempt to persuade the stranger his curiosity had abated. The stranger eyeballed him with a guarded look, seeing through the ruse.

The bartender stopped rubbing the bar top and returned the rag to its resting place. "Bryan? That's your name, right?"

Bryan took a long drag on the cigarette and let the smoke drift slowly between his teeth. "It used to be," the man replied dryly.

"Sorry, man, I didn't mean to get excited like that," the bartender explained. "It's just not often we get your kind around here." He flipped a thumb over his shoulder, toward the old man who, after returning from the bathroom, continued chugging shots of Crown Royal and muttering to himself. "As you can see, we get the regular dregs."

"My kind?" Bryan looked up slowly from his glass and placed the cigarette into a nearby ashtray. "What's that supposed to mean?"

The bartender offered a nervous smile in an effort to diffuse the situation. "Celebrities of course."

Bryan's sarcastic chuckle echoed throughout the bar. The old man glanced at them with mild curiosity. The couple in the corner glanced up from their drinks and eyeballed the man. Within the confines of the nearly empty tavern, the laugh echoed off the walls, however there was no hint of humor contained within.

"Celebrities?" Bryan rasped. "Sure, man, whatever floats your boat. Just keep the drinks coming and don't get all gushy on me. I don't sign autographs, unless you're a woman with big boobs, of course."

The bartender shook his head vigorously. "No, no, nothing like that! Sorry to bother you. How about this? Your drink is on the house and we'll call it even, okay?"

Bryan pointed his finger and cocked his thumb like a gun. "Now you're talking!" He offered the bartender a broad smile. With the reflection of the low lighting overhead, the smile appeared more demonic than merry.

The bartender practically tripped over himself to return to the old man. It seemed arguing about the city was better than dealing with a washed up, alcoholic has-been. Bryan didn't blame the guy; he would have done the same if roles had been reversed. He lifted the glass to his lips but stopped when a news report popped up on the television mounted over the "Town Tap" sign behind the bar. A masked figure, adorned from head to toe in black body armor, with various gadgets attached to a belt around his waist, dragged two handcuffed teenagers across the ground toward waiting police cars. The police trained their guns on the two teens while the masked figure adjusted a nylon tube attached to his wrist. The tube ran from the bracelet to a pack on his back. The scene cut away to a reporter who stood about a block from the action.

"*As you can see the hostage situation could have taken a deadly turn had it not been for the heroic intervention of Oracle. According to one eyewitness, the police failed to open a dialogue with the hostage takers who threatened to murder a woman and her unborn baby. Our sources have told us the two men who took her hostage were former members of the street gang 'The Raging 86's' and the woman was an ex-girlfriend of one of the leaders. Stay tuned for further details."*

Oracle stood over the squirming gang bangers while onlookers, crowded behind bright yellow police tape with adoration in their eyes, screamed his name. Their faces, flush with excitement, gazed upon the hero through bulging eyes as if he were the second coming of Jesus Christ.

Oracle had just started his term as the current hero. Normally, a hero served a four year term before passing on to the next. That safety protocol had been put into place when the Hero Factory was created in 1981. Brady Simmonelli, the Chairman of the Hero Factory, considered it the prime safety protocol. "Power corrupts and our goal is to prevent corruption," he said when the organization was founded. Bryan would never forget those words.

"Power corrupts indeed," Bryan muttered to himself as he watched the action unfold on the television screen.

Since 1981, the Hero Program had been extremely successful every year in existence. Crime had fallen seventy-five percent. In 1990 (during the term of *Twilight Shadow*) a police force had been established within city limits for the first time since 1976. The gangs had been decimated. The Hero Factory's reputation, considered an unparalleled success during its tenure, changed in 2014. Between 1980 and 2014, no city official nor their families had come under harm. The Hero Program's prime directive was to keep the people of the city safe but also maintain the city's government infrastructure in order to prevent the city from descending into chaos. Until 2014, when all that had changed. 2014 was the year someone bombed City Hall. Thirty-Five people had been killed including the mayor, the police chief and seven out of ten city council members. That year was a blemish in an otherwise spotless record of the Hero Factory.

Bryan drained the glass and placed it on the bar. With a scowl he replayed the event over in his mind until his anger reached the boiling point. The hero on duty at the time failed in his prime directive and was subsequently kicked out of the Hero Program. The event resulted in the biggest embarrassment suffered by the organization since its inception. Confidence in the leadership team of the Hero Factory had reached an all-time low, and the Hero Factory nearly shut its doors that year.

Bryan threw a wad of cash on the bar and chuckled. *A false tip.* That's all it took to throw the hero off the trail of the real perpetrators that day. The tip regarding criminal gang activity positioned the hero on the other side of town, about as far away from City Hall as one could get.

"Gang activity!" Bryan barked. "What a hoot that was!"

The bartender whispered to the old man and gestured toward Bryan. In unison they glanced at him nervously, as if he were about to lose it and shoot up the place at any minute. He didn't give a shit what they thought. Frankly, he didn't give a shit what anyone thought.

The gangs hadn't had any organized activity in years before that phony tip came in. If the hero on duty had his head screwed on straight, he should have caught on immediately. After the bombing was when the rumors started circulating. Some said the hero was drunk or on drugs at the time. Other rumors spread stating the hero was shagging a blonde stripper working down at the Double Deuce, located near that side of town. Bryan knew better. The reason was much worse. The hero on duty, haunted by his past, harbored a private vendetta against the gangs. Ghosts from the past betrayed the hero. Like a poltergeist, the ghosts tossed the hero's good judgement aside like a piece of furniture, and the city had suffered because of it.

Bryan stepped outside and inhaled the crisp evening air. It provided a welcome relief from the smoke-filled environment inside the tavern. In the distance, police sirens echoed off of nearby skyscrapers and vanished into the night. Across the street, a hooker and her john huddled together in the shadows as money changed hands. Despite the many strengths of the Hero Factory, this side of town remained its weakness. This side of town was a cesspool of junkies, whores and the con artists. Corruption on this side of town was rarely noticed by hero or cop alike. As he watched the hooker and her customer hop into a beat up blue pickup truck and speed off, his thoughts returned to that day in 2014.

"Heroes," he scoffed and reached for another cigarette. He shoved it into his mouth and retrieved the lighter. The red of the fire engine absorbed the yellowish color radiating from the sodium vapor street lights overhead. "Fuck them all."

Bryan turned his attention toward the next city block and shoved the lighter into his pocket. Stumbling a bit from his whiskey high, he shambled down the street before disappearing among the shadows.

The bartender and the old man emerged from the tavern and looked both ways, hoping Bryan was out of earshot. Convinced Bryan was gone, the old man turned to the bartender.

"What the hell was that guy going on about?" he asked.

The bartender looked down at his hand, clutching the bat he retrieved from underneath the bar. He was never one to take chances and wouldn't start tonight, with such a loose cannon running around.

"Zeke, you drank so much your brain is mush," the bartender grumbled. "Don't you know who that was?"

The old man shook his head. "You mentioned the name Bryan Whittaker before but it don't ring no bell."

"Do you remember when Soulfire was the hero on duty?" the bartender asked.

Zeke cocked his head but still looked confused, which only served to fuel the bartender's irritation further. He tapped the end of the bat impatiently against the pavement.

"Damn your worthless hide, Zeke. You don't remember shit!" The bartender lowered his voice, despite the emptiness of the streets. As stated, he was never one to take chances. His eyes turned glassy as he recalled the memories of those days. He pointed the bat in the direction Bryan had walked. "Are you telling me you don't remember him?"

The old man concentrated for a moment. The act twisted his face as if he were sitting on a toilet, suffering from constipation. Suddenly, Zeke's eyes lit up and the bartender dropped a hand on his shoulder.

"Exactly!" the bartender exclaimed. "Soulfire was the hero on duty when City Hall exploded."

April 3rd, 1979

The heavily armed men behind Pete "Shorty" Williams had itchy trigger fingers and prepared to shoot at the slightest provocation. As leader of the Street Kings, Pete realized these meetings, as short as they were, might result in bodies hitting the floor. His entourage understood the stakes of this meeting were high, so they came prepared to kill if necessary. Tensions had been at an all-time high since the police were forced from the city last year. Across the table sat the leader of Raging 86's, Brian "Buzzsaw" Kelly. Buzzsaw, the only Caucasian gang leader in Crystal City, stood at 5'8" with a slim build and black, slicked-back hair, giving him a boyish, 1950s mobster look. Pete underestimated no one and Buzzsaw would be no exception. The man didn't get his name from his charming good looks or his well-manicured nails. Many years ago he caught someone flirting with his wife and, in a fit of rage, grabbed a kitchen knife and sliced the man's balls off. Since that point, most people chose the safe route and avoided eye contact with his wife or any girlfriends he may have accompanying him. Pete never understood the man's uncanny ability to switch from calm to furious faster than one could flip a light switch. Buzzsaw was drumming his fingers on the table impatiently, which didn't bode well for the pace of this meeting.

"You called this meeting so let's get this show on the road already," Buzzsaw grumbled. He ceased drumming and leaned forward, a demonic smile spreading across his face. "I have this hot piece of ass waiting for me in the car, and I don't intend to leave her waiting for long, if ya know what I mean."

Pete forced a smile. He never let his disgust of the man show. "Of course."

A piece of paper sat on the table in front of Pete. He placed his hand over it and hesitated for a moment before sliding it across the table toward Buzzsaw.

Buzzsaw glanced down but made no move toward the paper. For a moment, Pete worried the outcome of this meeting would fall apart before it began. After staring at the paper for a minute, Brian dropped a finger on it and slid it closer. He picked it up and scanned the paper. As he read it his eyes narrowed.

"This is it?" Buzzsaw scoffed.

"I wanted to keep it simple," remarked Pete. "Ever since the cops left and the politicians fell under our thumb, we've been too busy killing each other to attend to more important matters. Our businesses have suffered. Too many good people lost their lives over a pointless war. Our real enemies are gone and its time we stop fighting each other." Pete leaned back and pounded his chest with a closed fist. "*We* own this city now. It's time we stop destroying it from within and turn it into the cash cow it can be."

Buzzsaw dropped his gaze to the paper. Pete folded his hands and waited for his response calmly. He realized a treaty between the gangs meant each leader would be required to relinquish a portion of their turf if this plan were to work. Pete understood this would be a difficult decision for all involved, but he needed to make everyone realize there would be a pot of gold at the end of this rainbow.

"It seems you put a lot of work into this." His eyes drifted from the paper and locked on Pete's. "I can respect that."

Buzzsaw dropped the piece of paper and reached into his sport coat. The action caused Pete's men to tighten their grips on their weapons. After briefly rummaging around inside his jacket, he pulled out a pen and held it up for all to see.

"I'll be honest with you, Shorty. I'm tired of all the bullshit too. Let's make us some money, shall we?" With a flick of the pen he signed the bottom of the paper.

Pete took the paper, folded it and shoved it into his pocket. He stood slowly because he didn't want to agitate the already frayed nerves of the armed men surrounding them. He extended his hand across the table.

Buzzsaw smiled at it. "Nice doing business with ya." He stood and accepted the outstretched hand, giving it a brisk shake before pulling away. "I'll see you soon to discuss the specifics, but now it's time for me to address more urgent matters." He winked and left the room with his foot soldiers in tow.

Pete looked down at his hand. For a second he was overcome with the overwhelming urge to douse it in soap and hot water and scrub until his skin was raw. Despite his revulsion he couldn't help but be filled with hope and excitement for the future of this city.

Nothing could stop them.

August 11th, 1980

When the door opened, two men dressed in black flak jackets and fatigues marched inside. M-16 assault rifles hung across their shoulders and belts filled with ammo clips showed they meant business. Their faces, obscured by tinted sunglasses, remained expressionless. Between the soldiers stood a stocky man with receding black hair and matching mutton chops. Clutching a black, leather-bound suitcase, he slid into one of the oversized leather seats parked in front of the desk. The guards hung back, flanking the doorway.

The man laid the briefcase gingerly on his lap and fidgeted with his silver cufflinks. He studied the armed men from the corner of his eye while shuffling uncomfortably in the chair.

"My associates informed me the police department had been disbanded. Even as I was about to board the plane, they remained steadfast in their opposition to this meeting for safety reasons." He flicked a thumb over his shoulder. "Perhaps my associates were incorrect. If there are no police, what would you call those two?"

The man seated behind the desk slid his glasses down the bridge of his nose and looked up. "They are my insurance policy, Mr. Simmonelli, and I assure you your associates' fears are not entirely misplaced. Safety is my primary concern since Crystal City has not had a police force in quite some time."

"Mercenaries?" Brady Simmonelli asked.

Mayor Randall Cogsburn shrugged. "Call them whatever you want. I assume, based on your expression, you disapprove of the protection provided to City Hall?" The mayor waved his hand in a shooing motion to the guards and they stepped outside. "Perhaps your associates didn't tell you the history why there are no police here?"

Brady Simmonelli folded his hands on top of the briefcase. "I'm a businessman, Mayor. Do not presume I would not do the due diligence required before attempting to undertake this endeavor. I'm well aware of this city's history, otherwise we wouldn't even be having this conversation."

Brady placed the briefcase on the desk, fumbled with the combo lock and popped it open. He retrieved a large manila envelope and placed it next to the briefcase. On the cover of the envelope was an emblem of a roaring head of a lion pointed skyward. He tapped the envelope with his index finger.

"Inside this folder are the costs and schematics for the factory as well as a detailed set of work instructions." He turned the envelope around and slid it toward the mayor. "You will see the first page contains a non-disclosure agreement and, as soon as that is signed, we can get down to business."

The mayor raised an eyebrow but did not move. "Do you really believe your idea will work for this city?"

Brady's face split into a wide grin. "I conceived my idea specifically for this city." He petted the envelope like a puppy. "Believe me, Mayor, when I say the details have been gone over a thousand times by myself and my associates. I guarantee an eighty percent drop in crime within the first four years of service or I will pay back every nickel this city invests in the operation."

The mayor opened the envelope and removed the packet of paperwork. He scanned the front page, tapping every word with the tip of his finger. As he read each word in the proposal, his grin widened like a kid who had just won a free shopping spree in a candy store. Once finished he grabbed a pen from a nearby jar and signed the bottom of the page.

"My God!" he exclaimed breathlessly. "This is ingenious. You never told me the level of detail contained within the concept model. If you explained this to me over the phone, I would have given you a verbal approval immediately."

Brady chuckled. "Sorry, Mayor, I don't work on verbal approvals.

The mayor stood and extended his hand across the desk. "Brady, you have a deal! When can you start breaking ground?"

Brady matched the mayor's smile, stood and accepted the handshake. "I can have my people begin the preliminaries tomorrow, if you'd like."

The Hero Factory had been born.

September 13th, 2013

Bryan stared at the mangled door jamb of the front door and sighed. Shattered glass and splintered wood littered the front porch. The barrel-chested man standing next to him had his arms folded across his chest, shaking his head in disbelief.

"It looks like your buddy H-Bar struck again," the man grumbled.

"H-Bar" was the name bestowed upon Bryan's friend and fellow firefighter, Terry Lincoln. Terry's overuse of the Halligan bar was the stuff of legend among most of the firehouses in the area. Many people believed he went to bed at night with the tool by his side. One time, Bryan overheard a fellow firefighter joke he once saw Terry caressing the thing in his bedroom one night. After the joke circulated throughout the ranks, the man standing next to him, Fire Chief Mackenzie "Mac" Shawnessy, gave him the nickname and it had stuck ever since.

"I think your pal has deep psychological issues," Mac continued. "This was a goddamn gas leak. Jesus, I swear to all that's holy, one day I will beat him to death with that thing!"

Bryan stifled a smile. If Mac saw it, he would probably beat him in Terry's place. Mac was a "by the book" commander and, although he occasionally found Terry's overuse of the H-Bar amusing, this was not one of those times. The homeowner would surely sue the department for damages.

When they stepped into the foyer, Terry emerged from the kitchen with the H-bar dangling by his side and a large scowl on his face. "Gas stove."

Mac flicked a thumb over his shoulder, toward the shattered door. "What about that?"

Terry shrugged. "Better safe than sorry."

Bryan could feel the heat of the Chief's rage radiating from Mac's body. If Terry kept pushing his buttons, Bryan was afraid this would escalate from a gas leak call to a homicide. Luckily Mac stormed out of the house before any bloodshed. Bryan whirled on Terry.

"One day he is going to shove that thing right up your ass."

"Well, I guess it will cure my hemorrhoid problem," he chuckled.

Bryan rolled his eyes and followed Terry out of the house. A crowd of neighbors gathered on the front lawn gawking at them, as if expecting the fire department to drag out a human body. It never mattered whether it was a four-alarm fire or pulling a cat from a tree, onlookers flocked to the flashing red lights like moths to a street light. Bryan noticed the Crystal City police cruiser parked behind their pump truck and frowned when he saw the cop talking with Mac. Mac turned to them with a grim expression and a sympathetic gleam in his eye when he noticed them approaching.

Mac's demeanor concerned Bryan. Although he was a usual grump most of the time, the somber manner in which he addressed them disturbed him. Mac usually kept his emotions in check.

"What's wrong, Chief?" asked Terry.

Mac ignored Terry and addressed Bryan. "I'm sorry, Bryan, but it's your wife and son."

Bryan removed his fire helmet and cradled it under his arm. "Alicia? Jackson? What's wrong?"

"I'm sorry, Mr. Whittaker," the cop answered with a look of sadness. "Your wife and son were the victims of a carjacking at the corner of Crescent and 8th. The perp was armed and shot your family before the responding units could get to them. They're at Mercy General in critical condition. I can drive you there if you need me to."

Bryan stood in stunned silence. That intersection was located near the Ironbound section of the city where no one but the dregs of society hung out. What the hell was she doing in that area?

"Was she lost?" Bryan asked the cop.

"I'm sorry?" the cop responded, looking confused.

Bryan felt his anger rising. "Was she *lost*? What the hell was she doing there?"

The cop shook his head. "I don't know, sir. We haven't been able to interview her in ICU."

"Take me to them," he demanded.

"Here, let me take that." Terry grabbed the helmet from Bryan. "Get out of here."

Bryan followed the cop to the car and slid into the passenger seat. They took off out of the neighborhood with lights flashing and siren blaring.

"By the way, my name is Hector Rodriguez," the officer said, keeping his eyes fixed on the road ahead.

Bryan remained silent. His thoughts focused on his family. The ride was a little more than eleven miles but it seemed like an eternity before they arrived at the hospital. When Officer Rodriguez finally pulled up to the hospital, Bryan stumbled from the vehicle before it came to a complete stop and rushed toward the emergency room doors.

Mercy General, smaller than most of the other city hospitals, never kept a full staff. Since the Hero Factory had been established, doctors trickled into the city but most set up shop in the larger hospitals where the cash flow was heavy. Mercy General, due to its size, was not the most appealing hospital for doctors.

Bryan burst through the doors and hurried toward the intake desk where a nurse sat, filing her nails and humming to herself.

"I'm here to see Alicia and Jackson Whittaker!" he barked breathlessly.

The nurse dropped the file on the desk and turned toward her computer. After a few keystrokes, she squinted as the data came up on the computer screen. "Gunshot wounds." She hesitated and looked up at Bryan. "Are you related to the patients?"

His heart beat so rapidly he thought it would explode from his chest. "I'm her husband and his father." His tongue felt twenty times bigger than normal and his throat felt as if he had swallowed a cocktail of sandpaper and broken glass. The way the nurse studied him offered little comfort.

The nurse turned to a phone next to the computer and picked up the handset. "Um, yes...Dr. Anderson? I have the husband and father of the patients in room 223 here in the reception area. You will be right down? Yes, thank you." She hung up the phone and motioned toward the waiting area. "If you can have a seat, the doctor will be right down."

When Bryan turned to the reception area, he observed Officer Rodriguez hovering near the entrance. The cop winced when he noticed Bryan studying him.

"It is pretty much the end of my shift so I figured I'd hang around to make sure everything was alright," he explained. "If that's a problem, I guess I can take off."

Bryan shook his head and fell into a nearby seat. Five minutes later a doctor, dressed in a white overcoat with a stethoscope hanging around his neck, ran across the hall toward them. When he reached the reception area, Bryan stood and watched as the doctor tried to catch his breath.

"Are they okay?" Bryan asked, panicked.

"You may want to sit down, Mr. Whittaker," the doctor gasped as he worked on catching his breath.

"I don't want to sit down! I want to make sure my family is okay!" Bryan shouted. Out of the corner of his eye he noticed Officer Rodriguez inching closer, ready to intervene if things got out of hand.

Dr. Anderson's mouth tightened into a thin pink line of consternation. He chewed on his bottom lip for a minute before speaking again. "I'm afraid I have some bad news. Your wife is in critical condition in our ICU but your son..." he trailed off.

Bryan grabbed the doctor's shoulder and squeezed. Officer Rodriguez's hand fell to the butt of his Taser. "What is it?"

Dr. Anderson sighed and diverted his gaze to the floor. "I'm sorry...your son passed away thirty minutes ago."

The news hit Bryan like a sledgehammer. His gut clenched and the room spun, becoming a kaleidoscope of colors. He reached out and grabbed the doctor's shoulder before falling to one knee. His breathing became ragged, like trying to suck a milkshake through a coffee stirrer. Everything around him disappeared into a fog and the only thing he could see was the innocent, gap-toothed smile and curly blond locks of his son bouncing in the breeze as he played with his soccer ball. That was the last time he saw him. Bryan never bothered to say goodbye when he left for his shift. Jackson looked like he was having so much fun that Bryan didn't want to bother him. Some downtown scumbag stole his son from him and Bryan felt the blood drain from his face.

Officer Rodriquez grabbed his arm and helped him into a nearby chair. "Hey, do you need me to get you a bottle of water or something? Whatever you need, buddy, I'll go get it."

Bryan looked at the officer fiercely. "What I need from you is to find the bastard who did this."

A look of resignation fell across the officer's face, which was all Bryan needed to know about the situation. Crystal City only recently budgeted for a police force. Filling the ranks took time and they didn't exactly have the pick of the litter. Some of the officers were seasoned veterans of other departments but most were rookies or unwanted cast offs from other departments who had to accept the job or risk having to find a new career. In the end, the city only had a budget for a police force of fifty officers. The city required triple the amount. They didn't have the manpower dedicated to give Bryan's case the attention it deserved.

"Let me go get you a bottle of water," the cop said before hurrying down the hall.

Bryan hadn't cried since he lost his mother twenty years ago. That streak ended on September 13th, 2013.

The Following Day

Alicia Whittaker passed away the next morning, which jumpstarted Bryan's descent into a pit of despair. After the doctor broke the news he became an emotional zombie, wandering the halls of the hospital mindlessly. While hospital staff prepared the forms he needed to sign, he haunted the waiting area, staring at the vending machine through glassy eyes. He wasn't hungry or thirsty, he just didn't understand what to do next. Terry arrived at the hospital twenty minutes later and found him in the same position, staring at the machine with a hollow look in his eyes.

"Bryan, I'm so sorry," Terry offered weakly.

Bryan said nothing but continued to stare at the machine as if he expected selection A1 to change from a bag of Doritos to an elixir able to resurrect his deceased family. Terry gently placed his hand on Bryan's shoulder.

"Come on, let's get you home."

"I can't leave yet," Bryan replied. "They are going to perform an autopsy and I have forms I need to fill out. Also, I need to collect some things and make funeral arrangements. So much to do…" His voice tapered off.

"Forget that for now," Terry pleaded. "You need to go home and rest. I promise I will help you with that stuff tomorrow."

Terry led Bryan to his car and opened the passenger door for him. On the ride home Bryan remained motionless, staring out the window in silence. They were about a mile from his home when Bryan turned to Terry.

"Where the hell was Spectre?" Bryan asked with an angry gleam in his eyes.

Terry wore a confused expression. "What?"

Bryan returned his gaze to the window. "Alicia was carjacked in the Ironbound section of the city. The Hero Factory had been promising to clean up that section of the city for months now. The heroes were supposed to be working with local police and ramp up patrols in the area. So where was Spectre? Where were the police?"

"Ironbound," a term coined by a police captain in 1966. The name stuck because of its heavy concentration of industry, focusing mostly on cast iron pipe and fitting manufacturing. Over the years the industry attracted undesirables, heavy drug use, and eventually the gang leaders. In 1970 the gangs decided to headquarter themselves in the region, pushing the honest workers out of the city. Soon afterwards, the city wasn't able to attract any honest people to the area, which turned the factories into nothing more than havens for the dregs of society. Most deteriorated and became havens for drug labs and dog-fighting rings.

"I don't have an answer for you," Terry replied. "Maybe he was somewhere fighting crime or saving babies or something." A weak excuse, but it was all he could come up with.

"Maybe," Bryan muttered.

Terry pulled the car into the driveway of a four bedroom, two bath bi-level located on the south side of town. At the end of the driveway stood a black mailbox with the word "Whittakers" stenciled in red. The house, once a joyous and welcoming place for Bryan and his family, was nothing more than a structure filled with painful memories. Memories of the squeals of his son playing in the yard, memories of his wife cooking his favorite goulash dinner, memories of holiday dinners with the relatives were nothing more than an archive of painful reminders of what had been lost.

Bryan stepped through the front door and paused. It was as if he could hear the sound of his wife shuffling down the hallway, ready to greet him with Jackson on her heels. After he came home from every shift, no matter what time it had been, his boy would be up and waiting for him to come home. Nothing but emptiness welcomed him home now. He dropped on the sofa and flipped on the television, cycling through channels mindlessly.

"Do you need me to get you anything? Food? Drink?" Terry asked.

. Terry witnessed a cold, hard look fall over Bryan's mood and he winced. When he glanced at the television screen he saw an image of a news reporter standing outside the open gates of the Hero Factory. A crowd had gathered and several people lined up near the front entrance, waiting to get inside. Terry slipped into the recliner opposite the sofa and studied his friend's icy demeanor with a touch of sadness. He had to do something before Bryan slipped into a dark void in which he would never emerge. Instead of dwelling on how powerless he felt to help his friend, he turned his attention to the TV.

Spectre was being interviewed outside the main hall of the Hero Factory. Behind the interview, the people in line conversed briefly with guards before continuing through a processing area single-file. As he watched the interview, an idea struck him like a lightning bolt and he sat up in the chair. He looked at Bryan's glum expression and hoped he could convince his friend what needed to be done to move forward with his life.

"I have an idea," Terry said. Bryan turned from the screen and cocked an eyebrow.

"Oh really?"

"You need to sign up for Hero Program!" Terry exclaimed, rubbing his hands in anticipation of Bryan's response.

Bryan's expression turned to one of confusion. "The Hero Program?"

"Yes!" Terry clapped his hands together. "I know you are upset with the Hero Factory and I can see the anger in your eyes as you stare at the TV. You've been questioning their ability to protect us since we left the hospital." Terry stood up and dropped his hand on Bryan's shoulder. "Now is a perfect time for you to make a difference. Spectre's term is ending." Terry pointed to the screen. "See the volunteers lining up to become the next hero? That could be you!"

Bryan laughed, but there had been no humor in it. "You must be crazy. I would never be accepted. The background check is very strict. I'm pretty sure men who are emotional wrecks walking around like mindless zombies wouldn't be first on their list of potential recruits."

"That's bullshit and you know it," Terry countered. "You've been a firefighter in this city for eleven years. You received a mayoral commendation for the house fire rescue in 2009. The Chief personally recommended you for the Arson Investigation program last year."

Bryan shook his head. "I have a criminal record. That's an automatic disqualification."

It was Terry's turn to laugh. "A pot charge when you were seventeen? You must be kidding. They will throw that shit out in no time. Hell, Volt was arrested for drunk and disorderly when he was twenty-one. They weigh the severity of the crime, my man!"

Bryan let out a long, drawn-out sigh because he knew Terry's words rang true. With his exemplary professional record in the city, the drug charge wouldn't even be considered. Perhaps there was a possibility for him to succeed where others had failed. One day perhaps he could prevent someone's wife and child from being murdered in the streets. There was one issue which made him nervous. He stood in front of the TV with his arms folded across his chest and tapped his foot, deep in thought.

"What's wrong?" Terry asked.

"What do you think they do to those people inside the Hero Factory?" he asked. "How exactly do they turn an ordinary person into one of them?"

Terry shrugged and turned his attention to the TV. On the screen, Spectre was all smiles, having the time of his life while being interviewed by a young, buxom reporter. Terry winced, knowing Spectre's nonchalant attitude would fuel the rage festering within Bryan.

"I have no idea," Terry responded. "Whatever it is, there doesn't seem to be any side effects except the ability to kick some serious ass and have pretty young ladies worship you." He offered Bryan a wry smile.

Bryan didn't look convinced and Terry sighed.

"Okay, okay you got me. I can't lie to you. There are side effects. Once you go through the process you come out with a four hour erection," Terry quipped.

Bryan cracked a smile. "I agree with you, this city needs someone who knows what they're doing. Maybe I owe it to my family or all the future wives and children who won't come home to their families."

Terry stood between him and the television. The frown on his face formed deep creases along the sides of his chin. "You don't owe them. If anything, this city owes you for all of your years of service. Nothing you do will bring your wife and kid back, man. That's the hard truth." He jabbed Bryan's chest with his finger. "The only person you owe is you. The only way you will ever make peace with the past is to embrace the future. You need this for yourself more than the city needs this from you."

After a long time pondering the pros and cons of applying to the Hero Program, Bryan relented and nodded his head in agreement. "Okay, you pain in my ass. You had me at four hour erection."

October 31st, 2013

Bryan arrived at the Hero Factory on the second day of processing. The crowd swarmed the complex, hoping to get a good look at Spectre who was there to welcome the applicants. Behind the wrought-iron gates stood several turnstiles with overhead metal detectors, manned by armed men wearing dark blue polo shirts bearing the emblem of the Hero Factory. Due to the size of the crowd, it was difficult to tell the difference between the applicants and the gawkers. Bryan studied the throngs of people, attempting to discern his competition from the crowd. Anyone who looked younger than twenty-one could be ruled out because of the age requirement. *Men, women, children.* Their faces all looked the same, blending into one another as his eyes skipped from one person to another. The anticipation was gnawing away at him like a dog on a bone. Before he could explode from anxiety, a hand fell on his shoulder.

"Excuse me, but you are an applicant, correct?"

Bryan turned to see a bald, muscular black man built like a horse wearing the same shirt as the guards inside. Bryan's gaze fell to the Glock holstered by the man's side.

"How did you know?" asked Bryan.

The man smiled, revealing gleaming white teeth. He stuck his thumb out and pointed it toward a group of people surrounding the gate. "You don't look like you came here for the tour."

Bryan chuckled. "Yeah I guess you're right. I think I'm lost, where are we supposed to go?"

The man motioned for him to follow. He led Bryan to a side entrance that had a control pad and digital screen mounted above it. The man punched in a code and pressed his face against the screen.

"*Welcome, James Stout*," a female voice responded. The gate opened and James motioned toward the entrance.

"After you, Bryan," he offered with a smile.

Bryan froze and the hairs on his neck stood. He eyeballed James suspiciously. "How did you know my name?"

The man's smile did not waver. "We know who you are. You came to us highly recommended." When he noticed Bryan was still not convinced, he clarified his remark. "Your boss, Mac Shawnessy, recommended you. Come with me, I'll explain everything on the way."

Bryan's suspicions faded as soon as Mac's name was mentioned. He followed James through the door and into the courtyard. The grounds of the Hero Factory, well-manicured and better than any he had seen within the city limits, spread across the front of the building like a blanket. Bent grass circled three flag poles in the center of the courtyard. Upon the top of each pole sat the flag of the country, under it sat the flag of the city and the flag of the Hero Factory sat below the others. The recently paved entranceway ran from the main gate to the entrance. A large private parking area ran adjacent to the side of the building and sat virtually empty with the exception of a handful of vehicles most likely belonging to the staff on duty.

They entered through the revolving glass door at the front of the building and approached an oversized mahogany desk adorned with three video monitors. The chair behind the desk sat empty.

"I guess Walt went to take a piss before we open to the public," James muttered. He pointed to an oversized log book on top of the desk and handed Bryan a pen. "Before we move on I will need you to sign in."

Bryan logged his name and current time and put the pen down. He studied his surroundings, marveling at the architecture of the main foyer. A dome ceiling decorated with crystal chandeliers marked the main welcome area. The walls and floors were constructed from marble, or at least made to look like it had been. If it was fake, it was the best imitation marble Bryan had ever seen. James led him past the hall toward the elevators. Next to the elevators, a bronze plaque hung on the wall with several names engraved upon its surface, the names of every hero to serve the city. Bryan ran his finger over the names, carefully tracing each letter.

"Maybe one day your name will be up there," James said.

Bryan quickly removed his finger, embarrassed that he had been caught ogling the plaque. He turned to James and shrugged. "Maybe."

The elevator doors opened and they stepped inside. James pushed the button for the 17th floor.

"The owner of this place sure didn't spare any expense with the architecture," Bryan remarked.

James chuckled. "You're right about that. Anyway, I promised I'd explain things so let me get started. Your boss came to see us right after your family died. At first he approached Mister Simmonelli angry about the events which led to your..." He trailed off, seeing the pained expression on Bryan's face from the memory. "Led to the unfortunate events," James finished. "Eventually Mister Simmonelli managed to calm him down and they spoke in great detail about you and what you have done for this city. Mister Simmonelli agreed it was hard to overlook your exemplary record."

"Was it hard to overlook my *criminal* record?" Bryan asked sarcastically.

James laughed. The deep, thunderous tone of his voice echoed off the elevator walls like a storm. "I don't know what they use as criteria for selecting the next hero, but I will admit I had never seen anything like it."

"Like what?" Bryan asked.

A digital 16 appeared on the screen overhead. "One more floor to go," said James. "I suppose I have enough time to tell you."

"Tell me what?" Bryan asked, slightly agitated.

"I had never seen any applicant selected for the final interview without at the very least meeting the team first," explained James. "I even asked Frank down in tech, who has been here longer than me, if he ever heard of anything like it."

"What the hell are you babbling about?" Bryan became irritated with the man's ambiguity.

The elevator dinged and the number 17 appeared overhead. The doors opened to reveal another hallway, filled with marble walls and floors, similar to the first floor.

James turned to Bryan. "You have been selected to proceed to the next steps. I am escorting you to meet with Mister Simmonelli so you can complete final testing."

Bryan stepped out of the elevator and stopped. "How is that possible? I thought there was some long, drawn-out process involved."

James nodded. "You're correct. Selecting the next hero is a three step process. There is the application and initial interview with the head of recruiting. After that an in-depth background check is done on each candidate. When I say 'in-depth,' I'm not kidding. They go balls to the wall, even background screening immediate family members. The third step is where you are right now." James motioned toward a thick wooden door at the end of the hall. "Come on, they are waiting for you."

Bryan hesitated. "Wait a minute, what about all those people outside?"

James smiled. "We have to keep up appearances." James knocked on the door. "And it's always a good thing to start screening people for the next term."

The door opened and a wiry man with silver hair and matching goatee stood in the doorway. He narrowed his eyes when Bryan stepped up next to James.

"So this is him, huh?" the man asked.

"Yes, sir," replied James. "Bryan, this is Donald Runnels, head of Research."

Bryan stuck out his hand. Donald curled his lip and eyeballed it as if Bryan just offered him the severed head of a baby seal. When he finally took hold of his hand, he gave it a single brisk shake before letting go. The man's grip was similar to a wet noddle. "Come inside."

Bryan entered the room which doubled as a conference room. A long rectangular table constructed from mahogany sat in the center of the room surrounded by ten leather chairs. A projection screen hung on the far wall and pictures of heroes adorned the walls behind the chairs. At the end of the table, opposite the projection screen, sat a plump man, with a thick brown toupee that looked as if a cat had died on his head and sporting wire-rimmed glasses. The man stood as soon as Bryan entered and hurried to greet him.

"Mister Whittaker, I heard so much about you from Mac Shawnessy. My name is Brady Simmonelli and I am the Chief Executive Officer of the Hero Factory. From what Mac told me, we worried you might not come." He motioned toward a nearby chair. Brady's face flushed with sympathy as soon as Bryan sat. "I want to extend my heartfelt condolences on your loss, but we hope to convince you today that you are making the correct decision."

"We tried to make this as informal as possible," Donald explained. "But as you may or may not be aware this is a rare occurrence for us. This is the first time in our history—"

Bryan held up his hand. "Yeah, yeah I know. James did a bang up job of explaining on our way here." He turned to Brady. "But I do have a question. Why me?"

"Because you are already a hero," a voice replied from behind. Bryan turned to the door and frowned when he noticed it was closed. There were no windows in the room and the walls seemed too thick to carry a voice from another room. Confused, he leaned forward with his palms flat on the table.

"Um...who was that?" Bryan asked.

A figure appeared near the projection screen. "Appeared" was actually not the correct term. The person entered the room "through" the wall, like a phantom. The person, adorned in white from head to toe, reminded Bryan of a ghost. A white hood covered his head and a shroud covered the lower half of his face, revealing only steely eyes gazing back at him. The man wore body armor underneath a cloak and a belt strapped around his waist. Several small compartments attached to the belt flanked a holstered 9MM handgun. Two oversized bracelets held similar compartments wrapped tightly around his wrists. Bryan recognized the man immediately.

"Welcome, Spectre, I was worried you wouldn't show up," Brady said.

Spectre stood between Donald and Brady and fixed Bryan with a hard stare. "As I was saying, you are already a hero," he repeated. "The staff here at the Hero Factory does not need to determine what kind of hero you would become because they already know what kind of hero you were. The first two phases of the hiring process would be a waste of everyone's time."

Bryan folded his hands on the table. "Firefighting doesn't make me a hero. It just means I was doing my job."

Spectre folded his arms across his chest and laughed. "What do you think this is? Your job is to protect the city. You have already been doing that. Your way is no different than mine. The only difference between the two is the amount of people you would be saving, and the reasons why. You will be given the tools to go above and beyond anything you have ever accomplished before."

"What exactly are these tools?" Bryan asked with suspicion.

"You will find that out when the time comes. Until you are officially appointed as Hero, you can consider that a trade secret," Donald replied.

Brady clapped his hands together. "First things first. Shall we go over the rules and regulations as well as the benefits associated with the job?"

"Sure, that sounds like a plan," Bryan replied.

Spectre held out his hand. "Good luck, Bryan."

Bryan tried to shake it but his hand passed completely through. It was like grabbing mist and Bryan stared at his hand in awe. While his hand passed through Spectre's, he felt a chill which permeated to the very bones of his fingers.

Spectre roared laughter. "I'm sorry, Bryan, just a bit of freshman hazing. I hope to see you at the introduction ceremony." He phased through the wall and vanished.

"Spectre has a strange sense of humor which I never quite understood," Brady explained. "Anyway, let's go to my office so we can prepare you for the final test."

They hopped on the elevator and took it down to the fifth floor. Bryan and Brady stepped off but Donald remained behind. "I need to return to the lab and run some diagnostic tests on the machines." He reached over and pushed the button, shutting the doors between them.

"Forgive Donald," said Brady. "He can be brisk at times."

"Really? I never noticed," Bryan replied with an eye roll.

There was no hall on the fifth floor. The elevator stopped and dropped them into a waiting area. A receptionist desk guarded a glass door with the words *Brady Simmonelli, CEO* etched on the front.

"Good morning, Mister Simmonelli," the perky brunette behind the desk drawled.

"Good morning, Brenda," Brady replied. "This is Bryan Whittaker. I will be administering the final test today."

Her eyes widened and she smiled. "That's wonderful news. Good luck, Mister Whittaker." Her scarlet lipstick glistened from the overhead fluorescent lights with some of it sticking to the top of her teeth.

"Have a seat, Bryan." Brady motioned toward an oversized leather seat parked in front of his desk.

The office, like the conference room, had pictures of heroes hung around the room. A large golden key, mounted on top of a plaque, sat at one corner of the oversized cherry wood desk. Brady caught Bryan staring at the trophy and smiled.

"The key to the city," he explained. "The city council presented it to me in 1986." From the desk drawer he retrieved a stack of papers, which had been stapled together in the upper left corner. He laid them upon the desk and placed his hand on top. "Before we administer the final test there is just one thing left to do. If this is really what you want, then all you need to do is sign these papers and provide a check or money order in the amount of five thousand dollars."

Bryan had started to reach for the papers but stopped when Brady mentioned money. "Um...I'm sorry, did you say five thousand dollars?"

Brady narrowed his eyes. His eyes grew cold as he stared at Bryan. "Yes, I did. You don't think we really select people based on their merit do you?"

Bryan had been so taken aback that his hand froze over the paperwork. Once the initial shock of what had just been said faded, he quickly pulled his hand back as if it had been burned and rose from the chair. Angrily, he jabbed an index finger in Brady's direction.

"I'm not sure what kind of operation you're running here, but I'm not about to pay you to become a hero. Is that what this is? A person has to bribe their way into the Hero Program?" Repulsed by what he had just been told, Bryan's stomach felt as if a flock of birds fought over a crumb of bread inside. He turned to leave.

"Wait a minute!" Brady beseeched. "I've never been turned down before. This...um...this is awkward." He reached over, opened a drawer and retrieved a stack of cash. "This conversation can never leave this room." He placed his hand on top of the pile. "This here is five thousand dollars. How about I just pay you and we pretend this conversation never took place?"

Bryan's hand fell on the door handle and his jaw fell. He couldn't believe what he was hearing. He had his doubts about the Hero Factory and its program but he never believed for a second the program itself was corrupt. Bryan may have laid blame at Spectre's feet regarding his failure to protect his family but would have never believed in a million years they were criminals. The news hit him like a punch to the jaw.

"Is that what the last hero paid you?" Bryan growled. "How about you take it, roll it up, and insert it in your ass!"

Brady stared at him with an icy contempt for a minute before his features softened and he broke out into a grin. He slid the paperwork across the desk. "Excellent."

"Excellent?" Bryan repeated with a confused look on his face.

Brady's eyes studied Bryan intensely. "You will not pay a bribe nor take one. Money does not seem to be your motivating factor. That's a good thing."

Bryan let go of the door handle. "What?"

Brady circled the desk and approached Bryan. "I guess you're too young to remember, but I'm not. Decades ago this city was a cesspool of corruption. Back then city leaders didn't make decisions, money did. Money ruled the streets as well as men's hearts and became the driving force behind every decision. The poor didn't have it, the gangs chased it while capitalists stole it. Back then you could buy power with cash, drugs or sex because everyone, and everything, was for sale. Men with machine minds and machine hearts treated the people of this city like cattle. I want a city where money may buy you things, but not people. I want a city where people can walk freely without being oppressed or peeking around every corner, scouring the shadows for boogeymen. I need heroes who cannot be bought and paid for. You can't ask that question on some written exam, the only way to measure how an applicant truly feels is to see it in action." Brady gripped Bryan's elbow. "Relax, you have proven yourself."

Bryan was too young to remember the old ways. Stories of the turbulent past of this city had been taught in school and he cringed when he thought about how the way must have been. Despite Brady's words, Bryan still held some doubts regarding his intentions.

"So what now?" Bryan asked.

Brady grinned. "The only thing left to do is to make sure you are physically able to accept the job."

Bryan narrowed his eyes. "You mean like a strength and conditioning test or something? You do know I graduated from the fire academy and ran into burning buildings for a living, correct?"

Brady's smile faded and his demeanor became serious. "I don't mean that, Bryan. I have no doubts of your strength or physical ability to handle the demands of the job." His eyes drifted toward Bryan's forehead. "We need to know if your *mind* can handle it."

Bryan started to ask another question but Brady stopped him with an outstretched hand. "I'll explain on the way. Let's head over to the lab."

They stepped onto the elevator and instead of pushing a button, Brady retrieved a key from his pocket and inserted it into a slot beneath the buttons. When he turned the key, the buttons lit up in unison. A voice spoke to them from an overhead speaker. "*Password please?*"

"Adjudication," responded Brady. The elevator doors closed and they descended. "As I was saying earlier, you have passed all of the tests except one. We are on our way to see Donald and lead scientist Doctor Wendy Markus. Wendy specializes in gene mutation."

"Gene mutation?" Bryan repeated with a touch of concern.

Brady smiled. "Let me finish. Dr. Markus will conduct some tests on your mind to make sure you will emerge from the process unscathed. Based on latest statistics over ninety percent of the human population can emerge from the gene mutation process mentally intact." The elevator stopped and he turned to Bryan. "I just want to make sure you are not one of the ten percent."

The doors opened and they stepped into a lab compete with stainless steel bioreactors, a filtration system weaved into the ceiling, beakers and shakers strewn throughout the lab and scientists wandering around the laboratory studying charts and crouching over various machines. As soon as they entered, an extremely attractive woman with long legs poking from a white lab coat and long black hair tied into a pony tail strolled over. The name plate on the coat read *Markus*. She offered them a welcoming smile.

"Hello, I'm Dr. Wendy Markus and you must be Bryan Whittaker." She stuck out her hand and Bryan hesitated, remembering what happened with Spectre. He mentally slapped himself for being stupid and took her hand.

"Yes I am," he replied.

"It's wonderful to finally meet you. I've heard so many good things about you," she said and motioned toward a reclining chair with something resembling a giant hair dryer mounted above. "I need you to step over here and sit please."

Bryan sat and placed his hands on the hand rests. Restraining cuffs mounted on the sides snapped over his wrists. He immediately stiffened and his internal alarm system began blaring.

"Relax, Bryan, this is for your own good. The test measures the ability of your brain to handle gene mutation. The restraints are there for your own protection."

"We don't need you flailing around and breaking your arm before you officially begin your duties, right?" added Brady.

"Flailing around?" Bryan croaked. "Does it hurt that much?"

Wendy grinned and placed her hand on his forearm in an effort to calm him. Her beautiful face, soothing voice and warm smile was all she needed to calm even the most savage beast. "Oh, nothing like that. As a matter of fact there is no pain at all."

"Then why would I be flailing?" he prodded.

"The mind is the most mysterious object within a human body," she explained. "We have yet to unlock all of its secrets. The test we conduct wakes up the brain in a certain way. With some subjects nothing at all happens, but others scream and try to fight the machine. We prefer to think that a human brain has two sides; the conscious side and the dormant side. It's the dormant side we worry about."

"Think of it like a roller coaster. Some people scream with joy, others cry with fear while others can sit and take it all in without uttering a sound," Brady added.

"Just remain calm, Bryan, this should only take a few minutes." Wendy moved toward a control panel. With a few button pushes, the cylinder above the chair lowered.

The cylinder covered Bryan's entire head creating darkness all around him. "Bryan, can you hear me?" asked Wendy. The cylinder muffled the sound of her voice but he understood her.

"Yes," he replied.

"The test will begin in 5…4…3…2…1…"

The darkness vanished and several images exploded into view. At first they appeared slowly, as if he were flipping through an old family album. After a moment the images gradually increased in speed. Most were images from his past. One moment he was with his mother and father during a trip to the beach when he was seven, and the next he was a teenager getting drunk with his friends. The happier memories soon merged with more sinister images. His memories faded and became someone else's. In one image he saw a homeless man being beaten by a group of teens. Another image showed a teller being pistol whipped during a bank robbery. Another image showed police lobbing tear gas into an angry mob, eventually morphing into a group of soldiers raiding a village in a third world country. Every moment seemed to be a scene from a movie, but they were too vivid. Too real. The images changed in rapid succession but none caused him to flail or cry out in terror. He wondered about the validity of the test until the final set of images. They slowed to a crawl and once again became images from his past. Unlike before, the memories were not so happy.

The death of his grandmother.

His marijuana arrest.

There were others but it wasn't until the final image emerged that he lost complete control of himself. The final image was an icy knife being plunged into his heart. The image of his wife and child, lying in a pool of their own blood, ripped out a piece of his soul. This image was more vivid than the others which only served to magnify the shock of their loss. The sheer violence of the scene caused him to cry out in terror. Bile rose into his throat as nausea took over. Every happy memory had been wiped as one would wipe a chalkboard. It was at that moment he realized why the restraints were in place. They pulled at his arms as he tried to break free of them. Veins popped from his biceps as he struggled unsuccessfully against the bonds. The urge to tear them off and rampage through the lab overwhelmed him but he soon tired himself from flailing uselessly against them.

Bryan did the only thing he could do at that moment. He *screamed.* It was the scream of a man tortured by loss and haunted by demons of despair. He screamed until he had no more air in his lungs. Even when his air ran out and his scream became nothing more than a choking gasp, he continued until he feared his voice box would tear apart. Mercifully, the images faded and the bucket over his head lifted.

Scientists gathered around him and that was when he felt the sharp pain in the crook of his arm. One of them inserted a needle and he forgot about the images. They disappeared as easily as someone flipping off a light switch. A burning sensation could be felt where the needle penetrated his skin before coursing throughout his body. What he thought was a sedative was actually something much more. The burning sensation moved up to his chest, followed by an inability to breathe. He gasped for breathe as his entire body burned from within. His jaw locked into place and his eyes felt as if they would pop from his sockets like popcorn. He wouldn't have been surprised if someone told him his eyeballs were rolling around on the ground like marbles.

"Vitals?" Brady asked.

"Blood pressure and heart beat are normal," Wendy replied. "Brain activity is off the charts, which is expected at this stage. But…" she trailed off.

"What is it?" Brady demanded.

"It's his body temperature."

Before Brady could ask for clarification, Bryan screamed. His entire body felt like it was engulfed in flame. His fists opened and closed rapidly, grabbing at something that was not there. He could almost feel his immune system fighting the substance they had injected him with. *Can someone feel their immune system?* When he looked at his hands his eyes widened and fear gripped him like a vice. They were on fire.

"Body temperature; one hundred and eighty degrees and climbing," Wendy shouted.

Bryan was surrounded by shocked faces. He was sure every scientist in that room gathered around him. When his hands lit up like fireworks, they took a step back and eyeballed him from a safe distance. The flames were climbing. They moved slowly from his hands to his wrists, consuming the restraints in the process and reducing them to piles of ash. The flames inched upward, licking at his forearms. Panicking, Bryan leapt from the chair and dropped to the floor in an attempt to put the flames out. As the flames continued to climb, his brain screamed "STOP! DROP! ROLL!" It did not matter, nothing he did would stop the flames from spreading.

"Body temperature is two hundred and thirteen degrees and climbing," Wendy continued, her voice becoming more frantic with each update. "Three hundred...four hundred!"

The flames climbed up his arms and engulfed his shoulders, slowly creeping toward his face. Bryan stopped rolling around on the ground as soon as he came to a realization. There was no pain. Despite the intense heat he couldn't feel any pain associated with the flames. If he closed his eyes, he would have thought he was doing nothing more than sitting in front of a fireplace. He picked himself up off the ground and watched as the flames continued to inch closer to his face. By the time they reached his neck they fizzled out, vanishing as if they were never there. He fell into the chair and turned his hands over, admiring their unblemished surface. *Were the flames nothing more than a dream?*

"Success!" Wendy cried. "Body temperature at the peak of the event registered seven-hundred and eighty degrees Fahrenheit! Current body temperature is ninety-nine point seven degrees." She hurried to Bryan and placed two fingers over his wrist and looked at her watch. "Pulse is elevated but otherwise normal."

"What the hell was that?" Bryan rasped.

Wendy and Brady exchanged a glance. Turning to Bryan, she smiled. "You have been injected with the mutagenic compound. As soon as it had been determined your mind would survive the transformation, we moved forward with the procedure."

Bryan ran his fingers through his hair and grimaced when they came back damp with sweat. "What the hell does that mean?"

Brady approached him and reached toward him but hesitated slightly before coming into contact with him. Satisfied Bryan wouldn't set him on fire, he dropped it onto his shoulder. "Congratulations, you have officially passed the Hero Program." Wendy tore a printout from a nearby printer and handed it to Brady. "You are no longer Bryan Whittaker."

"I'm not? Then who am I?" Bryan asked.

Brady folded the paper into a perfect square, placed it into Bryan's hand and locked eyes with him. The seriousness of his gaze caused Bryan to shift uncomfortably.

"You are *Soulfire* now."

Spectre

Halloween night

The two men huddled together, under the cover of shadows, in an alleyway behind Thompson Jewelers. This particular business held a special spot in Crystal City lore. After the famous gang purge of 1979, it became the first legitimate business to open in the city. The store continued to have a steady stream of customers throughout the years, ranging from love-struck teenagers shopping for engagement rings to corporate executives purchasing expensive yellow diamond trinkets for their mistresses. The business brought in cash by the truckload, which is why it became the target of the two men.

"You understand what needs to be done, right, Chip?" one man said to the other.

"Jeez, I got it already, Frank. You nag me more than my wife!" Chip slipped a cheap, dime store Halloween mask of Scooby Doo over his face. Choices were slim at every shop since the good masks had already been gobbled up for Halloween.

Frank's mask was nothing more than a generic clown face, but in the dimly lit alley, the shadows danced across its surface, causing its creep factor to go up a few notches. He shifted it around, trying to make it comfortable, but the flimsy rubber band kept pulling on his ear. He cursed under his breath.

"I have to nag you because you almost got us nabbed on the last job," Frank muttered as he wrestled with the mask. "It ain't like the old days, man. You gotta be careful now."

"Yeah, yeah," Chip grunted. He checked the magazine in his 9MM and shoved it into his waistband. "Are you sure Manny will be out front when the time's right?"

Frank nodded. "Yes, he is across the street right now, waiting for us to make our move." He shoved a snub nose .38 in his pocket. "Remember the plan. There's one customer inside being helped by the sales lady. The manager is probably in the back, so that makes three total we need to lock down before we smash and grab, got it?"

"Yep," Chip replied. "I take out the two cameras over the front door and you charge the sales lady. By the time they figure out what's happening, we will be on our way to the Caribbean."

A shuffling sound drifted from the darkness further along the alleyway, away from the main street. The two men froze and strained their eyes as they studied the murky gloom. Frank's hand fell to the butt of his weapon and he took a step forward. The sound receded, leaving silence in its wake. Frank relaxed his grip on the weapon.

"Like I was saying, we—" Glass shattered, stopping Frank midsentence. A metallic clank followed, like a bottle cap hitting the ground. Frank grabbed his weapon and Chip followed.

"Who's there?" Chip shouted.

Silence greeted them.

Chip continued toward the back of the alley, but Frank grabbed his shoulder roughly. "What the hell are you doing?" he whispered.

"I'm going to check it out. The last thing we need is a witness, right?"

Frank nodded in agreement and moved to follow. He stopped when the outline of a figure appeared from the darkness. It crouched low, inching slowly closer. Frank's eyes widened in surprise, and he aimed his gun. Before he could fire, Chip grabbed his wrist.

"What the—" he cried out in surprise.

"Look!" Chip gestured toward the figure.

Frank strained his eyes to see through the murk. The shadow emerged from the darkness, and he breathed a sigh of relief. He lowered his weapon as a cat jumped off a nearby dumpster and landed nearby, eyeing them warily.

A damn cat. He almost shot a damn cat.

"We gotta stop being so jumpy," he muttered.

Chip nodded in agreement. "Yeah, let's get outta here. This alley gives me the creeps."

They rounded the corner and scanned the area before entering to ensure there were no witnesses, with the exception of curious feline onlookers. At this particular time of night, traffic remained light, so no one lingered nearby with the exception of Manny parked under a street light across the street. When Frank saw the vehicle, he growled and clenched his fist.

"I told him to park *away* from the streetlights, goddammit!"

"That dunderhead," Chip muttered. "He might as well just drive a goddamn ice cream truck."

They continued toward the front of the building. The enormous storefront windows allowed them a view of the inside, where a middle-aged blond woman stood behind the counter using a loupe to examine a diamond ring. An older man with slicked-back silver hair, dressed like he just stepped out of a board room, stood opposite from her. Frank chuckled at the irony of the situation. The old man was trying to pawn the ring but instead of walking out of the store with some cash, he may be lucky to leave with his life.

Frank stuck up his middle finger and pointed it angrily toward Manny who simply flashed that stupid grin of his. Chip was the first through the door, and Frank angrily followed.

"DOWN ON THE GROUND!" Frank roared.

Before the older gentleman could even turn around, Chip smashed him in the face with the butt of his weapon. The unconscious man dropped to the floor, blood pouring from the corner of his mouth. Frank rushed the woman and shoved the barrel of his gun in her face.

"If I see your hands slide even an inch toward the silent alarm, I will blow a canyon through your forehead," he growled.

The threat worked. She threw her hands in the air as if someone had burned them. The loupe fell to the ground, cracking the lens. A horrified squeak escaped her throat, and her mouth formed a perfect O.

Frank looked at Chip and nodded toward the back of the store. "Go find the manager, I got these two."

Chip disappeared to the back of the room. Frank retrieved nylon ties from his pocket and tied the woman's hands behind her back. While he tightened the straps, the tears flowed from her like a river, her pathetic sobs carrying throughout the store. Her incessant squeaking sounded like nails on a chalkboard, and he wasn't sure how much more he could take. He leaned over her shoulder and whispered menacingly.

"Shut your trap before I shut it for you."

Frank had to give her credit; she did her best to suppress the sobs. The annoying squeaking stopped, but she shuddered uncontrollably, like a person with Parkinson's. He sighed, figuring it was better than having to listen to her. He grabbed the old guy's belt buckle and rolled his unconscious body over, tying his hands behind him. Once he finished, he dragged the man to the shuddering woman.

"You killed him!" she gasped.

Frank scowled. "No I didn't, now shut up!" He propped the guy against the jewelry counter. He snatched the ring the woman dropped and eyeballed it. With a satisfied smile, he glanced at the unconscious man. "Thanks!" he beamed before pocketing it.

Frank grabbed the jewelry case key from the woman and unlocked the showcases. He grabbed a plastic shopping bag from his pocket and stuffed several Tag Heuer and Rolex watches into it. He made his way over to the ring counter, where sat a four carat diamond. His hand froze on the ring when he heard a commotion coming from the back room. Realizing Chip had not returned, he became concerned that the manager had somehow overpowered him. Placing the bag on the floor, he retrieved his gun from the top of the counter. He took two steps toward the back of the store when a figure emerged from the back office. It wasn't Chip and it wasn't the store manager.

"Oh shit,' Frank uttered.

"Yeah, I have that effect on all scumbags," Spectre replied.

Frank was dumbfounded. They had been so careful to keep plans of this robbery between the three of them. Frank wanted this to go off without a hitch, so he went out of his way with excluding outsiders on this job. With Spectre here, it was safe to say this plan was now officially full of hitch.

Spectre strolled past the two people on the ground. Gripped in each hand were his trademark batons. Frank winced when he saw tiny droplets of blood dripping from them, splattering on the floor.

"How the hell…?" Frank asked.

If he expected a response, none was given. Spectre glided across the room like a ghost. Frank lifted his weapon and fired. The bullets passed harmlessly through Spectre, puncturing the wall behind him.

"Jesus Christ!" Frank muttered.

He turned and ran through the door, abandoning the loot. At this point Frank couldn't care less. There would be no way he could go toe-to-toe with Crystal City's resident superhero. He scurried across the street (nearly missing a passing Honda in the process). Frank scowled when he reached the car and saw Manny was not inside.

"Where the hell did that son of a bitch go?" he rasped, struggling to catch his breath. He grabbed the driver side door and threw it open, spilling Manny's unconscious body onto the ground.

"What the hell?" Frank cried out.

"You criminals are all the same. You guys talk a big game, but when it comes time to back it up, you're soft as marshmallows," a voice said above him.

Frank looked up to see Spectre crouching on the roof of the car. With eyes wide, he backed up several steps. Spectre sank through the car and walked through as if it wasn't even there. Frank's hand shook as he did the only thing he could think to do at that moment. He brought the gun up and aimed it at Spectre, who simply laughed and shook his head.

Frank knew how futile his attempt was even before Spectre's baton smashed the gun out of his hand, where it went skidding down the street. The second baton struck his jaw with a resounding crack. The last thing Frank saw were millions of stars rocketing across the night sky before he slammed his face into the pavement, ending his night prematurely.

Passing The Torch

Bryan opened his eyes and stared at the light streaks forming an *I* on the ceiling. The light trickled in from the streetlight outside, which Bryan prayed the city would move for some time to no avail. He sat up in bed and glanced at the clock on the nightstand: *3:30 am*. Ever since his family's passing, sleep had been a fleeting thing. Most nights, his mind refused to shut down and on those nights he found himself wandering the empty halls of his house like a ghost. In six hours he would officially become the new hero of Crystal City, which created enough excitement and anxiety to keep him awake for a week.

Bryan rolled out of bed and shuffled into the bathroom. When he flipped the light switch, a gaunt face peered back at him from the bathroom mirror.

"Jesus, I look like a ghost," he muttered.

Bryan winced and splashed cold water on his face. After running his hands through his hair several times in an attempt to make himself appear less zombie and more human, he returned to the bedroom and laid on the bed. It took thirty minutes but he eventually fell asleep again.

Bryan was stirred awake by the ringing of the doorbell. He rubbed his face groggily and shambled downstairs. He opened the door to see Terry's smiling face leering at him. His smile faded when he saw Bryan was still in pajamas.

"Why aren't you ready yet?"

Bryan rubbed the cobwebs of sleep from his eyes. "What time is it?"

"Dude, it's 9:30! You need to be at the Hero Factory in thirty minutes!"

"Aw shit!" Bryan exclaimed.

Bryan rushed upstairs, threw on a polo shirt and some khakis, hurried into the bathroom, brushed his teeth, and tried to make his hair as presentable as possible in thirty seconds. Satisfied he didn't look like he just crawled from a grave, he returned to the front door. Bryan found it amusing that Terry remained in the same spot on the front porch. *He's like a faithful hound dog.*

Bryan grabbed his car keys, but Terry stopped him. "Whoa, I didn't come out here to ride shotgun. I'm driving!"

"Hey, are you going to be my personal chef too? I expected groupies but I didn't think you'd be one of them," Bryan laughed. The laugh made him feel good. He hadn't laughed like that since his family died.

"Maybe, but don't expect sexual favors or anything like that. I pretty much draw the line at cooking," Terry replied.

They arrived at the Hero Factory ten minutes earlier than expected. Part of the reason they got there so fast was the lack of traffic on the road, but the main reason was Terry became the second coming of Dale Earnhardt. He seemed to believe the speed limit was only a guideline and sidewalks made great shortcuts. Bryan left fingerprint indentations in the dashboard and tasted blood when he bit the inside of his cheek from clenching his jaw so tightly.

"Jesus, I feel safer running into burning buildings," Bryan grumbled.

"Terry's Taxi Service is now closed for the day. This is where you get off," joked Terry. "I'll see you at the ceremony."

Bryan nodded and stepped out of the vehicle. As soon as his feet hit the pavement, he felt a burning sensation course through his body. It felt like having acid reflux, except the feeling traveled through his entire body. He looked down at his hands and flexed his suddenly stiff fingers. A burning flush crept through his cheeks, and he felt like he was sweating, but when he pulled his hand from his forehead it came back dry.

"Hey, are you okay?" A look of concern crossed Terry's face.

Bryan nodded slowly. "Yeah, I'm alright. Just nerves I guess."

"You'll be fine. You played with fire for a living, I think you can handle this."

Bryan returned the smile and closed the door, watching the dust trail as Terry drove off. He turned his attention to the front gates when he heard footsteps on the pavement. James approached him with a smile on his face.

"Welcome back," James said. "Everyone's inside making final preparations." His eyes drifted past Bryan toward the parking lot and watched vehicles trickling in. "We better get you inside before the paparazzi gets a hold of you."

James led him to a large auditorium. Folding metal chairs had been arranged in curved rows facing a podium. Behind the podium stood a large projection screen flanked by the American flag and a flag with the logo of the Hero Factory. In the corner of the room stood a marble statue bearing a likeness to the first ever hero of Crystal City, Illusionist. The similarity was uncanny. The sculptor even recreated the likeness of Illusionist's dragon head staff perfectly.

"Wait here," James said. "Mr. Simmonelli and the mayor should be down shortly. In the meantime make yourself comfortable." He pointed to a table against the wall filled with coffee pots and various pastries. "Feel free to grab a coffee and donut if you want."

Bryan wasn't hungry nor was he a big fan of coffee. Instead, he approached the statue and ran his hand across its surface. To his surprise, the surface of the stature was warm to the touch. He stepped back and cocked his head, marveling at the craftsmanship.

"The shit you must have seen back in the day. It must have been tough battling through all that adversity by yourself. You were a real hero," Bryan whispered.

"Yes, he was," a voice agreed from the doorway.

Startled, Bryan swung to see a stout, blond-headed fellow standing in the doorway. Bryan recognized him immediately and blushed from embarrassment.

"Mayor Stedson! Sorry, I didn't hear you come in."

The mayor held up his hand. "Please call me Harry, no need to be so formal here. Today is your day." He held out his hand. Bryan approached him and gave it a brisk shake.

"This mayor is always so modest. Unfortunately for me, my mayor was a pontificating windbag," a deep voice called from the other side of the room.

Bryan turned and nearly fell over with shock. Where the statue had stood now stood the real thing. Illusionist stepped off the pedestal, laid his staff against the wall and reached for the dark green hood covering his head. The loose folds fell to his shoulder, revealing a man in his 50s, with silver hair and deep wrinkles leading from his eyes to his sideburns.

"Illusionist!" Bryan cried with surprise.

He shook his head. "Not anymore. Nowadays I'm Chase Stinson, your friendly neighborhood street magician."

"Don't be so modest," the mayor chided. "Entertaining kids with terminal cancer is no street magician. You're still a hero." He clapped a hand on his shoulder and chuckled. "You just have a different audience now."

As the two men conversed, Bryan felt the familiar burning flush creep through his body again. He shut his eyes and rubbed his temples as the discomfort increased in intensity. When he opened his eyes, he noticed the mayor and Illusionist staring at him.

"Are you okay, son?" asked the mayor.

Before he could respond, Wendy Markus entered the room, followed by Brady Simmonelli. "It's a side effect of the serum." She placed her hand on Bryan's shoulder. "You will eventually learn to control it."

Bryan rubbed his chest like he had a bad case of indigestion. "What did you do to me?"

"We made you a hero," Simmonelli stated bluntly. "Let's head to the lab. I will explain everything."

When they reached the lab, Donald Runnels was waiting for them with a sour look plastered to his face, as if he were incapable of expressing himself any other way. He tapped a notepad with the end of a Sharpie and glanced at Wendy.

"Well?" he asked impatiently.

Wendy motioned Bryan toward a nearby seat. "Subject is experiencing a burning sensation along with some numbness in extremities." Donald wrote everything she said on the notepad. She stopped dictating and glanced at Bryan. "Anything else out of the ordinary?"

Bryan thought about it for a moment. "I feel like I'm sweating but I'm not. Headaches. Restlessness too, although that may not be out of the ordinary since I haven't been sleeping much lately."

Donald stopped writing and looked up. "Any chest pains or blurred vision? Heart palpitations? Any muscle fatigue?"

Bryan shook his head. "No, nothing like that."

Wendy pressed two fingers against Bryan's neck and looked at her watch. "Pulse is normal." She grabbed a blood pressure cuff hanging nearby and fastened it around his arm. She gave the pump a few brisk squeezes and monitored the gauge. "Blood pressure normal." She removed the cuff and set it aside." She ran her hand along Bryan's arm. "The skin feels unusually warm, comparable to a fever." She jammed a digital thermometer into his mouth. After a moment passed, she attempted to remove it but yanked her hand back so fast she dropped it. "OUCH!" she yelped.

"What's wrong?" Bryan asked, suddenly concerned.

Wendy opened her hand and held it out. Angry red streaks ran across the tips of her fingers. She looked at the thermometer on the floor as if it had bit her.

"The thermometer...it burned me!"

Donald dropped the notepad on the desk and brushed past her. "My God! Look at it."

When Bryan looked down, his eyes widened. *I'll be damned!* The white thermometer was charred black in areas and its twisted plastic shell was barely recognizable. Before he could get up and grab it off the floor, the arms of the chair started smoking. Panicked, he leapt from the chair.

"What's happening?" he shouted. The burning sensation within him intensified to the point where he could barely stand it. He shifted his feet uncomfortably and started breathing rapidly, nearing the point of hyperventilating.

Wendy held out her hands. "Calm down, Bryan. It's just your power."

"My power?" he wheezed. "How the hell do I stop it? What's it doing to me? Help me, goddamn it!"

"Calm down," she repeated. "Close your eyes and think of something cool and relaxing."

"Cool and relaxing?" Bryan breathed. "Like what?"

"Think something you may find relaxing. Think of taking a dip in a cool ocean at night with a full moon overhead or envision yourself sitting poolside during a Caribbean cruise. Relax yourself…that is the most important thing."

Bryan closed his eyes and pictured the Disney vacation his family had taken two years ago. The resort where they stayed had a lazy river wrapped around the pool area. He would never forget how cool the water had been despite the Florida heat, and he could almost feel the water running through his fingers as it splashed over his face.

"I think it's working," he said, opening his eyes.

The burning sensation ebbed as the heat surrounding him slowly dissipated. Bryan looked at his hands and, even though they had an angry red tint about them, he didn't feel the heat coming from them anymore. Wendy reached out tentatively and touched the back of his hand.

"It is," she agreed.

Donald picked up the notepad and started writing again. "So would you say Class Three, Doctor Markus?"

Wendy glanced at the mangled thermometer lying on the floor and shook her head. "No." Her brow furrowed as she fell into deep thought. "Class Four."

Donald froze and looked at her with an expression of bewilderment. Brady Simmonelli sputtered and coughed repeatedly as the water he had been sipping traveled down the wrong pipe. The Mayor stepped forward with widening eyes.

"Are you sure?" he gasped.

"Wait a minute," Bryan interrupted. "What does Class Four mean?"

"It's a basic ranking system," Wendy explained. "Once the mutagenic compound has been introduced into the host, it creates a reaction in the subject on a simple scale we devised. You witnessed the reaction firsthand. The scale goes from one to five with one representing basic augmentation like heightened senses, increased endurance and strength. Five represents..." she stopped and glanced at Donald.

"Let's just say Class Five is a unicorn," Donald finished for her.

"A unicorn?" Bryan repeated.

"He means it doesn't exist," Wendy replied. "Not yet, anyway."

"Am I the only one?" asked Bryan.

Wendy looked confused and cocked her head to the side. "Excuse me?"

"Am I the only Class Four?" Bryan clarified.

Wendy smiled and shook her head. "Don't worry, you're not some unique freak of nature. Hex was also a Class Four."

"Class Four ranking means you have powers outside of basic mutation and/or combat training," Donald added. "Hex has the psionic ability to manipulate probability and affect her target with negative energy. Further research into her classification revealed a dormant mutant gene had been activated by our mutagenic agent."

"We believe this is a possibility with any applicant. Currently there is no way to diagnose someone who may have dormant mutant genes," Wendy explained.

Bryan looked down at his hands and flexed them repeatedly. The burning sensation returned. Before it could course its way completely through his body, he closed his eyes and calmed himself.

"So are you saying I have some sort of mutant gene inside me?" Bryan asked.

Wendy did not respond. Instead she grabbed his wrist. "Your heart is racing." He removed her hand and looked at Donald. "We better get him into his suit before he burns his clothes off." Donald nodded and left the room.

"My suit?" Bryan cocked an eyebrow.

Donald returned carrying a costume on a wire hanger. The suit was Arctic blue with the exception of red and yellow flames descending from the chest to the feet and along the arms.

"What the hell?" Bryan exclaimed. "That costume looks like the world's worst set of spandex footie pajamas. I'm not wearing that thing."

Donald narrowed his eyes and draped the costume over a chair. "I have some bad news for you. You *will* wear it because you have no choice in the matter."

Wendy's response was less crass. "This suit was designed by our research team and constructed from unstable molecules that allow the fabric to conform to the powers of the person wearing it without detrimental side effects. We have also designed a data processing and telemetry system into its fabric on a molecular level, which, in short, turns it into a wearable computer."

"While on duty, heroes are implanted with a tracking chip to monitor their activities and to check on their welfare," Donald added. "The cost of surgically implanting these chips as well as surgically removing them became too costly and also risked potential medical side effects. With suits similar to these, there will be no need to surgically implant chips into a hero's body any longer. We started a similar prototype with Spectre."

Bryan approached the suit and ran his hand across its fabric. "It feels like a wetsuit," he remarked.

"Why don't you try it on?" Wendy gestured toward a door at the back of the room. "Use my office, where it's private."

Bryan grabbed the costume and slung it over his shoulder. He was surprised at how lightweight it felt. *All that technology embedded into it and it weighs no more than a feather.* It was a shame the Hero Factory couldn't use their advanced technological research to cure cancer or solve world hunger.

Bryan entered Wendy's office and hung the suit on a coat rack near the door. It looked as if a tornado blew through her office. Stacks of papers were strewn across the desk while empty take out containers overflowed the trash can. Her computer was on but the Hero Factory logo screen saver was active. At least twenty Post-it notes were fastened to the front of the monitor, and Bryan wondered how Wendy could even see the screen through the mess. His attention turned to a framed degree hanging on the wall behind her desk. *The George Washington University, Doctor of Philosophy awarded to Wendy Markus.*

"Philosophy? Are you trying to get into my head, Dr. Markus?" Bryan muttered.

Bryan stripped to his underwear and put on the costume. Bryan was in peak physical shape from all his years carrying fire equipment up and down stairs, but it still felt like trying to stuff a sausage. Once he finally got the costume on, he flexed his arms and legs to work out the kinks. The suit was tight, but it was the feet that took some getting used to. He expected the material to be flimsy and thin at the bottom of the feet but it was the exact opposite. It felt more like wearing work boots. The soles were well protected, and he could barely feel the floor at all. He sat on the desk and lifted one foot up and studied the bottom. *No difference between the suit itself and the feet.* The craftsmanship of the suit was ingenious.

A knock at the door interrupted his newfound foot fetish. "Are you okay, Bryan?" asked Wendy.

Bryan folded his clothes and tucked them under his arm. His hand hesitated on the door handle, slightly embarrassed to be dressed up like a comic book hero from the 60s. He drew in a deep breath and opened the door. Wendy smiled as her eyes drifted up and down, studying him. She looked up and blushed when she noticed Bryan looking at her.

"I guess I got caught up in the moment," she apologized. "You look good!"

Her eyes twinkled, and Bryan wondered for a moment if she was hitting on him. When she started writing in her notebook, Bryan blew it off as a misinterpretation.

"I feel like a damn pig in a blanket," Bryan grumbled.

Wendy stopped writing and smiled. "The suit will conform to your body over time, making it more comfortable." She gestured toward his clothes. "You can go ahead and leave those in my office. We need to conduct one more diagnostic test before the official ceremony."

Bryan dropped the clothes on her desk and followed her into the lab. She led him to a room surrounded on all sides by glass. Cameras had been mounted in every corner of the room. Outside the room stood a control panel with several digital displays and gauges. Between two of the displays was a microphone.

"This is our observation chamber. I will need you to step inside for observation purposes. The room is surrounded by six-inch thick bulletproof Plexiglas able to withstand temperatures up to five thousand degrees Fahrenheit," Wendy explained.

"Why?" Bryan asked, suddenly alarmed.

Wendy offered him a reassuring smile. "Don't worry. It's more for our protection than yours. Hero powers can be unstable and hard to control during the transition period. We need to be able to see what you are capable of without putting the research team in harm's way." Wendy punched some commands into the control panel and the door swung open.

"So what do I do?" he asked.

"Once the door closes, I want you to clear your mind and concentrate," she explained. "Focus on the burn as it flows through you. Basically, do the complete opposite of what we asked of you earlier."

Bryan stepped into the room, and the door closed behind him. Through the window, he watched as Wendy fussed with the control panel. She leaned over the microphone and locked eyes with his. "Simulation will start in twenty seconds. Try to relax and concentrate."

"*Twenty... nineteen... eighteen...*"

Bryan closed his eyes as the countdown continued. The burning started from his chest and coursed through his body. He held his hands tightly against his sides and focused on it, imagining himself running into a burning building and allowing the heat to envelop him. The burning increased, becoming a river that washed over his entire body.

"*Five...four...three...two...one...*" The countdown stopped. "Bryan open your eyes," Wendy commanded.

Bryan opened his eyes and panicked. His body exploded in flame. He thrashed around in an attempt to douse the flames; when that didn't work, he fell to the ground and rolled around. *Stop, drop and roll.*

"Bryan, get up!" Wendy's command floated through the overhead speakers. "Calm down, you're okay."

Bryan stopped thrashing about and realized, despite the heat, he felt no pain. His breathing slowed, and his heart rate followed. He stood and looked down at his hands, which were aflame but not *burning*.

"Criminal Program, Level One engaged," Wendy barked through the microphone.

Before Bryan could ask what she meant, a holographic image of a young man appeared before him. He was dressed in jeans and a white t-shirt. His head was covered by a scarlet bandanna with an 8-ball logo, the gang symbol of the Raging 86's street gang. He held a pistol in front of him and pointed it toward Bryan menacingly. Bryan looked toward Wendy for guidance. She held her hands up and cocked her head. *Go get him*, her eyes told him.

Being unarmed, the only thing Bryan could think of was to close his hands and point his fists toward the gunman hoping fire would shoot from them and incinerate the guy. Nothing happened.

What the hell?

Bryan opened his hands. The flames licked the palms and encircled his fingers, generating heat but causing no pain. With all of his years of fire training, he realized what made the flames unnatural. Fire needed oxygen or at least an accelerant to burn. The flames continued to dance around him as if they were a living entity. He decided to try something a bit unorthodox. Lifting his hands, he pointed his fingers toward the holographic image; but this time he concentrated, willing himself to control the flame. To direct it. At first nothing happened, but as he continued to concentrate, the flames reached out, yearning to free themselves from his fingertips. As they spread outward from his hands they created fiery tendrils measuring around four feet in length before dropping to the floor. He approached the image and snapped his arms forward violently, causing the fiery whips to slash through the image. With a flicker, the image vanished before the tendrils hit the floor. With a quick snap of his wrist, the tendrils fell from his fingers, becoming fiery serpents slithering across the ground, attacking the area where the man once stood.

"Holy shit," Bryan muttered, watching in awe as the snakes continued to slither over the spot where the image used to be. After a moment passed, they extinguished into smoldering piles of ash.

The burning sensation subsided, and soon the flames surrounding Bryan were extinguished. He rubbed his hands together briskly as he pondered the events that had just transpired. Fire shouldn't work that way. It went against every physical law he had ever learned about fire.

"The flames...they were *alive*," he gasped.

The door open and Wendy rushed in, clutching a piece of paper in her hand. "Did you see that?" She realized the question was dumb as soon as it left her lips and she blushed. "I'm sorry, of course you did." Awkwardly she thrust the paper toward him. "This is a printout of your recorded vitals during the test. Everything was normal except your body temperature."

"What was the reading?" he asked.

"At the time the snakes hit the floor, your body temperature hit seven hundred and eighty degrees."

Bryan looked at the paper in her hand but didn't reach for it. He had no desire to take it. For some odd reason he felt frightened by it, as if it would explode simply by touching it.

"So what does this all mean?" he asked.

Wendy swallowed audibly and folded the paper in half. "When you caught fire back at the lab, I assumed that was your power. But I was wrong, it's so much more."

Bryan eyed her warily. "More?"

"Your body has the ability to create fire, yes, but the mutagenic compound we injected inside you gave you the ability to do more. You can psionically control it and manipulate it."

"Like turning it into whips and little fire snakes," quipped Bryan.

"Yes." She reached out and touched his body suit, running her hand down his arm. Her smile widened. "It's cool to the touch; feel it yourself."

Bryan traced the area where her hand was. "Wow, you're right. I guess you have to hand it to modern technology, huh?"

Wendy's smile faded, and she glanced at her watch. "Damn, I was so caught up in the test I forgot we have a schedule to keep. Come, follow me. We have very little time to prep you for the ceremony."

Bryan followed her to the auditorium where he had met Illusionist earlier. Brady and Donald were in the middle of conversation, but they stopped as soon as they entered the room. Brady's harried look vanished when he spotted Bryan in his new costume.

"Look at you," he beamed. "You will make one fine hero."

Donald didn't seem to share his mood. "You're late!" He glanced at Wendy. "You will need to prep him quickly."

Wendy waved her hand dismissively. "I realize time has escaped us, Donald. I don't need to be reminded." She turned to Brady and quivered with excitement. "Wait until you see what he can do!"

"I look forward to it." Brady looked at Donald and motioned toward the door. "Let's get out of here and let her do her thing."

They left the room, and Wendy grabbed a clipboard from the podium. "Unfortunately, I will need to rush you through the ceremony, but you'll be okay." She looked down at the clipboard where several sheets of paper had been attached. "First, we will introduce all the former heroes in order, starting with Spectre. They will come out one by one and line up on stage where you will eventually join them."

Bryan's eyes lit up as Wendy read off each hero's name. He would get the chance to be on stage with every hero that had ever served Crystal City. He looked forward to meeting Spidermancer. Just thinking of her brought a smile to his face. He had just graduated from high school when she began her service, and he was reminded of his immense crush on her when Wendy came to her name on the list. The excitement faded a little when he remembered why he was here in the first place. He wasn't here because of childhood crushes or delusions of grandeur. Those days were long gone, and he needed to remind himself he was here to do a job, not reminisce of happier times.

Wendy snapped her fingers in front of his face, jolting him from his thoughts. "Hey! No day dreaming!" she barked. "After the heroes are introduced, the mayor will introduce you. You'll come out, wave to the crowd and smile. You can even do a little trick with your powers if you want." She winked. "Just don't go setting anyone on fire."

"Where's the fun in that?" he joked. "What happens after all of that?"

She looked down at her watch. "I will have to explain after the ceremony. We need to go."

Wendy escorted him toward the front entrance where James, the head of security waited. Outside the front door, a canopy tunnel had been erected leading from the door to a set of stairs leading up to the stage. At the end of the tunnel all of the heroes were huddled around each other deep in conversation.

"Welcome back!" James said and gestured toward the door. When he turned, his jacket drifted aside, revealing a very large handgun sticking from a shoulder holster. Bryan wondered why he needed to carry a weapon with so many heroes loitering about, but decided not to press the matter.

Bryan drifted toward the door and listened as the ceremonies began. From his vantage point, he couldn't see much because the walls of the tunnel obscured most of the stage, but he could hear the mayor giving a speech accompanied by thundering cheers. To Bryan, it sounded like a million people were out there, which did nothing to help calm his nerves. A thousand butterflies fluttered in his gut. He was never a big fan of speaking before large crowds.

Wendy must have sensed his nerves because she laid a hand upon his shoulder. "Are you okay?"

Bryan smiled and waved her off. "Yeah...nerves, that's all."

She opened the door and returned the smile. "You'll do fine. Come on, let's go."

Bryan followed her down the tunnel. It felt like the longest walk of his life. By the time he reached the other heroes, the mayor was in the middle of discussing the history of the Hero Factory to the crowd. Although Bryan had never attended a hero induction ceremony before, he felt this was the spiel the mayor gave every four years.

"Look who it is! We meet again." Illusionist stepped away from the group and shook Bryan's hand. "Welcome to the club, son."

"Yeah, right!" added Spectre with a smile. "I'm just glad I don't have to worry about this shit anymore. I'm going on vacation after this. The next time you people see me, I'll be lounging on a beach somewhere sipping a margarita and chumming with hot blondes in tiny bikinis."

Every hero came adorned in their trademark costume, which was customary during induction ceremonies. Illusionist fumbled with a clasp shaped like a beetle at the top of his cloak. When he noticed Bryan eyeballing him, he smiled weakly and shrugged.

"I only wear this thing every four years. I guess time hasn't been kind to me. I have gained some weight since my younger days," he admitted.

"It might have something to do with all those slices of pizza you shove in your mouth," Volt quipped. He was dressed in his signature black tights with yellow lightning bolts adorning the arms and legs of the outfit. He picked at the oversized bracelets attached to his wrists and tapped his foot impatiently, glancing intermittently toward the stage area.

Illusionist shrugged. "All heroes have their weaknesses."

"I hate wearing this damn thing. I can't believe I put up with it for four years," Indigo Queen muttered. She wore her signature leather pants, knee-high boots, gloves and half shirt. The entire ensemble was purple in color. She stuck a finger inside the neck of her shirt and pulled at the collar. "This damn thing is so itchy."

"At least you have a costume," scoffed Vertex, who wore nothing but a pair of brown cut off shorts and heavy work boots. Tattoos covered every inch of his skin from the neck down.

For years Bryan admired these heroes on television as he was growing up. But listening to them complain made him realize behind every guise of the hero was a real human being, with real feelings and emotions.

The mayor introduced Brady Simmonelli to the roaring crowd. Bryan turned and pushed past the heroes in order to get a better look at the stage.

"Hello, ladies and gentlemen!" Brady addressed the crowd. "It is once again time to introduce your new hero. But before we bring all of the heroes out here, I just wanted to let you know that it has been my personal pleasure to pilot the Hero Program into the 21st century. For thirty-two years, heroes have patrolled these streets, driving the crime rate down to record lows. I know I speak for the mayor in extending our congratulations to Ray Soderberg who has just been named the first police chief in Crystal City since 1978." A booming round of applause coupled with raucous cheers filled the parking lot of the Hero Factory. When it died down, Brady continued. "It brings a tear to my eye to think how far we have come. Our resolve to cleanse these streets of the criminal element is absolute. Our heroes will not be discouraged. I will not be discouraged. Ray Soderberg and his police force will not be discouraged. We will continue striving for improvement in the way our heroes perform in meeting their goals and objectives. Well, without further ado, let us bring out our heroes who have served us faithfully throughout the years."

The air filled with thunderous applause. Each hero stepped on stage as their name was called. The latest hero was introduced first and the rest were brought out chronologically. The final hero, Illusionist, received the loudest and longest applause of them all, which he rightfully deserved. He took a city on the verge of collapse and turned it into a respectable place to live and do business. The man deserved most of the credit bestowed upon the Hero Factory, because he had the hardest job of them all. When he stepped onto the stage, Illusionist turned into a winged horse to the delighted squeals of the children before changing back and joining the other heroes.

"Now for the moment you have all been waiting for," Brady boomed. "Our newest hero is no stranger to serving the public. He comes to us as a former fireman for the city."

"I'm so excited for you," Wendy whispered in his ear. "Go out there and show them what you got."

Brady turned toward the back of the stage, looking directly at Bryan. "I introduce to you, *Soulfire!*"

Bryan climbed the stairs, and it felt like he was moving in slow motion. Every step he took was like walking through a pool of molasses. Once he stepped onto the stage, however, all of his reservations vanished. The look of reverence the people offered him gave him comfort. Toddlers sat upon their father's shoulders with mouths agape. Women squealed and took pictures with their smart phones. Men smiled and a few even gave him a thumbs-up. Bryan glanced at the front row where Terry and Mac sat side by side. Mac wielded a crooked grin, looking amused. Terry beamed and seemed ready to rush on stage and envelop Bryan in one of his patented bear hugs. Bryan waved to the crowd, and they went nuts. As the noise died down, Bryan looked toward Wendy while the crowd waited with bated breath.

Go ahead! She mouthed.

Bryan had almost forgot! *A trick. Entertain them.* In his excitement, he nearly forgot her instructions. Turning to the crowd, he closed his eyes and let the familiar warmth wash over him. When it bloomed into a feverish burning which seemed to originate from every pore in his body, his eyes flew open. Several gasps escaped from the crowd as they watched Bryan set himself on fire. The flames swirled around his body, eagerly licking the air around him. His eyes scanned the audience. Everyone looked on him in a daze, entranced by the scene unfolding before them. Bryan smiled. *Now it's time for one final trick; the coup de grâce.*

Bryan held out his hands with his palms turned toward the audience. The flames danced in eager anticipation. They understood it was time to put on a show, but he struggled with what he should do. It wasn't until his eyes fell on the Hero Factory flag in the courtyard that he came up with an idea. He grinned and focused on the image.

The flames churned between his hands, merging with one another. They grew bigger and bigger until a shape started to form. At first it was nothing more than a ball of fire turning between his hands. Soon a mouth began to form in the flames, followed by a snout. Bryan concentrated harder, controlling the flames with his mind, forcing them to take shape. Curves formed around the snout, eventually giving way to two eyes of swirling flame. The head floated in mid-air, no more than six inches from Bryan's outstretched hands.

The head of a lion.

The audience stared, wide-eyed at the spectacle before them. They stood, slack-jawed and silent, filled with awe. Bryan glanced sideways at the heroes, who seemed to have fallen under the same spell as the crowd. Bryan spread his hands apart, and the lion opened its mouth in a silent roar. Tiny slivers of fire streamed from its mouth and fell to the ground where they fizzled. Bryan turned to Wendy to see her smile was as wide as his. She tossed him two thumbs up.

Soulfire was born.

October 17th 2014

The traffic light changed to red, and Sarah Harding slowed the car to a stop. She mouthed a silent curse and looked back at her three-year-old son strapped in the car seat. Already running late to drop him off at daycare, a red light was the last thing she needed. Her annoyance faded when he flashed one of his innocent smiles. Unlike some kids, he always enjoyed going to daycare and playing with the other children.

"We're almost there, Anthony," she assured him.

When she turned back to face the road, a tall, burly Hispanic man with a bushy goatee, shaved head and teardrop tattoo under his left eye stood in front of her vehicle, studying her and licking his lips. The hair on the back of her neck stood at attention. Panicked, she leaned over to push the automatic lock on the car door. Before she could do so, the man rushed to the driver side of the vehicle, threw open the door and shoved the barrel of a handgun in her face.

"Move the fuck over!" he shouted, shoving her violently into the passenger seat. Anthony started bawling. The man looked at her angrily. "You better shut that damn kid up before I do!"

The man threw the car in drive but froze on the gas pedal. He gripped the steering wheel tightly, his knuckles forming tiny white dots against the black leather cover of the wheel. Sarah followed the man's gaze and screamed.

A wolf, as big as any she had ever seen, stood on the hood of her car. The animal sighting would be shocking enough in itself within city limits, but what made the encounter even more bizarre was the fact it was on fire. The animal's mouth opened eagerly, revealing rows of fiery teeth which ebbed and flowed in conjunction with the flames surrounding its body. Tiny sparks, like miniature fireflies, escaped from the animal and landed on the hood where they extinguished, becoming nothing more than wisps of smoke carried by the wind.

As silent as a shadow, a man appeared beside the driver side window. The would-be carjacker took one look at him before fear filled his eyes. Sarah's hand flew to her mouth, and she uttered one muffled word.

"*Soulfire.*"

The word invigorated the carjacker. He tightened his grip on the gun and shoved the barrel in her face. "Get that...that...thing outta here before I blow this bitch's brains out!" he shouted out the window.

Soulfire slumped his shoulders and sighed. It was the same with every criminal. They all thought he would back down just because they are carrying a gun, knife, baseball bat or whatever the weapon of the day was. It's as if every criminal in the city attended the same "How to Be a Criminal" seminar. Soulfire glanced at the wolf. Although the animal was nothing more than a fiery apparition created by him, it was completely under his control. It was as intangible as fire itself and just as deadly. Soulfire worried about attacking the perp directly because he was too close to the woman and child. He realized the collateral damage would be great if he risked an attack.

"Listen, pal, it's in your best interest to put the gun down and let these people go," he stated matter-of-factly, hoping the guy would listen to reason.

Unfortunately, the guy didn't. In response, the man placed the barrel of the gun against the woman's forehead. A horrified gasp escaped her lips, and Soulfire clenched his fists.

"Listen... *pal*," the man mimicked. "It's in your best interest to back the fuck off before you find yourself cleaning this lady's brains off the street with a soup ladle."

Soulfire held up his hands as if to surrender. He took one step back and turned to the wolf, nodding slowly. The wolf backed off the hood and padded away from the vehicle. The criminal smiled and relaxed his grip on the weapon, lowering it in the process.

"I knew you'd see it my—" he started to boast, but never completed his sentence.

Soulfire's power was in his fire, but he chose to approach this situation without being aflame in order to sneak up on the perp. Without flame he was just a normal man. Over the past year he had practiced perfecting his control over fire in all forms. It took his body several minutes to generate the heat required to create flame, but just because he chose the safe route this time did not make him vulnerable. Soulfire could manipulate fire and his fire source was slowly backing away from the vehicle. He reached out with outstretched fingers and summoned the fire of the wolf to his hand. The wolf vanished and within seconds his hands were ablaze. Before the crook could react, Soulfire tossed small strands of flame through the open driver side window.

The flames were no bigger than Twizzlers, but they were effective. They caught the man in the eyes and he screamed. He dropped the gun and his hands flew to his eyes, but it was too late. The fire already burned his retinas, blinding him. Soulfire took this opportunity to throw open the driver-side door, grab the guy and toss him to the ground. By the time his face connected with the pavement, police cruisers surrounded them.

"Better late than never," Soulfire muttered sourly.

The first officer on scene tossed handcuffs on the perp and took him into custody. Soulfire used this time to check on the woman and her son. She struggled with her child's seatbelt, which was caught in the car seat. She wrestled it free and snatched her son in her arms, tears streaming down her face.

"Are you okay, miss?" Soulfire asked.

Sarah turned to him and looked at him with an expression mixed with anxiety and fear. When Soulfire saw her son, he nearly fell over.

The child bore an uncanny resemblance to his son. Even the part in the kid's dirty blond hair was similar to Jackson's.

Soulfire reached out and touched the side of the boy's cheek, wiping away the tears. "Jackson?"

"What?" the woman asked.

Her words snapped him from his trance. "I'm sorry, miss. It's just that your son looks like someone I used to know." He quickly changed the subject. "Are you two okay?"

She nodded her head. "Just a bit shaken up, but we will be alright."

A police officer approached them. "Everything okay over here?" Everyone nodded, and the officer turned to the woman. "Ma'am, if you could please remain here for a few more minutes. We have a detective on the way to take your statement."

The resemblance to Jackson unnerved Soulfire. Even what just happened bore some similarity to the night of his wife and child's murder. In the end he welcomed the intervention of the police so he could compose himself.

"Thanks, officer," Soulfire said. "I will be on my way."

The officer nodded. "Thanks again for your assistance."

Soulfire watched the officer escort the woman and child over to a group of waiting police officers while another officer loaded the carjacker into the back of an awaiting cruiser. A group of gawkers had gathered curbside to grab a sneak peak of a hero in action. In the beginning, he relished their attention and embraced their adoration. Over time the attention grew tiresome. Sometimes the crowd gathered before he even arrived on scene. They preferred watching the action unfold rather than stopping the crime from happening. As a former firefighter who put himself in harm's way to save strangers on a daily basis, things like that did not sit well with him. Women in the crowd swooned over him, the children looked up to him, and the men yearned to be him. He used to stick around, sign autographs and pose for selfies, but today he just wanted to go home. He hurried to his car and hopped inside, pressing his thumb against the digital fingerprint reader embedded in the steering wheel. The car roared to life and he took off. The thumb print reader was a perk installed by Wendy's research team as a matter of convenience. Unfortunately, Hero Factory-issued costumes didn't come with pockets, and since he couldn't fly around the city like Superman, they had to do something so he could get around the city.

As soon as Soulfire arrived home he tossed his costume aside, threw on a pair of sweatpants and an old t-shirt and became Bryan Whittaker again. He dropped onto the sofa and grabbed the TV remote but froze with the clicker pointed at the TV. His thoughts drifted to the woman and her child's eerie resemblance to his own son. *Was it fate that caused me to be there at that very moment?* He didn't receive a call to that location, he just happened to be in the area because there was an awesome bagel place nearby. Did God somehow intervene and allow him an opportunity to redeem the Hero Factory for its failure to save Alicia and Jackson? He stared at the blank TV screen and shook his head. *No, their ghosts will forever haunt me.* The blame didn't belong at the Hero Factory's doorstep.

Bryan sighed and turned on the TV. His random flipping through channels was interrupted by a knock at the door. He tossed the remote aside and answered the door. Terry stood on the porch with a six-pack of beer in his hand.

"Celebration time?" he beamed.

"For what?" Bryan asked.

"Do you really need a reason to drink?" Terry replied. "I guess we can celebrate the fact that you saved someone today."

Bryan shrugged and stepped aside to let Terry in. "Yeah, I suppose so."

Terry placed the six-pack on the kitchen counter, removed a bottle and tossed it to Bryan who caught it and popped the top.

"I guess I need this after today." Bryan lifted the bottle to his lips and took a swig before setting it down on the counter. Reaching inside his pocket, he produced a pack of cigarettes.

Terry was in mid-swig when he eyed the cigarettes. He lowered the bottle slowly. "I thought you quit?"

Bryan lit one and inhaled deeply, letting the smoke exit between his teeth. "I did," he replied sourly. *That was before the pressures of being a superhero became a bit too much to bare.* He kept that thought to himself.

Terry was a longtime friend, and he knew by the look Bryan gave him it would be a sore subject to discuss, so he changed the subject.

"So now that you're done busting bad guys, how about we head over to Roscoe's? It is ten cent wing night and dollar drafts. I'm buying."

Terry flashed a wry smile which Bryan had seen a thousand times before. The phrase "I'm buying" usually meant he would buy until he got drunk. By then he would be too busy hitting on all the waitresses to worry about paying for drinks. When that time came, Bryan would be required to take over the purchasing duties until the manager booted them or last call, whichever came first. The last time Terry had that look on his face, he got so drunk he got into a heated debate with a bar patron over who the better captain was on Star Trek, followed by Terry throwing a steel-tipped dart into the guy's leg. To this day, Terry is still not allowed in the place.

"Alright, fine," Bryan reluctantly agreed. "Let me go get changed."

Terry pumped his fist in victory. "Now you're talking!"

Before Bryan left the room, his phone rang. It wasn't his cell phone; it was his *other* phone sitting on the kitchen counter next to the beer. Terry turned to it and scowled. *The party was over before it even got started.*

Bryan answered it on the third ring. "I'm here."

"*Soulfire, we have a problem. We received a call; there is possible gang activity off of West 8*th *Street near the old Genworks Foundry.*" The man on the other end of the phone sounded as concerned as Bryan felt. There hadn't been any reports of gang activity in years.

"That's the Ironbound section, dispatch," Bryan replied. "Please confirm this is where you actually need me. That location puts me on the other side of the city. Is Chief Soderberg okay with this?"

"*He believes the report to be credible. All of our units are tied up with other calls, but we will get backup out to you as soon as possible.*"

Bryan frowned and hung up the phone. He didn't feel comfortable with this at all. His primary objective was to keep the city's citizens safe, but he was also tasked with remaining in close proximity to City Hall, the court house and the city schools. Ironbound was an area still under improvement and far from any of the important infrastructure of the city. No one but criminals and vagabonds lived out there. On the other hand, reports of gang activity were serious business. It was the one thing to bring the city to its knees. He would be lying to himself, though, if he didn't relish the chance for vengeance. Gang members killed his family, and he wouldn't want to pass up a chance for retribution.

"So, I guess we need to put the celebration on hold, huh?" Terry had a sullen look on his face.

"I'm afraid so, buddy. This could be a serious problem."

Terry held up his hand. "I don't want to know. Your business is your business." He grabbed a beer and tucked it under his arm. "I'll take one of these for the road, thank you very much. Call me when you get back."

Bryan gave him a thumbs-up as he walked out the door. He ran his hand through his hair and looked at his bedroom door, where he left his costume. "Time to stuff the sausage," he groaned.

* * *

Soulfire pulled up to the foundry. As the sun settled above the building, its shadow crept toward the vehicle. He parked the car and stepped out, carefully surveying the area. The building represented nothing more than a hollowed out shell of its former self. Genworks had pillaged every asset it could when it pulled out of the city decades ago. He tossed his phone on the seat and shut the vehicle door.

The area seemed too quiet for his taste, and he decided to approach the building cautiously. The only thing echoing through the empty building was the traffic sounds from the interstate slicing across the city beyond. The large sliding door to the main shipping and receiving bay was open, allowing him a view of the inside. Dark, ominous shadows greeted him. Inside offered many great places to hide, especially with dusk fast approaching. He took one step forward and narrowed his eyes, straining to see within the confines of the shipping area.

Nothing. No activity at all. Soulfire began questioning the validity of the call. *What kind of witness would even be out here to see any activity?* He worried about a trap inside the gloom of the building. Closing his eyes, he concentrated until becoming fully engulfed in flame. The police would, at best, be twenty minutes away. If this was a trap, than he figured it would be better with a few friends along for the ride.

Soulfire held out his hands, palms facing each other, spaced approximately a foot apart. The flames from his hands began to merge, forming a ball of fire no bigger than a soccer ball. As he pulled his hands further apart, the ball increased in size, eventually becoming a sphere roughly five feet in diameter. He dropped the ball on the ground and it split in half, forming two fiery birds the size of falcons. He pointed toward the foreboding, dark recesses of the building. The birds took flight, hurling themselves in the direction he pointed. When they entered the building, the shadows dispersed, revealing dust and cobwebs along the way. Along their path they dropped small balls of flame, about the size of golf balls. Instead of fizzling out, they remained illuminated, allowing a runway of light for him to see as he entered the building. The two birds perched themselves high atop rusted scaffolding at the far end of the building.

The place was empty with the exception of rusted scaffolding and carbon steel pipe racks bolted to the walls. Along the far wall was a long, rectangular window and a door. When he tried the door, it was locked. The corner of the window was broken, but he could see there was nothing more than empty offices inside.

"What the hell?" he muttered. After searching the building, he exited and the birds followed. As soon as he stepped outside they merged with him, once again becoming part of the flame which surrounded him.

Soulfire was confident he had searched every inch, from the loading docks to the surrounding offices and even the foundry itself. By the looks of the layers of dust and cobwebs, no one had traversed this area in some time and most of the remaining machinery had rusted long ago.

Concerned, Soulfire returned to his car. He grabbed his phone with the intention of calling police headquarters and telling them to recall the backup. Before he dialed, he noticed his text message indicator was lit. He opened the phone and read the message. When he finished, he dropped the phone in shock. *It couldn't be!* His initial assessment of the situation had been correct. The call was indeed a trap, except not for him. He picked up the phone and read the message again, staring at it and hoping he had misinterpreted the message. The message did not change, the context remained the same. There would be no reason to call and delay the backup because backup would not be coming. Brady Simmonelli's text message was the worst news he had received since the death of his family.

Bombing at City Hall. Police Headquarters gone. Many dead. Report to Hero Factory ASAP!

The Aftermath

Bryan winced when he heard the shouts coming from the other side of the door. Simmonelli's secretary busied herself by filing her nails but stopped when she saw Bryan approaching. She set the file aside and her eyes filled with sympathy. *The shit has hit the fan,* her look said. Bryan placed his hands on the desk and leaned forward, feeling emotionally drained.

"You can go in, they are waiting for you," she said.

As if on cue, the shouting in the room intensified. The secretary turned her attention elsewhere, choosing to shuffle papers rather than carry the conversation to its inevitable unpleasant conclusion. When Bryan opened the door, the shouting ceased.

Brady, Wendy, Donald and the mayor stood in a semicircle around Simmonelli's desk. Brady sat with his hands folded calmly in front of him. Donald and the mayor appeared flushed and disheveled. It seemed they were the source of the shouting. Wendy looked at Bryan through sorrowful eyes.

"Bryan, come on in and have a seat," Brady said, gesturing toward the leather bound sofa in the corner of the room.

Bryan, not Soulfire. He hadn't been called Bryan by them since he was an applicant. *This was going to be a very unpleasant conversation,* he lamented. He slumped on the couch and braced for impact.

"What the hell happened out there?" The mayor asked.

"That's what I'd like to know!" Bryan responded a bit more defensively than intended. "I was dispatched to an abandoned warehouse on the other side of town with reports of gang activity, so how about filling me in with the details of what happened."

"Gang activity?" Donald scoffed. "There hasn't been any organized criminal activity in this city for years."

"Now hold on, Donald. Let him finish," Brady commanded.

Bryan did not desire to be subjected to an inquisition. He shot from his seat, his face flushed with anger.

"Don't you think I know that? I told the damn dispatcher as much. The dispatcher told me the witness was credible, so I went where I was dispatched. You know what I found?" He paused and looked at each of them as if waiting for an answer despite the question being rhetorical. "Nothing!" he shouted. "I didn't find a goddamn *thing*!" He slammed his closed fist on the desk, startling them.

Wendy placed a hand on his shoulder. "Calm down, Bryan. Let's try to figure out what happened." She turned to Donald. "Let's get the dispatch transcripts and see who sent him out."

Donald nodded and brushed past Bryan roughly. The look of skepticism on his face couldn't be more obvious. It seemed abundantly clear no one in the room believed him.

"While he does that, does someone want to tell me what the hell happened at City Hall?" Bryan demanded.

A solemn look passed between the mayor and Brady, and Bryan wondered if they would even answer the question. The mayor drew in a deep breath and answered the question.

"Someone planted several explosives in the tombs of city hall."

"The tombs?" asked Bryan.

"The tombs were jail cells used back in the 50s," explained the mayor. "It was used for storage when City Hall was renovated in 1993 and the inmates were transferred upstate. Once the renovations were complete, they sealed off the tombs for good."

"Whoever sealed it off did a piss poor job," Bryan remarked. Hanging his head dejectedly, he let a long, drawn-out sigh escape his lips. "What is the casualty count?"

"Seventeen wounded and at least thirty dead, including Chief Soderberg and seven out of ten city council members." The mayor paused and collected his thoughts. "At least that was what the last count was. The casualty count is still coming in."

"Jesus Christ," Bryan muttered. "I don't mean to sound insensitive, but what is the city's current government infrastructure right now?"

With one finger, the mayor slid his glasses higher on his nose. "You are looking at our infrastructure, son."

Donald burst through the door with a stack of papers in his hand. He dropped them on the desk with a resounding thud. "These are the transcripts from today's dispatch log. There is no mention of gang activity at all!" He turned and poked an accusing finger in Bryan's direction. "As a matter of fact, you weren't dispatched for anything at all around that time!"

Bryan narrowed his eyes with his hands clenched tightly by his side. He scowled so hard Donald's eyes widened, and took a defensive step back.

"I don't like the tone of your voice. Are you accusing me of something?" growled Bryan.

Brady stood and waved his hand in an attempt to diffuse the situation. "Now, Bryan, no one is accusing you of anything. Surely you had reason to be out there." The mayor shook his head slowly, and Brady rubbed his hands nervously. "With that being said, I have been put in the unfortunate position of choosing between maintaining the integrity of the Hero Factory and giving one of my heroes the benefit of the doubt."

"What's that supposed to mean?" Bryan asked.

"This is bullshit!" Wendy blurted. Her face turned the color of a ripe tomato. "I'm not going to sit here and watch you make the biggest mistake of your life!" She fled the office, slamming the door behind her.

A somber expression crossed Brady's face. He pursed his lips as if he had just swallowed a lemon. "I'm sorry, Bryan, but we need to move on from this unfortunate incident. It's important we maintain positive publicity for the company."

"We hope you will understand," the mayor added. "It is extremely important for the success of this program that public trust remains high."

"Are you firing me?" Bryan asked in disbelief.

Judging by the looks on their faces, he already knew the answer. Bryan grabbed the stack of dispatch logs and flipped through them. The entire day had been filled with routine dispatches for minor incidents. The most serious call was an armed robbery which the police had handled.

"This can't be," Bryan mumbled and dropped the stack of papers. "I want to speak with the dispatcher on duty during the second shift yesterday. He will tell you exactly what happened!"

"He?" A confused expression crossed Brady's face, and he flipped through the papers on the desk. "According to yesterday's schedule, the dispatcher on duty was Mary Jensen."

Bryan felt like he had just been transported to the Twilight Zone. Reaching into his pocket, he produced a pack of cigarettes and signature firetruck lighter. He shoved a cigarette between his lips.

"There is no smoking in this building," Donald huffed.

Bryan pushed the button on the lighter, lit the cigarette and inhaled deeply. He calmly returned the pack and lighter to his pocket. With a deadpan expression, he turned to Donald.

"What are you going to do, fucking fire me?"

Everyone in the room stood in stunned silence, mouths agape. Bryan realized he was about to become the first disgraced hero in the history of the Hero Program, so he didn't give a shit what they thought of him now.

"I'm sorry we had to do it this way," Brady offered apologetically. "I'm a businessman first and foremost, and had to make a decision based on the best interests of the business."

"We needed to assure the public we have contingency plans in place," the mayor added. "A hero's job is to protect the public. We have to prove to the constituents this program can protect them from events such as these."

"You and I both know I'm being set up," Bryan countered. "I was sent out to that warehouse on purpose. If I find out who it is, God help them."

The mayor's lips formed a tight white line and he shook his head slowly. "I'm sorry, son, but there is just no evidence to support your claim. The decision has been made and a replacement hero will be identified shortly. I'm truly sorry."

Bryan sucked on the cigarette and blew a cloud of smoke into Donald's face. "Yeah, I'm sorry too." He turned to the door and stopped with his hand resting on the door handle. "I remember this one time when a hero failed in his duty without suffering any consequences," he added but did not turn around.

"What are you talking about?" Donald choked, waving the remaining smoke from his face. "The Hero Program has been a complete success until now."

Bryan lowered his head and clenched his teeth, nearly biting the cigarette in half. He no longer cared what these people thought of him. No longer would he bite back any scathing criticism of the company, the people who ran it or the program itself.

"Oh really?" Bryan asked, feeling the rage bubbling underneath his skin. "Try telling that to my wife and son."

Upstate

Tyler McDermott traveled these halls twice a week for the past thirty years. He hated the smell of the place, but it was the least he could do for his older cousin who practically raised him when his parents were killed in a bank robbery gone wrong. *Wrong place at the wrong time*, the cops told him at the time. That was the best the cops could offer, and he hated them for it, which is the primary reason the prison turned his stomach.

When Tyler turned seventeen his cousin had been convicted and placed within the confines of this prison for life. At the time, Tyler made a promise to his cousin he would visit him regularly. This particular visit, however, differed from all the rest. This day he strolled through the halls with a smile on his face and pep in his step, even when he had to check in with the desk guard on duty.

"You're early today, Tyler," the guard remarked.

Tyler looked at his watch and signed the visitor's log. "Well look at that, you're right."

The guard picked up the receiver on the desk phone. "Visitor for Pete Williams." He replaced the receiver and flipped his thumb behind him, toward the visitor area.

Tyler took a seat in front of the Plexiglas wall and waited. The hard, plastic visitor chairs were not exactly the most comfortable for a man built like him. He weighed two hundred and sixty pounds, primarily muscle, and built like a dump truck. If he was any bigger, the tiny plastic chair would be climb up his ass and find out what he ate for lunch that day. A few minutes after he sat down, Pete "Shorty" Williams entered the visitor area and lowered himself into the seat on the other side of the glass.

Over the years, Pete had lost weight but aged fairly well since his incarceration. His smooth, ebony skin remained mostly wrinkle free despite his sixty-three years of age. His facial hair grayed significantly over those years, so he decided to shave his beard last week, giving his face a more youthful appearance. He followed it up with shaving his head simply because he was tired of having to deal with it. Pete picked up the handset next to him.

"Hey, look here!" Tyler exclaimed. "It's the newest eight ball from Cell Block C."

Pete did not smile, instead he fixed Tyler with a hard look and tapped his index finger against the handset impatiently. "Someone in this place told me a story the other day of a fox and a henhouse. It went something like this:

For weeks a fox continued to raid a chicken coop until one day a farmer built a trap. One day the fox came along, like usual, but got caught in the trap. "Help! Help!" cried the fox. "Help me out of here!"

"Are you kidding?" shouted a rooster. "You will pay with your life when the farmer gets his hands on you."

"Oh, no, please don't let the farmer catch me. I'll do anything you say," said the fox.

The rooster laughed. "Of course, you'll do anything to save your life, now that you've been caught."

All the chickens agreed and began making fun of the fox. However, one of the mother hens stepped forward. "Just a minute. I have a question. Mister Fox, you said you would do anything to save your life."

"Yes, anything you ask," answered the fox.

"Well," she replied, "if you will do anything to save your life, will you do anything to save our lives also?"

"Of course I will," said the fox.

"*Very well,*" said the hen. "*If we set you free from this trap, will you remain here in this chicken coop and protect us from any other foxes that try to get in?*"

The fox was surprised at such a question, but his life was at stake. So he quickly shouted, "Oh, yes, I will! I'll stay in here for the rest of my life and protect you."

The chickens were happy to hear his reply, but they were not sure they could trust him. After all, foxes are known to be very foxy. However, after much discussion, they decided to set him free. They pecked away at the netting until it fell apart. The fox hopped out.

To everyone's surprise, he kept his promise and remained in the coop as their protector. When the farmer came the next day, he could not believe his eyes. There was the fox playing with the chickens and protecting them from all outsiders. Never before had anyone seen such a sight.

Tyler cocked his head, wondering where his Uncle was going with the story. "I assume there is a lesson to be learned from this?"

Pete smiled. "Nobody is really sure how the fable ends. It seems like a happy ending, but what if it isn't?" He turned to see where the guard stood. Confident he was out of earshot, he lowered his voice and continued. "What if the fox was playing the protector temporarily, biding his time until the farmer left the farm to go pick up chicken feed, or go to church or wherever farmers go to get out of the house for a while."

Tyler's smile widened. "And the fox strikes without fear of reprisal."

Pete holds up his index finger. "Exactly. I heard a rumor from D-block. It seems a fox got into Crystal City's henhouse."

Tyler nodded, his smile unwavering. "The chickens are scattered."

Pete's expression softened and he grinned. "That's very good to hear." He glanced at the door guard as he approached. He waited until the man passed before continuing. "Tell me everything."

"The mayor is working on putting together a new city government. Soulfire has been booted from the Hero Program." Tyler pulled back his suit jacket and removed a small notepad. His fingers scanned through the notes as he read them off. "The police chief and city manager are dead, as are half the city council members."

Pete smiled and leaned in closer, eagerly absorbing every bit of news. "Has Simmonelli named a replacement?"

"They have, much quicker than I had anticipated."

"Who?" asked Pete.

Tyler flipped through the notebook. "His name is Sam Fowler, co-dename *Oracle*. The only information I found so far is that he was adopted at the age of five, is twenty-seven years old and was a stunt man for many years before becoming a theatre performer." Tyler retrieved a photo from his jacket pocket and held it up to the window.

Pete reached into the single pocket of his prison jumpsuit and retrieved a set of glasses. He put on the glasses and squinted at the picture. "It's about time a black man became a hero," he chuckled.

"Yeah, affirmative action at work," Tyler laughed.

The chuckles died on Pete's lips when he studied the picture further. He placed his index finger on the glass and traced a circle around a small, diamond birth mark underneath the man's left eye. He tapped the glass, deep in thought.

"What's wrong?" Tyler asked.

"It can't be," Pete gasped. "What are the chances?" He scratched the side of the head, deep in thought, and studied the picture further. After several minutes of examination he turned his head and rubbed his chin with a dazed look in his eyes.

Tyler returned the picture to his pocket. "Are you okay?"

"Continue with the plan," Pete commanded. "But first, slide me a piece of paper."

Tyler tore off a sheet from the notepad and slid it through the slot under the window. Pete grabbed a pen hanging near the phone and wrote. The guard eyeballed him, making sure no contraband passed between the two. The guards only watched but never intervened unless they had to. Most meetings through the wall took place between a lawyer and their client and all communication was considered privileged. That rule did not normally apply to prisoners and general visitors, but the guards rarely bothered Tyler.

Pete stopped writing and slid the note to Tyler, who picked it up and read it. When he finished reading it his eyes widened with surprise. "Are you serious?"

Pete's lips tightened and he lowered his voice. "I need you to do this. I need to confirm, because if it's true, this changes everything." He glanced at the guard whose gaze moved on to another prisoner. "Inquire. That is all I want you to do. Do not reveal our intentions yet. I need to think about things further." He pointed at the slip of paper. "I need you to get as much information as possible from our contact about the new hero."

Tyler looked down at the paper and tapped it with his index finger. "What if it's true?"

Pete's smile returned. "If it's true, then we set the wheels in motion earlier than expected." He pointed toward the paper in Tyler's hand. "If it's true, Crystal City will be ours once again."

Tyler read the note again. "I will do as you ask." He stood and shoved the note into his pocket. He turned to leave but Pete stopped him.

"Tyler…I think we found our fox."

Tyler nodded, his smile splitting the lower half of his face. "Now it's time to distract the farmer."

Sally Bradford (Spidermancer)

While Bryan Whittaker was sitting at the end of a bar and drinking himself deeper into despair, Sally Bradford was just finishing up her shift at work. After her retirement from the Hero Factory she decided to return to her law enforcement career as a forensic entomologist. She held seven years of experience under her belt assisting with homicide investigations for the Cullen County Sheriff's Department before her application to the Hero Program. A recent murder investigation involved the study of blowfly larvae which had been recovered from the victim, and she had been called to assist. She was studying one of them under a microscope when a knock interrupted her.

"Yes?"

The door opened and in walked Detective Chet Walker, the lead investigator on the case. "How's it going, SB?"

Sally had worked with Chet on so many investigations they were practically brother and sister. She pushed away a lock of auburn hair from her eyes and smiled. "It's going well. Based on this little guy, I believe we can put the timeline of death between two and three days."

Chet returned the smile. "I think we have our man. The victim was last seen with her boyfriend two days ago. Guess who can't seem to locate an alibi?"

"So what's your gut telling you?" Sally asked.

"My gut is telling me to get the paperwork for a subpoena started," Chet chuckled. "Thanks, baby doll! Tell your husband we're on for bowling Friday. I hope he's ready for another ass kicking." He winked and left the room.

"Oh shit!" Sally exclaimed, looking at her watch. Speaking of her husband, she was running late; she had promised to meet him at TGI Fridays at 7:00, and it was already 6:45.

With a pair of sterilized tweezers, she snatched the larva and placed it into a vial of ethyl alcohol. She marked the vial with the case number and locked it in the evidence locker before leaving the office.

Sally's car was the only vehicle left in the parking lot. Dusk cast gloomy shadows across her Honda Accord. She loved her job but the downside of working for a smaller police department was budgeting. The forensics team needed to be housed in a separate building, away from the main department due to space constraints. Calling the forensics area a building was a bit of a stretch; it was more of a trailer than an actual building. Before she locked the door, she shouted in the empty hall.

"Hello, I am leaving, is anyone still here?" Due to the empty parking area she expected no response and received none. She locked the door and crossed the parking lot to her car.

Sally unlocked the vehicle remotely but paused with her hand on the door handle. She observed movement from inside the lab and turned toward the trailer. The sun settled behind the building, causing the fluorescent light over the door to cast a shadowy trail across the front of the building. After no further movement came, she chalked it up to her imagination.

After stepping in the vehicle, Sally adjusted the rearview mirror to check her makeup. Behind her in the back seat sat a hooded figure, peering back at her through the rear view mirror.

"Jesus Christ!" Sally shouted and spun around, completely startled.

The stranger held up his hands to show he was unarmed. "Hello, Spidermancer."

"Who the hell are you and what are you doing in my car?" Sally demanded.

The man chuckled. "My name isn't important, but my mission is."

Sally inched toward the glove compartment. Although she had been retired from the Hero Factory for nearly ten years, she still kept her arsenal of venomous darts inside. The poisons contained within ranged from incapacitating to deadly.

The man recognized her intentions and slid forward. "Don't think I don't know what's contained inside the glove compartment. I'm afraid if you open it, you will be extremely disappointed."

The man leaned back in the seat, allowing her the time to check. She did such and was disturbed to see he spoke the truth. The darts were a large part of her arsenal, but she was also well-trained in hand to hand combat. For that, she needed to get the man outside. Throwing open the driver side door, she jumped out of the vehicle. The man hesitated, but eventually stepped from the vehicle with a resigned sigh. His bulky, hooded sweatshirt and baggy jeans did not allow her to identify him, but from what she could see it appeared he carried no visible weapons. Despite his apparent vulnerability she would not underestimate him. On the back seat she spotted her darts, but she could not get to them without going through him.

"So, Spidermancer, we meet again," he said and quickly shut the back door, shutting her off from her weapons. "That is such a cheesy comic book line, don't you think? *WE MEET AGAIN, MWAHAHAHA!*" he mocked, waving his hands in the air for dramatic effect.

"What do you want from me?" Sally formed a combat stance. Her preference was to not fight in her expensive high heels and slacks, but she wasn't sure what the man's intentions were.

The man noticed her change in posture and shrugged. "I hoped there wouldn't be a fight, but I should have known better. You were always such a firecracker." He leaned against the vehicle and crossed his feet at the ankles, leaving himself in a completely vulnerable position. This threw her off and she relaxed slightly, perhaps misunderstanding the man's original intentions.

"As I was saying," he continued. "I'm here on a mission."

"Oh," she asked with one eyebrow cocked. "And what mission would that be?"

"To change this city," he replied. "I need to cleanse this city from the blight the Hero Factory brought upon it." The man stood and lifted his sweatshirt up, revealing a belt containing several compartments. He opened one of the compartments and produced three of her darts, turning them over in his hands. "I took these three assuming they were potent neutralizers. But I admit you're better at identifying the symbols written upon the darts, so I apologize in advance if I screw this up."

Sally stiffened and resumed her defensive posture. With a subtle shuffle, she slid closer to the driver side door.

Without saying another word the man flicked his wrist, sending the darts airborne. Sally had been out of action for years but her reflexes were as sharp as ever. She grabbed the door handle and pulled the vehicle door toward her. The darts embedded themselves into the inside of the door with a dull thud. Without missing a step she reached around, yanked the darts from the door and fired them toward her assailant. Back in the day, Spidermancer was deadly accurate and had never missed her mark, until now.

With lightning fast reflexes the man batted them aside with the palm of his hand. Sally had never before seen a person with such reflexes except heroes. There would be no time to dwell on the identity of her attacker, because he reached for another compartment on his belt. She followed up her attack with a quick thrust of her right leg. Her shoe came off and flew toward the man, but he batted it aside with ease. Sally knew better than to underestimate her opponent. A flying shoe attack was not her primary attack, but merely a diversion. Losing the high heel shoe allowed her to plant her foot firmly on the ground and throw a round house kick, connecting with a reverberating smack against the man's jaw. He fell backward, hitting his head against the pavement in the process. Although she heard a loud crack, it didn't resemble a sound a skull would make when hitting pavement. It seemed too loud. When she straddled him for a finishing blow, she noticed his hood had slid off, revealing a helmet with a microphone attachment she immediately recognized. Her fist hung frozen in midair.

"No, it can't be!" Sally gasped.

The man took advantage of her distraction and removed another dart from his belt. With a swift stabbing motion he jammed it into Sally's outer thigh. Within seconds her face froze and her entire body became rigid. She fell to the ground, completely paralyzed.

The man stood and pushed the hood aside. Brushing himself off, he chuckled. "Luckily for you, that was a nonlethal dart." He yanked it from her leg and tossed it aside. "It would have been very disappointing had I injected you with a lethal dose before having the chance to explain." He squatted beside her and gently brushed a tuft of hair away from her eyes. "I wanted you to know this is not personal, nor did I single you out among the other heroes. You were the most convenient, but fear not, the rest of the heroes will join you soon enough."

With a gentle stroke of his finger, he caressed her cheek. "You were always so beautiful, Spidermancer. I was nothing more than a teenager when you became this city's hero, but I'm not afraid to admit I had a crush on you."

The man retrieved a six-inch blade from his belt and ran his thumb along the side of the steel, slowly and methodically. He leaned forward and whispered in her ear. "I'm a bit embarrassed to admit that I masturbated to your picture on more than one occasion." He lowered the blade to her throat, the highly polished silver contrasting sharply with her smooth, well-tanned skin.

A tear left her eye and slid along her cheek before falling to the pavement. Her body shuddered with fear. The jerky movements meant the poison was slowly losing its hold on her, and she would soon regain control of herself.

"I take no joy in this," the man continued. "But I cannot continue with my plan for this city if I have you guys standing in my way." He touched the tip of the blade to her jugular.

With a quick snap of his wrist the blade bit her throat. A gurgling, choking sound escaped her lips, which was all she could do under the effects of the poison. Her mouth filled with blood, spilling to the ground and merging with the blood pouring from the gaping wound in her throat. He wiped the blade on her shirt and returned it to his belt. As he stood and watched her lifeblood spill onto the concrete, he wiped away a tear. Her death would be the most difficult to watch, and he had realized this before setting out on his plan. His feelings toward her never faded.

Long after she died, he remained by her side. The guilt he felt was not of her passing, but the lie he spoke. In truth he didn't pick her because she was the most convenient, he picked her because he needed to test himself. He needed to know if he was really the man to complete the mission. If he was capable of killing a woman he had loved and admired, than he should have no issue with killing the rest of them. Satisfied he passed the test, he leaned over and gently kissed her forehead.

That would be the end of the tears.

Karl Mintz (Twilight Shadow)

The car dealership's service department was rather busy for a Monday. Karl wrapped up his sixth oil change and tire rotation before the Service Manager approached him.

"Karl, there is some hottie in the waiting area asking for you by name," he said with a sly grin on his face. "Should I tell your girlfriend you'll be late for your date?"

Karl rolled his eyes and tossed an oily rag at him. "Whatever, John. Maybe my oil change left a lasting impression on her."

"Yeah right. Something left a lasting impression on her, alright," John replied.

Shaking his head, Karl left the garage and entered the waiting area. It was empty, but when he approached the service counter he spotted Wendy Markus pacing impatiently. He smiled and tapped her on the shoulder.

"Hello, Wendy."

Wendy turned and the expression on her face caused his smile to fade. Her face twisted with distress and the dark circles under her eyes told him she didn't sleep well last night. The glassy, hollow look about her unnerved him. She tried to force a smile but failed miserably.

"Hello, Karl," she said weakly and wiped at the corner of her eye. She appeared to have been crying.

"Are you okay?" he asked, suddenly concerned.

Wendy shook her head. "No." Her voice cracked and she took a moment to compose herself. "I'm sorry to bother you at work, but we have a problem."

Karl folded his arms across his chest. "We? When you say 'we,' do you mean the two of us or do you mean the Hero Factory?"

Wendy closed her eyes and ran her fingers through her hair. During the time when Karl was the hero on duty, she interned at the Hero Factory. She was young at the time and fell for his good looks the moment she laid eyes on him. It was nothing more than a celebrity crush, but when he reciprocated her advances, she took it further. Even though he was ten years older, the sex was much better than she had imagined. Over time, the lust wore off and they grew apart but remained good friends. Based on the look he gave her now, he was probably wondering if her feelings had changed and she wanted to rekindle something. She almost wished that was the reason for her visit, because it would have been much better news to report.

"Sorry, Karl, I meant The Hero Factory," Wendy replied apologetically. "Spidermancer was found dead last night."

Karl's jaw dropped. The news hit him extra hard because he was Spidermancer's mentor. His term had ended when hers had begun, and the shock of the news hit him in the gut like a battering ram.

"How?" he sputtered.

Wendy drew in a breath before letting it out slowly. She reached into her pocket and produced a piece of paper, folded neatly into a square, and shoved it into his hand. "The police are investigating but we managed to get ahold of this crime scene photo."

Karl unfolded the paper and saw it was a copy of a picture. His eyes widened and he leaned against the counter as the strength in his legs gave out. In the photo, Spidermancer was tied to the hood of her car, arms and legs spread to form an imperfect X. Her throat was sliced open, forming a second mouth in her neck. A single word was written in a rusty colored ink on the side of the driver-side door: *Revolution*.

"Is that blood?" Karl asked, trying to bite back the bile that accumulated in his throat.

"Yes," Wendy mumbled.

Slowly he folded the picture and handed it to her. "Revolution," Karl repeated. "What do you think it means?"

"I don't know," Wendy admitted. "Brady will be holding a press conference in the morning, followed by a memoriam." She looked at Karl through moist eyes. "We never had to bury one of our own before."

"I realize what happened to her is tragic and I feel bad for her family, but why come to me?" From the corner of his eye he noticed John eyeballing him and tapping his watch impatiently. "I don't want to sound insensitive but my boss is staring daggers at me right now."

"I'm sorry, I probably should have called, but I needed to see you. Soulfire's ejection from the program was a black eye but this is so much worse. If we cannot protect one of our own, how can we protect the city?" Wendy held up the paper. "Oracle has been our lone bright spot lately. He personally volunteered to lead the investigation into her death." She noticed Karl's eyes drifting between her and his boss. "Sorry, I'm rambling. I guess the real reason I came here was to ask you to be careful. We're not entirely sure this was a random incident."

Karl cocked an eyebrow. "What do you mean?"

Wendy stared out the window where a mechanic jockeyed cars between the bay and the parking lot. She remained silent for a moment before looking at her watch. "Maybe I'm just being skittish. Listen, I have to run and it looks like your boss is about to beat you with a tire iron. Just promise me you'll watch your back."

"I will," he replied.

Before Wendy left, she mentioned one last thing which Karl wish she hadn't. "I'm sorry it didn't work out between us. I never stopped caring about you, I really mean that."

"Your work always took precedence over our relationship," Karl replied flatly. "It was who you were and I don't blame you for it."

She nodded. "Goodbye Karl."

Through the front window he watched her get in her car and drive off. Footsteps approached and knew who it was before he even turned around.

"Are you done flirting with the customers?" John asked, his words dripping with sarcasm. When he saw the expression on Karl's face his smile faded. "Are you okay?"

Karl nodded slowly. "Yeah, I guess so."

John glanced at the bays. "The others can finish with these cars. We have nothing more than oil changes and brake jobs for the rest of the day anyway. You look like you just seen a ghost. Go home and relax, but your ass better be here first thing in the morning!"

* * *

Karl drove home in a daze. His thoughts had been muddled with everything Wendy told him. Murdering Spidermancer was no easy task. No one excelled at hand-to-hand combat more than her. Whoever murdered her must have somehow caught her off guard or come at her with an army.

By the time he pulled into his driveway, he forced thoughts of Spidermancer from his mind. He had a date tonight and wanted to focus on something more cheery, because the last thing he needed was to be a downer tonight. He paid good money for the tickets to the comedy club and he wasn't about to let the news spoil it.

"Put on your big boy pants and suck it up," he told himself as he unlocked the front door and stepped inside his house.

Karl took a shower, picked out a clean pair of jeans and polo shirt, got dressed and examined himself in the bedroom mirror. The hot shower did him a world of good. He felt much more relaxed and ready for a wonderful date night. While in the middle of brushing his hair, his cell phone rang and he grabbed it on the third ring.

"Hello?"

It was his girlfriend, Carla. "*Hey Karl, it's me. What time do you want me to come over and pick you up?*"

"Oh, hey, babe." The digital clock on the nightstand read 6:25. "The show starts at 7:30, so how about you swing by in about a half hour?"

"*Sounds good,*" she replied. "*See you later, love you.*"

"Love you too." Karl placed the phone on the dresser and returned to the bathroom.

"To love another person is to see the face of God," a voice muttered from his bedroom.

Karl swung around and saw a hooded figure blocking the door leading into the hall. His arms were folded nonchalantly across his chest and he rocked back and forth on his heels.

"What the hell?" Karl exclaimed and placed his hand on his chest. "Jesus Christ, you nearly gave me a heart attack!"

The man chuckled. "Well, I certainly wouldn't want that. That would ruin the touching moment I have just witnessed between a man and his love." He crossed his feet at the ankles and leaned casually against the door frame.

The man's odd demeanor caused the hair on Karl's neck to stand at attention. In the top drawer of his dresser, buried underneath the underwear, were two icepicks and a blackjack he used during his time as the Twilight Shadow. He inched toward the dresser until his hip bumped against it. The man either didn't see his subtle movement in the dimly lit room or he didn't care.

"I'm just gonna ask you one more time," Karl growled. "Who are you and what the hell are you doing in my house?"

The man uncrossed his feet and straightened. Karl quietly opened the top drawer just enough to reach inside. Without betraying his intentions, Karl's hand explored the drawer hoping to brush across the weapons.

"My name is unimportant, Twilight Shadow," the man replied. "I'm here because I'm on a very important mission."

The more the man talked, the more his voice sounded familiar to Karl. He couldn't shake the feeling he had met this man before, but the hood and the gloom offered no hints as to the man's identity.

"What kind of mission?" Karl's hand brushed across the blackjack, and he slowly lifted it from the drawer.

"I won't bore you with the details." The man stepped forward. "I was hoping you would make this easy, but judging by the weapon you have concealed behind your back, I guess I have my answer."

Karl brought the blackjack up and rushed the stranger, but before he could reach the man a sharp pain radiated from his chest above the heart. He looked down to see one of his icepick handles sticking from his chest. The man had been so quick Karl never saw him throw the weapon.

"Impossible," Karl gasped. *Nobody was that fast.* He fell back against the bed with blood pooling around the blade.

"Sorry," the man apologized. "I grabbed that from the drawer, fearing you might have been tempted to use it."

Karl's first instinct was to remove the icepick, but he realized the object was hindering the blood from escaping his body so he kept it in place. *I need to buy myself time.* Karl stood up, blackjack in hand, and rushed the now unarmed stranger. Like Spidermancer, his reflexes had not atrophied over the years, and despite the blood loss his strength remained. He jumped on the dresser and used his foot to propel himself off the wall toward his target. Karl was fast, but the man was faster. He slapped the kick casually aside. Karl didn't expect it to strike its target because it was a simple distraction. His true intention was to crack him upside the head with the blackjack. When the man dodged the kick, he stepped into the path of the blackjack. The weapon caught him on the side of the jaw, sending him backwards into the hallway.

Karl landed on his feet but stumbled. The blood loss made him weaker every second. It was imperative he finished this battle fast before weakness overcame him. Mustering inner strength, he charged into the hall and threw a roundhouse kick. With lightning speed the man caught his leg in midair and kicked him inside his left knee, connecting squarely with the joint. Bone snapped and searing pain rocketed through his leg toward the spine. His knee, now disfigured, turned an angry purple color. Already an ugly purple bruise encircled the area. *There is no getting up from this*, Karl lamented. He dropped the blackjack and clutched his knee, clenching his teeth so hard he thought they would crack.

"*Fuck!*" Karl screamed out with a mixture of pain and rage as he grabbed at his ruined knee.

"I could have made this painless for you, Twilight Shadow," the man said, approaching him and leering down at Karl. "Instead your people insist on making it hard on themselves. I hope the rest of them see reason."

"I'm not fucking Twilight Shadow anymore," Karl spat. "Maybe you haven't heard the news, but I'm retired."

The man produced a dart which Karl recognized as one belonging to Spidermancer. "You will always be Twilight Shadow," the man replied. "Putting on the costume of Karl Mintz doesn't hide who you truly are."

Realizing the man had been Spidermancer's killer filled Karl with a rage unlike any he had ever experienced. With his final ounce of strength, he yanked the icepick from his chest and slammed the blade into the man's foot. Blood poured from the wound like beer from a freshly tapped keg. The man screamed in pain and dropped the dart, which landed beside Karl's head. The man responded by slamming his boot into Karl's face. Now he had a broken jaw to match his broken knee.

"Fucker!" the man cried out in anger. He reached over and grabbed the dart off the floor. Karl was too weak from pain and blood loss to fight over it. The man yanked the icepick from his foot and threw it down the hall in anger.

"You're going to pay for that," he scowled. Karl felt a sting in his neck as the man jammed the dart into it. As if to add insult to injury, the man mocked Karl.

"I picked Spidermancer first for personal reasons. I picked you second because you're weak. You were the laughing stock of the Hero Program."

Karl's body stiffened and he found it difficult to move, like trying to move in a sea of molasses. From the neck down he was paralyzed. The man leered at him and removed his hood. Karl's eyes widened, and he tried to wiggle away from the man but his body would no longer respond to his commands. He tried to speak but his tongue was numb, as if he swallowed a pound of Novocain. He became a prisoner trapped inside his own body.

"Class one, am I right?" the man asked rhetorically. "Extensive hand-to-hand combat skills, small arms expert." He tapped his lips with his index finger as if deep in thought. "What did they say...oh yeah, that's right: extremely agile with high mobility were the words they used to describe you." He limped in a circle around Karl. "What a joke that had been."

"Fuck... *you*!" Karl coughed the words out before he lost complete control of his voice.

"But you were always a fighter. Despite your weaknesses, you always battled back, no matter the odds. You threw caution to the wind, which is what I most admired about you." He looked down at his foot and pointed at the wound. "As much as that pisses me off, it proves my point." He pulled up his sweatshirt, revealing a belt with assorted compartments. Inside one of the compartments, he retrieved a flexible wire with two wooden knobs, one at each end. He clutched the knobs, one in each hand, and bent down near Karl's face. "I would love to hang around and reminisce but I have people to do and things to see, buddy."

The man placed the wire against Karl's throat and wrapped it tightly around his neck. With as much strength as he could muster, he pulled. Karl let out a raspy, choking sound but the rest of his body remained limp, out of his control. Spidermancer's paralytic dart was very potent, but unknown to Karl's assassin was that the dart would have killed Karl Mintz eventually. By the time the final breath escaped Karl's lips, the stranger was smiling.

Two down, seven more to go.

Gene Montgomery (Spectre)

Gene gazed at the computer screen and frowned. He rubbed his eyes and tried to massage the headache away from his eyeballs. The staff accountant paced irritably behind him, rubbing his hands briskly together like Dr. Frankenstein waiting for his undead creation to rise from the gurney. On the computer screen, the Windows main screen had flipped upside down. The taskbar currently sat at the top of the screen while all of the accountant's program icons were flipped upside down on the right side of the screen.

"One of you guys must have been screwing around with my computer," the accountant barked.

Gene rolled his eyes and glanced at his watch. *7:15.* Just his luck. His help desk team had already left for the evening so it was up to him to deal with the stupidity. Being the IT Manager had its perks (like salary) but also had its drawbacks (irritating accountants). Accountants were wizards when it came to financial numbers but jesters when it came to computers.

"Well?" the accountant grumbled.

"Sir," Gene sighed. "I assure you none of my people were working on your machine." He pointed at the keyboard. "This particular issue has an easy fix. All you need to do is press the CTRL and ALT keys while pressing the UP arrow." Gene pressed the keys and the screen returned to normal.

"How did it happen, then?" the accountant folded his arms across his chest and looked down at Gene in a scolding manner, like a parent admonishing a child.

Gene shrugged. It was most likely caused by a spazzy accountant banging keys like a deranged monkey, but he wasn't about to say that out loud. He didn't want to hang around longer than necessary.

"Gremlins," Gene replied gruffly and left the office, leaving the accountant muttering curses under his breath.

Gene's office was located on the other side of the building. By the time he reached it, most of the office personnel had gone home for the day. He entered the office and noticed the only person left was the janitor hovering near the cubicles emptying trash cans. Maintenance and cleaning services had been negotiated into his company's lease, so the company who owned the building provided everything. They didn't seem to mind the terms, because the building was located in the posh Riverside district and along with upscale locations came upscale rent.

Vince had been the janitor of service for sixteen years and rarely took a sick day, however the person dumping the trash was not Vince. The janitor was a tall, middle-aged black man with a thick mustache and dark hair tucked underneath a ball cap, while Vince was a squat, white man who was two years from retirement.

"Is Vince not feeling well today?" Gene asked the man.

The janitor looked up from a trash bin he held and shrugged. "Yeah, I guess you can say that." He returned to dumping trash into his cart.

Gene narrowed his eyes. The odd response caused him to pause in the doorway. The janitor smiled, tossed the last bit of trash into his cart and pushed it to the end of the hall out of view. Gene followed the janitor with his eyes, but the ringing of his office phone distracted him. He picked it up on the fourth ring.

"Hello, this is Gene."

The line went dead and he lowered the handset into its cradle. Gene wasn't overly upset at missing the call, because at this late hour it was most likely another aggravating, last minute call to fix something ridiculous like before. Gene enjoyed his work in the IT field, but some people's stupidity tended to rub him the wrong way. He massaged a knot from his neck and glanced at his email. He groaned when he saw thirty new messages. Before he could click on the first email, a news alert flashed on the local news widget installed on the computer. Clicking on the icon, he pulled up the local news webpage. At the top of the main page, a ticker scrolled across the screen.

BREAKING NEWS: Former hero Twilight Shadow found dead inside his residence. No details yet. Hero Factory expected to release a statement shortly.

Gene stared at the screen in stunned silence. *First Spidermancer and now Twilight Shadow.* When the news broke of Spidermancer's demise, he chalked it up to local thugs catching her off-guard. Could it be a coincidence? A home invasion gone awry? He found these reasons difficult to digest. *Two murdered heroes in two days could not be a coincidence.* Gene produced a key from his pocket and unlocked the middle drawer of his desk containing his utility belt and two redesigned 9MM handguns. The redesigned clips held twenty shots each and the utility belt contained compartments with everything from concussion grenades to grappling hooks inside.

Gene checked to make sure the clips were full but before he could return the weapons to the drawer his office door opened.

BAM!

A bullet passed through the top of his head and embedded itself in the wall behind him. The shot echoed through the office and came from a gun clutched by the janitor in the doorway. Spectre hadn't been retired long and was not as rusty as other heroes. He knew something was wrong as soon as the door opened. His ability to phase quicker than one could flip a light switch saved his life many times before and tonight was no different.

"I figured it wouldn't be that easy," the janitor grumbled.

With lightning-quick reflexes, Gene removed both guns from the drawer and fired. The janitor moved faster than anyone he had ever seen and dodged the shot before running into the hall. That was when Gene knew the man was the same person who had killed Spidermancer and Twilight Shadow. Without hesitation, he phased and leaped through the wall into the hallway.

The cubicles, referred to by the management as the "bullpen" area, surrounded him. The janitor vanished. Thinking the man must have ducked behind one of the cubicles, Gene approached carefully. With his weapons aimed outward, he trained them on each cubicle hoping his opponent got antsy and revealed himself prematurely. When his adversary failed to appear, Gene tried a more unconventional method.

"I guess this is where I'm supposed to provide some witty banter, perhaps asking why you are doing this. Is that what I'm supposed to do?" Gene asked, hoping to draw his adversary out. His voice echoed through the empty halls, and he strained to hear any sound that would betray the man's hiding spot.

"Really, Spectre?" a voice called from behind him, further down the hall. He swung his weapons around but no one was there. "I never believed you to be so naïve."

"Spectre's retired, buddy," Gene replied, moving slowly toward the source of the voice. "Maybe you haven't heard, but I'm just plain old Gene Montgomery now."

The janitor's voice came from the far cubicle, closest to the exit. Gene drifted toward the sound, his weapons at the ready.

"No, Spectre, you are incorrect. You will never be Gene Montgomery again. As soon as you entered the Hero Program, you killed Gene Montgomery. I'm here to finish what you started and kill Spectre."

The janitor laughed, but when Gene descended on the last cubicle, the laughter died. He rushed around the corner and pointed his guns into the cube.

It was empty. The computer on the desk was on but sat idle at the main screen. Gene scowled when he noticed an oval speaker plugged into the USB port.

"*Oh I'm sorry, were you expecting someone?*" the voice from the speaker asked, followed by more laughter.

His adversary was fast, but Gene was faster. Two bullets rocketed harmlessly through his phased torso. Gene whirled and fired. The janitor dove behind the far wall and Gene rushed after him. He rounded the corner but found the area empty.

"This guy is too damn fast," Gene muttered, his aggravation level beginning to rise. This cat and mouse game wouldn't end until one of them was dead.

As if reading his thoughts, his adversary taunted him from the speaker. "Peekaboo, I see you."

"How about you stop dancing around and come out and face me like a man," Gene growled.

"Oh, Spectre, I'm not that stupid," he replied. "I realize the folly of engaging you in a straight fight."

Gene decided he wasn't going to play this guy's game anymore. He returned to his office, opened the drawer and retrieved the utility belt. He placed one of the guns in the drawer to allow him a free hand. From inside one of the belt compartments, he retrieved a flash bang grenade and a wrist restraint, a device he could fasten to his wrist and allow him to fire a bolo while on the move. If his opponent wasn't going to show himself voluntarily, then Gene would flush him out and restrain him.

"I hope you retrieved enough of your toys, because I won't be allowing a second trip," the man's voice taunted from an area further down the hall, near the administrative offices.

"Suck on this, asshole."

Gene tossed the flash bang toward the sound of the man's voice where it exploded into a cascade of light. He designed it to be silent but effective. The janitor revealed himself, diving from a nearby cubicle with his arm draped across his eyes. Gene seized on the advantage, firing the wrist restraint. Two steel balls ejected, spreading apart until they revealed a cable. The weapon hit its mark perfectly, catching the man in the legs below the knees. The steel balls encircled the man's legs and tightened with a resounding *CLACK!* The janitor fell on his stomach where he remained face down.

"Not so cocky now, huh?" Gene grabbed the man by the back of the neck and rolled him over onto his back.

With a snap of his wrist, the man grabbed Gene's left hand and slapped a small dome-shaped object onto his left wrist. As soon as the man let go, intense pain shot into Gene, coursing through his entire body. Gene convulsed repeatedly before dropping to the floor.

The man removed a knife from a sheath strapped to his leg and cut the bolo wire, freeing himself, while Gene continued writhing on the ground. After several moments the convulsions ceased, but he found himself unable to move or speak.

"To answer your question, Spectre, yes, I'm feeling pretty cocky right now." The man kicked Gene's gun down the hall and removed the wrist restraint and tossed it away. "My mission is to eliminate you people one by one. Do you think I would be able to accomplish any of that without studying you?" He crouched over Gene and leered. "I know everything about each and every one of you. I have been studying you for months, learning all of your tricks. Each of you will die by my hand."

Gene closed his eyes and concentrated. If he focused he could phase himself through the floor and fall through to one of the offices downstairs. He would crash on something and it would hurt, but he would survive, which was probably better than the alternative right now. As he concentrated, sweat trickled from his forehead but no matter how hard he tried, he couldn't make his body become intangible. The man noticed his struggle and chuckled.

"I get this sneaking suspicion you're trying to get away," he mocked. "Unfortunately for you, that's not going to happen. You see the contraption I slapped on your hand? It doesn't really have a name, but I call it the dazzler, just for the hell of it. I built it myself," he boasted. "It's like a Taser except it doesn't shoot thousands of volts of electricity into your body. I'm sure right now it may feel like it did, but what I actually built is something else entirely." He stabbed the air with an index finger, pointing it toward Gene. "I built it just for you, Spectre. I won't bore you with details, but to make a long story short it interferes with your phasing ability. I used your DNA to find out what makes you tick and created a serum to counteract it. All I needed was about a teaspoon of the serum which happened to fit quite nicely into that capsule right there." He pointed at the top of the device, near a slot containing a pill. "You should feel special; this thing won't work on anyone else."

With derisive laughter, the man reached up and pulled at his hair and beard, revealing them to be fake. He tossed them aside and straightened out his real head of hair while picking fake whiskers off his top lip.

Gene's eyes widened with surprise when he recognized his attacker. He blinked rapidly and struggled mightily but couldn't move no matter how hard he tried. His body was useless. The device attached to his hand turned him into nothing more than a useless pile of flesh.

"Don't worry, Spectre. The solution will only keep you immobile for a limited period of time." He narrowed his eyes and surveyed the room, focusing on one of the cubicles. He ran his hand across the top of the cubicle wall and closed his eyes. "This should be just long enough for me to complete what I have started."

In the corner of the room stood a twenty-four inch paper trimmer sitting beside a copy machine. The man strolled over to the table and eyeballed the trimmer. He grabbed the handle, raised it up and slammed it down, looking at Gene through the corner of his eye.

"Do you want to know how I knew where to strike you with the dazzler?" Gene was unable to answer, but the man didn't seem to expect one "Your hands are your weak spot. Your Achilles palm," he chuckled at the wittiness of his own joke before continuing. "I knew you'd be unable to phase your hands if you needed to hold onto something, otherwise it would simply slide through your hand. It's why I let you go back to your office. I knew it would be safer for me to approach you with that wrist contraption attached to your hand rather than a firearm." He tossed him a demonic smile and Gene's heart sank.

The pinky on Gene's his right hand began to twitch, followed by his index finger. He was regaining sensation in his fingers. He hoped his adversary would continue talking, buying him precious time to summon his strength and strike while he was preoccupied. When the man stopped talking and turned to the paper trimmer instead, his hope faded.

The man lifted the handle and slammed it back down. "It's time for me to finish what I started." He slammed the blade down again. The trimmer was bolted to the desk but the man lifted the bladed handle and yanked it sideways with such force that it broke off like a branch from a dead tree. He turned to Gene and nodded slowly. "This will do quite nicely."

The man crept forward, wielding the steel blade like a machete.

The Scourge

Brady Simmonelli returned to his office, collapsed into his desk chair, and stared at the computer screen. During his time away from the office, his email box had reached capacity.

"Son of a bitch," he muttered.

An employee had found Spectre's body at 7:00 AM. The scene had disturbed the unfortunate secretary to the point she required sedation when the first paramedics arrived on scene. Someone had wrapped a computer cable around Gene's neck and hung him from an overhead light fixture like a slab of meat. Both hands had been severed and tossed into a nearby trash bin. The person scrawled a message on a nearby cubicle wall in Spectre's blood.

The revolution has begun.

This, combined with the destruction of City Hall, could be the one-two knockout blow for him. The Hero Factory had dealt with killers before, but nothing like this. The inability to protect their own would surely evaporate any confidence the people had in the program. Brady sighed and turned toward the window overlooking the courtyard. Already, beyond the main gates, a crowd was gathering. Every major news agency was outside with reporters shoving each other out the way in order to grab the best spot for their story. The news of Twilight Shadow and Spidermancer's passing had barely passed the twenty-four mark, and he was now expected to give a statement regarding another dead hero. The citizens of Crystal City were getting restless.

One hero's death was a tragedy. Two was a shock. Three was a catastrophe. It was time for damage control.

"They are ready when you are."

Brady turned around to see Wendy looming in the doorway. "Let them wait a little longer. I'm trying to figure out what the hell I am going to say."

Wendy looked down and fiddled with a loose thread on her suit jacket. She had dressed to impress today. The look would work in front of the cameras, especially when they were about to admit to the world they had no idea what to do. Behind Wendy stood Oracle, looking morose. Beard stubble grew in mangy patches around his chin, and he looked as if he hadn't slept in a week.

"Do we have any leads?" Brady asked him.

Oracle shook his head slowly. "Nothing. It couldn't be an organized gang hit. I couldn't locate any sort of gang activity to suspect otherwise. If someone was methodically planning to off every hero, I would have heard of it by now from my informants."

"It has to be multiple people," Wendy argued. "A single-person sneak-attack might have been plausible in Spidermancer's case, but Twilight Shadow…" she trailed off.

Brady remembered the history between Wendy and Twilight Shadow and gave her time to compose herself. God knew they all needed some time to compose themselves.

"Spectre too," she continued. "There is no way a single person could have taken either of them out."

Oracle pinched the bridge of his nose and rubbed, as if warding off a migraine. "I disagree. I took the liberty of reviewing the arrest records of everyone those three had put away, and the perps were either nonviolent offenders or minor players in small gangs. No one had the muscle or the clout to pull off something like this. And trust me, when I say *gangs* I mean four or five kids with nothing better to do outside their parent's basement." Oracle shook his head. "No, this was done by one, maybe two people, looking to make a name for themselves. Probability is high that these suspects have some sort of military background with access to specialized weaponry."

"Why would someone do this?" Brady asked. "What is their motivation?"

"Anarchy," Oracle replied.

Brady turned his attention to the crowd outside. "I suppose this was bound to happen eventually. This city was a cesspool when I found it. I'm amazed we were able to maintain civility for this long."

"So what's the plan?" asked Wendy.

"We will call it a freak accident and feed that to the media, which should placate them for the moment. The details of Spectre's death are not public except to a heavily sedated secretary, which should buy us enough time to get to the bottom of this." Brady turned and pointed at Oracle. "It's your job to find the perpetrator and put an end to this. I am giving you carte blanche to bring them down by any means necessary!"

Oracle nodded and left the room. Wendy glared at Brady. "A freak *accident*? Surely you can't be serious! What if we don't find the person responsible before the secretary decides to talk?"

Brady matched her stare. "Money is a powerful motivator. I'm confident we can buy her silence in the matter." Wendy continued to glare at him which only served to irritate Brady further. "What do you propose I do? I can't go on record telling the people that someone is stalking our heroes and slaughtering them like cattle. Their perception would be we are weak, unable to protect the city. The city government would lose confidence in our ability to protect it. It would be a public relations nightmare of epic proportions."

"Really, Brady?" she said. "You're afraid of a PR problem?"

"PR is the lifeblood of this company, Dr. Markus. Without it, we would not be in business very long. How long do you think this company would last if the public feared our heroes could no longer protect it?"

Wendy didn't respond. Instead she turned toward the window and looked beyond at the mass of huddled bodies outside clamoring for a statement. "Whoever is doing this has some sort of vendetta against us. They want to see us fail."

The implied meaning of her statement did not escape him. Brady knew of only one man with a vendetta against the Hero Factory. "You think Soulfire is responsible?"

"Who else has a reason to destroy our reputation? Who else has the ability to overpower three heroes?"

Brady pinched his chin, deep in thought. "Their wounds were not consistent with his abilities."

"Perhaps that's simply a red herring. He could be using other means as a ruse, something to throw us off his trail."

Brady nodded reluctantly and picked up the phone. Tommy Stamper was named the new chief of police not long after Chief Soderberg's death. Brady had known Stamper since he was a patrolman, and he needed someone who could handle this request with the care it deserved. The last thing he needed was the city's police force engaged in a witch hunt. He punched the numbers to the Chief's private cell phone.

Stamper picked up on the third ring. "*Chief Stamper.*"

"Hello Chief, this is Brady. I need you to do me a favor."

"*What is it?*" he muttered impatiently.

It seemed the murders in his city took a toll on the police force's public relations as well as the chief's patience level. Brady would need to dance on eggshells around the man or he might just explode.

"I need you to issue an arrest warrant for Bryan Whittaker."

There was a long pause on the other end of the line. The silence broke with an exhaled gust of breath. "*I suppose it's too much to hope you mean a different Bryan Whittaker than the one I'm thinking of.*"

"Unfortunately, no," replied Brady.

"*What's the charge?*"

"Three counts of murder."

"*Jesus Christ,*" the Chief gasped. "*This won't be easy. Is there any chance I can borrow Oracle for this one?*"

"Yes, I will let him know immediately." Brady hung up the phone and glanced at Wendy.

Exhaustion was written all over her face. She ran her hand through her hair and returned her gaze to the crowd outside. For several moments, she remained silent, simply staring at the people while deep in thought.

"God help us if you're wrong about this one, Wendy," Brady said.

"If I'm right..." Wendy turned her head to the side, peering at him from the corner of her eye. "Then God help us all."

Soulfire

After wrapping up a twelve hour shift at work, Bryan looked forward to coming home. When he arrived home, he observed Jackson riding his big wheel in the driveway while Alicia sat on the porch talking on her cell phone. When he had been spotted coming up the driveway Alicia smiled and waved. He loved and hated her smile. The smile made her even more beautiful than she already was, almost angelic, but it also had a downside. Her smile could disarm him whenever he was angry, and he never won an argument whenever she armed herself with that smile.

"With the workload you have been having lately, I thought I wouldn't see you until tomorrow," she said when he stepped from the car.

"Hi, Daddy!" Jackson shouted and waved. He made no move toward Bryan, though, because he was having too much fun on his ride.

"Miss me?" Bryan wrapped his arms around her and squeezed. When he pulled away, his wife looked past him. Her eyes turned glassy and an expression of horror dawned on her face.

Concerned, Bryan spun around and followed her gaze. Behind him next to the garage, lying face down in a pool of blood, was his son next to the big wheel which flipped on its side. Bryan rushed to him and rolled him over. Instead of a blood-stained face, Bryan came face-to-face with a skull, blood-free and unmarked with the exception of a bullet hole in the right temple. With tears streaming from his eyes, he turned to his wife. Instead of her, he came face-to-face with a rotting corpse. A blood-less hole wept dirt and grime in the center of its forehead. Startled, he jumped back. The tears in his eyes caused his vision to become blurry, giving the corpse a wisp-like appearance. When he brushed the tears aside, the corpse opened its mouth, and a writhing ball of maggots spilled out. Bryan's stomach heaved. He turned away and vomited. As soon as he was done purging his evening meal, the corpse screamed.

"AVENGE US!"

Bryan's eyes flew open and he shot out of bed. Dripping sweat, he glanced at the digital clock on the nightstand and groaned. *4:45 AM.* His mouth was dry and his tongue felt like sandpaper. A sour taste, a combination of stale cigarettes and cheap whiskey, filled his mouth. He didn't remember driving home from the bar last night. His head pounded, and it felt like someone was trying to yank his brain through his sinus cavity.

The nightmares came more frequently and vividly in recent days. He would prefer blaming the alcohol, but he knew the true reason. *Guilt.* It was like a parasite coursing through his veins, threatening to eat him alive. Before his time with the Hero Factory, he had been a friendly, personable guy. These days, he was nothing more than an emotionless husk of flesh. A real life zombie, if you prefer. He found it more difficult each passing day to find any joy in the world. It was as if all pleasure had been sucked out with a giant vacuum forged from depression and broken promises. All around him he saw nothing but darkness, no matter the time of day.

After splashing handfuls of cold water on his face, he shuffled into the kitchen to fix breakfast. He fried up two eggs and placed them onto a slice of toasted rye bread, his usual post-drinking binge meal of choice. He plopped into the recliner and flipped on the television. The first thing that popped up was the local news in the middle of reporting the weather. The leggy, blonde weatherwoman in their employ droned on about an incoming warm front and severe thunderstorms forming off the coast.

Bryan cut off a piece of egg and shoved it into his mouth. Before he could swallow it, a breaking news update flashed across the screen. As the ticker rolled across the bottom of the screen, he swallowed so hard he almost choked. The headline read of a murder that had occurred in the city yesterday. He had been so drunk yesterday, Martian strippers could have landed on Earth and danced the Macarena on his front lawn and he would have been oblivious. The news flashing across the screen was not quite so amusing. It was a news piece regarding the death of Spectre.

Three heroes dead in three days. He dropped his fork onto his plate and set the entire thing aside. Suddenly his appetite vanished. As he continued watching the ticker roll across his screen, very few details regarding the incident were revealed. The news hadn't specifically called it murder, but the coincidence was too great to ignore.

"What the fuck?" he muttered.

"They are going to blame you for it," a voice called near the front door.

In an instant Bryan was out of his seat and turned toward the location of the voice. A shadowy silhouette stood near the front door. Pale moonlight drifted into the room through the partially open blinds that covered the front window. The light failed to penetrate the gloom and reveal the intruder. Despite an inability to identify the person visually, Bryan recognized the voice.

"Illusionist?" Bryan asked.

Illusionist closed the door and stepped inside. When he stepped into the lit hallway, his face was revealed. Gone was the jovial expression Bryan had seen on his induction day. The poor fellow looked as if he had aged ten years. Lines of exhaustion crossed his pinched face. A baseball cap hung low on his head to match the New York Yankees jacket he wore. His jeans were wrinkled and looked like they hadn't been washed in weeks. He seemed as excited as someone about to give a eulogy at a funeral.

"Jesus Christ, you nearly gave me a heart attack," Bryan groaned. "What the hell are you doing here?"

Bryan's internal alarm system switched to DEFCON 2. He hadn't seen Illusionist in a long time and found it quite odd he would be paying a visit at this hour after all this time.

Illusionist removed his hat and ran his fingers through his hair. Bryan noticed it had grayed significantly since their last meeting.

"I apologize for coming here at this hour." He glanced at the television and winced.

"What did you mean when you said they are going to blame me for it?"

Bryan clenched his fists and started to concentrate. Although he hadn't used his powers since leaving the Hero Program, he refused to be caught off guard by Illusionist. The act of concentration made his head pound harder, as if someone were playing bongo drums on an endless loop inside his skull.

Illusionist noticed Bryan form a defensive stance and sighed. "There's no need for that. I'm not your enemy." He moved to the couch and sat, placing the palms of his hands on his knees, showing he was no threat. He nodded toward the television. "The Hero Factory is going to blame you for that."

"For murdering Spectre?" Bryan questioned. "The hell they are! I'm not gonna be their fall guy for that. They can go fuck themselves."

"Let me be perfectly clear." Illusionist's expression turned deadly serious. "A *hero* did this, make no mistake about it. No one could take down three heroes in three days with perfect precision and execution. As a disgruntled former employee, they *will* assume it was you, and they will come for you."

"Let them come," Bryan growled.

"NO!" Illusionist shouted, which startled Bryan. The outburst was out of place for the normally soft spoken magician. "That is what they want, to divide and conquer us. We must stand united!"

"That is what who wants?" asked Bryan.

"The people behind this. I have my suspicions regarding the person running the operation, but I can't say until I'm absolutely sure. I do know *this*, war is coming to Crystal City."

Bryan shrugged. "So get Oracle to take care of it. That's his job after all, isn't it? To *protect* the city."

Illusionist remained strangely quiet. He stood and pulled aside the curtain covering the front window. The single streetlight at the end of his driveway illuminated a portion of the front yard and sidewalk. Bryan's sad lawn hadn't been tended to in weeks. The grass used to be the color of emeralds, weed free and well-manicured. Now it was nothing more than a haven for dandelions and mud wasps.

"I will need to gather the other heroes," Illusionist said without turning from the window. "Will you help me?"

Bryan laughed humorlessly. Illusionist turned and faced him with a surprised expression.

"You have got to be kidding me," Bryan scoffed. "You guys failed to protect my wife and son. The Hero Factory abandoned me when I needed them the most. Now you come to me for help? You want me to save them?" Bryan stood and frowned. "You heroes and your program can go take a flying leap off a tall building. Fuck you and fuck your city. The care train left the station long ago, pal; maybe you should get out of here and go catch it. I'm not your guy, nor am I going to be your patsy. You can run back and tell the Hero Factory if they come looking for me, I'll be here, ready for them."

Illusionist sighed and shook his head slowly. "I'm sorry to hear that, Bryan." He moved to the front door but stopped with his hand resting on the doorknob. "You were a firefighter, if I recall. A very dangerous job indeed. I can only imagine what kind of person would apply for such a suicidal job. Running into buildings, saving complete strangers for very little compensation while putting yourself in harm's way seems a strange way to make a living. A person would either need to be extremely crazy or extremely large-hearted to do a job like that. There's no glory nor financial gain from it. It's as if a person would need to have a desire to save lives and benefit society over their own well-being to even consider applying for such a dangerous profession." He turned and looked sideways at Bryan and paused before adding, "Go figure, huh?" He walked out without saying another word.

The pounding in Bryan's head ceased. Thank God for small miracles. The pain in his head may have faded, but it had been replaced by the sting of Illusionist's words. He dropped onto the couch and placed his head into his hands. His hatred for the Hero Factory festered like an open sore, but he couldn't deny Illusionist's words. Deep down, through the festering swamp of hatred, anger and despair swam the real Bryan Whittaker, the man who had become Soulfire. No matter how much he had endured, he could never bury what he truly was.

Another breaking news alert scrolled across the screen. Bryan read the ticker at the top of the screen, and his eyes widened as big as saucers.

Melissa Zampelli, also known as Indigo Queen, found murdered in her home along with her husband Zachary and her two teenage sons, Greg and Tyler. Updates to follow at the 6 o'clock hour.

Bryan's cell phone rang, startling him out of his daze. His eyes moved toward the kitchen counter, where he left his phone last night. He grabbed it off the counter and answered it on the third ring.

"Hello?"

"Do you believe me now?" Illusionist said.

The line went dead before Bryan could respond.

The Revolution Part 1

"*Two more down,*" the voice on the other end of the phone boasted.

Tyler smiled. "That's excellent news. The Hero Factory is weak; now's the time to strike at the core."

"*Are you sure? Don't you think I should eliminate the rest before moving to the next phase?*"

Tyler chuckled. "The remaining heroes should pose no challenge to you now; there's no point in delaying. Once we hold the Hero Factory, the remaining pieces will fall into place."

"*Okay, do what you need to do. I will meet you at the rendezvous point once it's done.*"

Tyler pocketed the phone and drew in a deep breath through the open car window. The air outside the city limits smelled much fresher than the carbon dioxide infested inner city, and he relished moments like these when he could escape the urban jungle. Throughout his life, Tyler had been a spiritual man. He believed everything from the sun to the lowliest of insects as God's handiwork. To him, everything was infallible, except people. Sometimes people needed to be lead back to the path of righteousness, which was the primary reason for working with Pete on this project. The stories he had been told about the old days disturbed him in the beginning. Tyler didn't want anything to do with what he believed to be a cesspool of sin, but when Pete explained how the city had been run, it had piqued his interest. Cleansing this city of sin and corruption would allow them to move onto other cities, indoctrinating people on how to live better.

"Come, ye children, listen to me. I will teach you the fear of the lord," he whispered.

* * *

Mayor Stedson entered Brady's office and lowered himself into one of the oversized leather chairs. With a long, drawn-out sigh, he rubbed his left temple. "What the hell is going on in my city, Brady?"

Brady hadn't slept well over the past few days, and he looked the part. His bloodshot eyes told the story. He didn't even bother putting on a suit today, instead opting for a sweater and a pair of jeans. No reason to be formal today, not with all hell breaking loose in the city.

"Oracle is working tirelessly to find the people responsible, Mayor." Brady removed a manila folder and dropped it on the desk.

"What's that?" the mayor asked.

"Ares Protocol." Brady opened the folder, revealing a stack of papers. A picture of Oracle was located in the upper right corner of the page. To the left of the picture was his contact information as well as a detailed breakdown of his abilities, his past employment history and emergency contact names and addresses.

The mayor leaned over and scanned the document. "Ares Protocol?" he repeated.

Brady closed the folder. "It is a contingency plan in case an event proved too difficult for a single hero to handle. I won't bore you with the details, so I will summarize the essentials. Basically, if we encountered an event that became too difficult to handle with current resources, we would re-enlist all prior heroes who could still physically perform their required duties. For example, we would eliminate any heroes who have aged to the point they would become a hindrance more than an asset. Also eliminated would be those who had become infirm or handicapped for one reason or another. Fortunately for us, all heroes who had served with the Hero Factory are more than capable of handling re-enlistment."

"Those that are still alive, you mean," the mayor responded dryly.

Brady frowned. "Yes, of course."

The mayor tapped the folder with his index finger. "It sounds like a good plan. When are you planning on implementing it?"

"I already have," Brady replied. "Wendy and Donald are working on contacting the surviving heroes as we speak."

"What do you need from me?" the mayor asked.

"That's a good question. First I need you to contact Chief Stamper and ask him to place protective details on the homes of every hero."

"That will seriously inhibit the effectiveness of our current police force," the mayor argued.

"I understand that," Brady countered. "However, I believe the activation of all the remaining heroes will offset any loss of police force."

Mayor Harry Stedson begrudgingly nodded his head. "I suppose. Speaking of our police force, I'm afraid they came up empty on leads. Has Oracle located any suspects?"

Brady was careful with his response. He could not tell the mayor he suspected one of the Hero Factory's own. The city had to believe the Hero Factory was infallible; otherwise, the program could suffer serious setbacks.

"Oracle has identified some leads." Brady replied. "I'm afraid I have some bad news, however. Oracle encountered gang activity in the Ironbound section where a large group of criminals converted an abandoned factory on the corner of 7th and Park into their headquarters."

The mayor's eyes glazed over, and he rubbed his chin, deep in thought. "Are you sure they were gang members. Perhaps it was just a group of transients?"

Brady shook his head wearily. "I don't doubt Oracle's assessment and neither should you. I'm sure he is more than capable of telling the difference between the two."

"Point taken," the mayor replied. "I will notify Chief Stamper. Our police force is small and will be much smaller after the special details, but the budget gods have smiled upon us and left us a bit of extra money in the coffers. I will authorize the OT and make sure Oracle has the full support of the police."

Brady nodded. "Thank you, Mayor. The help will be appreciated."

"Just make sure you squash this thing before it gets out of control," he replied angrily. "The last thing I need is to be known as the mayor who let the city descend into chaos."

"You won't have to worry about that." Oracle strolled into the office with a handcuffed man in his late 60s with silver hair and goatee to match.

Brady stood when Oracle tossed him face first against the wall. "Who is this?"

Oracle smiled and clapped the handcuffed man on the shoulder. "This here is the ever-elusive Brian Buzzsaw Kelly, infamous leader of the Raging 86's. Long time no see, Buzzsaw?"

"That can't be possible," Brady gasped. "I thought he was dead!"

"Yeah well, life is a funny little bitch, ain't she?" Buzzsaw chuckled. Oracle smacked him in the back of the head.

"Shut your trap."

"How the hell has he eluded us all these years?" asked Harry.

Oracle produced a folded piece of paper and tossed it onto the desk. "Apparently our friend here has been holed up in that warehouse I mentioned. He must have been feeling nostalgic, because all these years, he has been a busy little worker bee rebuilding the old gang."

"Yeah, I missed our Tuesday night spaghetti dinners and our Friday night bingo sessions," Buzzsaw mocked.

The mayor turned to Brady. "I will send Chief Stamper over there with the entire force, if necessary. We will have that place cleaned out by tomorrow."

Oracle waved him off. "That won't be necessary."

"Why not?" asked Brady.

Oracle produced a small, cylindrical steel tube from his pocket. He placed it against. Buzzsaw's handcuffs and pushed a button located on the side. A thin red laser light exploded from it, landing on the center of the handcuffs. With a click they unlocked and fell to the ground. Buzzsaw flashed an evil grin.

"Because the police department's services will no longer be required." Oracle pocketed the cylinder and produced a dart, which Brady recognized immediately as one of Spidermancer's.

"What the hell is going on?" Brady exclaimed.

Oracle noticed Brady eyeballing the dart and chuckled. "Yeah, that's right. I grabbed a whole bunch of these right before I killed her."

With lightning speed, Oracle dashed across the room, wrapped his arm around the mayor's throat and plunged it deep into his jugular. The mayor's eyes widened with fear, and he raised his hands and tried to swat the dart away, but Oracle was too powerful. The mayor batted weakly at the dart and emitted a mewling sound, like an injured cat.

Brady rushed over to help, but Buzzsaw's fist smashed into his jaw. The sickening sound of crunching bone resonated through the room, and he dropped to the floor, barely clinging to consciousness.

The mayor ceased struggling and his eyes slid shut. Oracle released him and his body slumped to the floor. Slowly, he turned to Brady.

"The Hero Factory has been a blight to this city since its inception." Oracle gestured toward Brady. "You people have been running it like your personal profit center. This city has been pissing funds into your bank account for over thirty years while riding the backs of the people who actually do the grunt work. The Hero Factory is no better than the gangs. The only difference is you claim it as legitimate enterprise."

"It's a fucking shame is what it is," Buzzsaw drawled with contempt. "At least we rewarded the people who put in the work. They were all well-compensated; and, from what I recall, the murder rate was lower than it is now. Murders didn't happen without the bosses signing off on it." He crouched over Brady's prone form and sneered. "We only killed people if we had to. We served justice. Now you have people running around killing people for sport and pleasure. That's no way to run a city. You fucks don't give a shit about anyone but yourselves and your pockets."

Oracle leaned down and yanked the dart from the mayor's neck. Green ooze leaked from the tip of the dart and mixed with blood trickling from the wound. He looked down on the body with contempt. "Your mayor is dead. Crystal City is officially under new management."

Brady started regaining his senses. Fortunately for him, Buzzsaw's blow knocked him close to his desk. Years ago, for security purposes, he had a silent alarm mounted underneath. If pushed, it would alert the police, the hero on duty, and James, his head of security. While their focus was on the mayor's body, Brady crawled toward the button. He spat a bloody wad of phlegm onto the floor before reaching up and pushing the button. After pressing it, he fell backwards and hit the floor hard enough to draw attention of the two men in the room.

Oracle wandered around the desk and smiled when he spotted the silent alarm. "I'm afraid that's not going to help you very much."

James Stout entered the room with two security guards behind him. Each of them had their service 9MM Glock's out, which they quickly pointed at the two men. James eventually lowered his weapon and looked toward Brady. James shook his head slowly, and the look on his face sank Brady's heart faster than the Titanic.

"The fact you didn't know this was coming only proves Oracle was right about the whole thing."

"What about the cops?" Buzzsaw asked.

"Most of them are on board," replied James.

"What about Stamper?" Oracle asked.

James shook his head. Oracle sighed and stared at the floor, pondering his next move. After a few minutes of wrestling with his thoughts, he turned to Brady.

"I have good news and bad news for you, Brady. The bad news is you have been fired."

Brady looked at him with contempt. "Go to hell."

A pained expression crossed Oracle's face. "That stings, Brady. Does this mean we can't be friends anymore? If I thought you weren't my friend, I'm just not sure I could bear it." Oracle rifled through the compartments on his belt, taking inventory of Spidermancer's remaining darts. "Anyway, as I was saying, the good news is you get to live."

Buzzsaw laughed and folded his arms across his chest. "I'm not sure he wants to be your friend anymore, Oracle. Look at his face. He's mad at you, buddy."

Oracle did not laugh. Instead, he eyeballed Brady with the same pained expression. He slid an index finger slowly across his throat, signaling to Buzzsaw to cease his incessant laughing. Once he stopped, Oracle took a step towards Brady.

"This is not personal. This is business. You did well in the time you had, but now your time is up. It's our turn now. I'm letting you live, because I need someone to run this place."

"Why keep the Hero Factory?" Brady asked. "I'm sure you will run the city like a dictator. There will be no need for the Hero Factory."

Oracle chuckled. "Oh, Brady, why are you so cynical? The world will always need a hero, I simply want to keep my finger on the switch." He turned toward the window with his hands clasped behind his back. "You probably think I'm crazy and the old way of doing things was archaic. You would be correct, of course." He turned to James and his security team. "Go outside and make sure we remain undisturbed."

James nodded and left the room with the two security personnel in tow. Oracle returned his attention to Brady and continued.

"These are the reasons why I'm taking control of it all. Now, you're probably thinking one hero cannot control the eventual tidal wave of criminal elements sure to sweep in and wash away all that is good in this city. You fear the gangs will run wild, killing each other and putting innocents in harm's way. That's where you're wrong."

"No, you are wrong!" Brady contested. "The first chance they get, they will overpower you and take control for themselves! The city will be worse than ever before!"

Oracle's smile faded and his lips tightened into a thin white line. "That will not happen. There is something you don't know about me."

He leaned in closer. "Do you want to know how I was able to take out the other heroes so easily?

Brady turned away, ignoring the question. Oracle responded anyway. "It's because I am the only Class 5 in the history of the program."

"That's bullshit!" argued Brady. "We classified you at intake as Class 2."

At first Brady felt confident such a thing was impossible, but when Oracle's smug smile returned, he started doubting his belief. Never in the history of the program had they encountered a Class 5, but he would admit the classification itself remained an enigma to his research team. The team did not fully understand the scope of power contained within a Class 5 mutation. The more Brady considered it, the more he believed Oracle could be telling the truth. Oracle, if he was indeed a Class 5, could possess the power to manipulate the test itself, throwing off the measurements completely.

"I see by the look on your face that you are beginning to doubt the validity of your statement. Good. I didn't want to prove my point."

Oracle turned to Buzzsaw. "Head over to the police station and round everyone up. We will move on to Phase 2."

"Phase 2?" asked Brady.

Oracle rubbed his hands together eagerly. "Now comes the fun part!"

Darren Jones (Volt) and Brock Schutt (Vertex)

IHOP, corner of 17th Street and Main

Darren Jones had been a lineman for Crystal City Power and Light for decades, ever since his retirement from the Hero Program. The closest he came to danger since his retirement was a downed power line during the storm of '96. The department believed the juice had been cut off to that sector, but when he tried move the line from the road, 100,000 volts of electricity passed through his body. Normally, that would have been enough to deep fry any man. Luckily for him, he was not just any man and had brushed it off like it was nothing.

Brock Schutt, on the other hand, had been a personal trainer since his retirement in 2005. He enjoyed helping people improve themselves physically, as well as feeling better about themselves. His time at Shockey's Gym had been enjoyable and the closest he came to danger since his retirement was stepping on a stray Lego piece left behind by his six year old son. For the two men, however, the danger they currently faced was greater than anything they had ever encountered.

"Thanks for meeting me," Darren said.

A waitress approached them, notepad in hand, with a warm smile on her face. "What would you gentlemen like today?"

"Just coffee for me, thanks," Brock said.

"Eggs, sunny side up, with a side of bacon and rye toast," Darren said. "Oh, and a coffee, as well."

While she wrote the order down, Brock scanned the restaurant looking for the slightest sign of trouble. Both of them took off from work, and since it wasn't prime time, the place was nearly empty. Inside, only an elderly couple sat near the entrance. When she left, Brock scowled at Darren.

"Did you know that for every piece of bacon you eat, nine minutes is taken off your lifespan?"

Darren rolled his eyes. "Well then, my friend, according to my math, I should have died in 1732." He grabbed three sugar packets from a cup parked near the window and placed them in front of him. "We have more important matters than a couple clogged arteries to worry about."

Brock shrugged and rolled up his sleeves, revealing a snarling panther tattoo on his left arm and a hawk with outstretched talons on the right. "What did Illusionist say when he called you?"

"He told me Ares protocol had been initiated. It appears we need to watch each other's back. He said sticking together is top priority right now."

Brock nodded. "Yeah, he said the same thing to me. Have you spoken to Hex or Soulfire yet?"

"Hex has a meeting this morning, but she said she'll meet us here in forty minutes." Darren grabbed a sugar packet and fidgeted with the corner. "To be honest, I think Soulfire is a lost cause."

The waitress placed an empty coffee cup in front of each of them and filled them from a decanter. She placed the decanter on the table between them and smiled at Darren. "Your food should be right up, honey."

Darren returned the smile and watched her as she returned to the kitchen. He felt like he couldn't trust anyone these days.

"Lost cause?" Brock asked.

"Illusionist told me he wasn't on board. He despises the program, and his anger hasn't faded over time, unfortunately." Darren dumped the sugar packets into his coffee and sipped gingerly.

Brock scowled. "I never agreed with Brady's decision to can him." He poured two creamers into his coffee and took a sip. "Not one of the company's finest hours, I suppose."

"You're right about that." Darren took another sip and put his cup down but kept his hands wrapped around it as if seeking comfort only the warmth could provide. "I don't blame him, but we're going to need all hands on deck for this if everything Illusionist told us is true."

Brock swallowed some more coffee and set it aside as the waitress placed Darren's bacon and eggs in front of him. He glanced at the bacon and frowned. "Rough."

Darren was in the middle of unwrapping his silverware from their napkin cocoon but stopped. "Don't judge. I can't help it if you choose to live on tofu, bean sprouts and protein shakes. Honestly, if I had to eat that crap, I would kill myself."

"I'm telling you that shit will—" Brock stopped. His eyes locked on the front door.

Darren stopped unwrapping the silverware and turned around. Three men entered the restaurant. Although one was Hispanic, one was Asian, and one was black, that was where their difference ended. Each wore street clothes with a tiny skull tattoo under their left eye. Darren was a history aficionado in school and recognized the marks immediately. The tattoo represented membership in The Kings.

Brock recognized the tattoos as well. He remembered seeing them on several prisoners during tours he took with the warden. Brock also recognized the bulge coming from their waistbands. It wasn't from excitement of going out to eat. They were packing guns, and it was clear they were not out for an afternoon stroll. The Hispanic turned toward the two men and pointed in their direction. The others followed his gaze and they smiled in unison. They briefly chatted with each other before approaching.

Brock studied his surroundings. Unfortunately, the restaurant had become more packed over time. The elderly couple near the entrance was still present while another table filled up with a party of five dressed in suits. They sipped coffee and engaged in conversation, oblivious to the scene playing out before them. A mother and her teenage son sat at the counter munching on some pastries. To Brock, it all equated to too many people in the line of fire for his comfort. Darren turned toward Brock with a concerned look on his face. Apparently, he felt the same way.

The three men stopped at their table with their hands resting on their waistbands. "Listen to me, bro," said the Asian. "We can do this the easy way or the hard way."

"Don't be stupid, man," added the Hispanic. "You heroes don't want to get no innocents killed now, do ya?"

Darren turned to Brock. "I'm confused, what are we supposed to do Brock?" He folded his hands on the table. "Is there anything in the Superhero Guide for Dummies which could help with this situation?"

Brock smiled. "Listen, fellas. It's probably in your best interest to go back to whatever sewer you crawled from before you get yourself hurt. I'm afraid Medicare doesn't cover accidents incurred during a bout of stupidity."

"Man, fuck you!" The black guy roared and removed a .38 special from his waistband. The other men followed his lead, drawing their weapons.

Their waitress happened to come over to check on them and when she saw the weapons, she screamed. The fresh pot of coffee she carried fell to the floor with a crash. The noise brought the attention of the other customers, and that was when all hell broke loose. People panicked and in a blind frenzy, the five businessmen trampled one another as they rushed to the exit. The elderly couple stood and watched in shock, either unable or unwilling to move. The mother at the counter grabbed her child and ducked behind it. Amidst the chaos, Brock's smile never wavered. He knew this fight would end before it really began; the thugs just didn't know it yet.

The Hispanic man stood a foot away from Darren, which was all the distance he needed. He reached out and grabbed the guy's left wrist, the one not holding the gun. Before the guy could turn and point the weapon, 10,000 volts of electricity passed from Darren's body into his. The gun fell to the floor and the guy followed, flopping on the floor like a fish out of water.

While everyone's attention turned toward the flopper, the hawk tattoo on Brock's arm sprang to life. It detached itself from his arm with a wet, tearing sound and dove straight for the Asian man. The bird's talons extended before viciously clamping down on his throat. It happened so quickly that the man never had a chance to raise his weapon in defense. With a scream, he dropped it and flailed at his assailant. In his frenzy to get the bird off of him, he tripped over a chair and fell backwards, becoming nothing more than a pile of flailing limbs and bird wings. Brock stood, and the final man took a step back, the hand holding the weapon visibly shaking.

"Did you really think it'd be that easy?" asked Darren, stepping beside Brock.

"Um…b-b-but," the guy stuttered, quickly backing toward the kitchen area.

"I would have been very disappointed if it was that easy," a voice called from the entrance. Both men turned to see Oracle standing in the doorway.

"Oracle?" asked Brock. "You're late, but I think we got this."

"Well, Vertex, since I am the current hero on duty I feel I should at least make an effort here, right?"

The usage of his hero name unnerved Brock. It was normally customary for the current hero to call retired heroes by their real names. His unease increased when he noticed several of Spidermancer's darts strapped to Oracle's belt. When he glanced at Darren, he noticed the same look of concern pasted to his face.

"What are you doing with those?" Darren asked, pointing at the darts.

Oracle chuckled. "Mementos." He rolled up his sleeves to reveal a hawk tattoo on his right arm and a panther tattoo on his left, exact replicas of those on Brock's arm.

"What the hell?" Brock muttered, feeling an icy stab of dread creeping up his spine.

"I just got them," Oracle boasted. "Let me see if I can do this right."

Oracle looked at his left arm and narrowed his eyes. The panther tattoo snarled and tore free from the arm. As soon as it hit the floor it increased in size until it became the size of an actual panther. It turned its steel gaze toward the duo and snarled.

"What the hell?" Darren echoed.

In the corner, the Asian guy stopped struggling and fell still. The hawk turned its gaze toward its master and returned to Brock's arm. The third thug looked at the scenario unfolding in front of him and decided it wasn't worth whatever he was being paid. He tripped over a fallen chair in his rush toward the door and smacked his head on the door frame, knocking himself unconscious. Brock stepped over Asian and stood between the panther and Darren. He removed his shirt, revealing more tattoos.

"So you're the bastard who killed the others," Brock growled.

Oracle lowered his head in a mock bow. "Guilty as charged."

"But why?" asked Darren.

"Because they would have tried to stop me."

"Stop you from doing what?" Darren asked.

Oracle remained silent, and the panther lunged for Brock. Even though Darren had been out of action for years, his reflexes had not faded over time. Thousands of volts of electricity passed through the air like lightning bolts, striking the panther and knocking it into the kitchen. The crashing of the panther's body was followed by a scream and the cook ran out, pale as a ghost. He looked around the room, noticed the carnage, and vanished out the front door.

Brock used the distraction to spring into action. The largest tattoo on his chest, a skeletal reaper draped in black, leapt from his body. It grew to a height of seven feet and retrieved a three-foot scythe from within the folds of its robe. It swung the weapon violently, causing Oracle to leap to the right to dodge the blow, which only missed its mark by inches. The panther emerged from the kitchen, snarling with hatred in its eyes, and turned its gaze on Darren.

"I guess I'll be animal control," Darren said to Brock. "You keep Oracle busy."

Brock nodded and advanced on Oracle. Lightning shot from Darren's fingertips, which caused the panther to retreat into the kitchen. Darren chased it inside, leaving Brock outside with Oracle.

The reaper readied another blow, but the hawk tore free from Oracle's arm and attacked. The reaper flailed wildly at its newest adversary and clipped a wing, however the bird refused to let up on its ferocious assault. The curved blade swung through the air for a follow-up attack, but the bird grabbed it in its talons and flew off. The apparition turned its empty eye sockets toward the fleeing bird and shook its fist in fury. Oracle used the distraction to recover his senses. He pulled a modified .40 caliber pistol from its holster and fired multiple times with deadly precision, hitting the reaper in the chest with every shot. The reaper twitched with each shot until it collapsed in a cloud of black smoke. Brock cried out from the psychic bond he shared with the tattoo and fell to one knee. The reaper tattoo returned on his chest and Brock placed his hand over it. Although there was no physical damage to Brock, the psychic pain was real.

Oracle calmly approached Brock and placed both hands on his face, one on each side, like a lover's embrace. "I wish it didn't have to be this way, Vertex. I originally dreamed of running this city with each of you by my side, as I created our utopian paradise. Just think of it... no crime, no corruption and no need for money. Everyone helping everyone else, like civilized society should be."

Brock coughed and struggled to catch his breath. "And you think this is the way to do it? What makes you so special? What makes you God?"

"The Hero Factory made me God," Oracle said with a chuckle and pressed tighter on his face.

With a flash of light and crackle of energy, several thousand volts of electricity rocketed through Brock's skull. His screams echoed off the walls of the restaurant and became louder as Oracle increased the voltage. Soon the odor of burnt hair and flesh filled Oracle's nostrils which caused him to gag, but he never let up. He continued pumping electricity into his victim until nothing more than a blackened skull stared back at him.

As Oracle pumped electricity into his foe, a sudden sharp pain shot through his arm, and he looked down to see the panther had returned to its place. He let go of Brock and looked toward the kitchen. Darren stood in the kitchen doorway, smoke drifting from his fingertips. His jaw hung open with dawning horror as he looked upon the corpse of his fallen comrade.

"You killed him, you son of a bitch!" he roared. Electricity arced from his fingertips toward Oracle.

The blast caught Oracle on the shoulder, and he shrieked in pain. He fell into a nearby table, knocking it over and sending several water glasses crashing to the floor. Darren advanced on him with rage burning in his eyes. Holding his hands six inches apart, he allowed electricity to build up between them, forming a ball roughly the size of a softball. The ball increased in size until it became the size of a soccer ball. With the intention of blasting Oracle with the ball, he circled the fallen table toward the prone form of his adversary. Before he could toss the ball of certain death forming between his fingertips, a shot echoed through the restaurant, and it felt like Darren had been hit in the back with a sledgehammer. He looked down at blood pouring from a ragged hole in his chest. Slowly, and in extreme pain, he struggled to turn and face his newest adversary. Brian Kelly stood by the entrance, clutching a shotgun with smoke trickling from the barrel.

"It seems you heroes aren't as tough as I thought."

Darren fell to his knees and the electric orb fizzled out. Oracle recovered and approached him, clutching his smoldering shoulder. Limping from his previous encounter with Twilight Shadow and holding his now wounded shoulder, he stared at his fallen adversary with hatred in his eyes. He placed the barrel of his weapon against Darren's temple, but instead of pulling the trigger, he looked at Brian.

"Make no mistake, Buzzsaw, just because you shot a man in the back doesn't make him any less tough. It only makes you look like a coward."

The smile melted from Brian's face. "What did you say to me?"

Oracle pulled the trigger, blowing half of Darren's face off. The viciousness with which Oracle pulled the trigger startled Brian. His eyes widened and he took a step back. Oracle pointed the gun at him and narrowed his eyes.

"I said your actions make you look like a coward. Don't ever interrupt me during a battle again."

Brian frowned. "He was about to fry your ass. I just saved your life, you ungrateful son of a bitch!"

Oracle holstered his weapon and shook his head. "No. The only thing you did was cast doubt on whether or not I was strong enough to defeat both of them."

Brian tapped the shotgun against his leg nervously. "You're crazy, you know that?"

"Am I?" Oracle scratched his chin. "Maybe it's society that's crazy. Maybe I'm the only sane one in this fucked up world."

As Oracle strolled through the restaurant toward the exit, he passed a waitress cowering inside a booth. He stopped and looked down at her.

"Please don't kill me," she whimpered.

His scowl faded. "I'm not going to kill you. I'm trying to save you."

Oracle left the restaurant, leaving Brian alone surrounded by Darren's blood. Long after Oracle left, Brian continued to stare at the empty doorway.

Brian reloaded the shotgun and sighed. "This guy will be the death of me."

To The Gates of Hell

Terry rang the doorbell again and tapped his foot on the porch impatiently. After a minute passed, he rapped on the door, but a minute passed with no answer. Finally, he banged on the door.

No answer.

Terry's watch read 10:15 AM. Bryan's car sat in the driveway, so Terry concluded he was either in the shower or passed out drunk. He hadn't spoken to his friend in a while and became concerned for his welfare which had been the reason for his visit. Terry worried Bryan would drink himself to death if he continued spiraling into depression.

Terry turned the doorknob, and found it only mildly surprising that it was unlocked. Bryan rarely locked the door because, according to his words, he had nothing left to steal. Terry opened the door and stepped inside. Despite the morning sun, the inside of the house stood dark and gloomy. Every curtain had been closed and every shade drawn while several dirty dishes sat abandoned in the kitchen sink. Empty takeout containers had been piled into the garbage can until the bag threatened to burst. The eerie silence of the house bothered Terry, and the first thing he thought was that Bryan's depression had overwhelmed him and he had killed himself.

"Bryan?" Terry called out.

When no one responded, he focused and listened for anything such as the shower running, sounds from a radio or even a TV set running to give him some hope nothing more ominous had happened. When nothing but silence responded, he called out again.

"Bryan?"

When he received no response, Terry stepped into the living room and peered into the darkness. Once his eyes adjusted to the gloom, he stumbled toward the sofa to see if Bryan had passed out on it. Bryan normally passed out on the sofa when he was so drunk he found himself unable to climb stairs. When Terry noticed the sofa was empty, he returned to the hall. Before he could head up the stairs, he was stopped by a voice.

"Well, this is disappointing."

Terry stiffened and turned toward the voice. A shadowy outline sat in the recliner next to the window. Despite a trickle of light floating in from the side of the curtains, Terry could not see the man's face.

"Bryan?"

"Nope, I'm afraid not. I believe our mutual friend took a walk or something. When I arrived, he wasn't here, so I took the liberty of grabbing a seat in the hope he would return soon. I assumed he had fallen so far down the rabbit hole of despair that no one would come visiting him. Unfortunately, I had miscalculated."

"Who are you?" asked Terry.

The man switched on a nearby table lamp, bathing his face in soft white light. Terry recognized him immediately and relaxed.

"Oracle? What are you doing here?" When his eyes fell on the gun in Oracle's hand, his body went rigid once again.

When Oracle saw Terry eyeballing his weapon, he quickly holstered it. "I apologize, I didn't mean to scare you or anything. I came here to warn Soulfire."

Terry cocked an eyebrow. "Warn him? By pointing a gun at him?"

Oracle rose from the seat and smiled. "I'm sure you heard what happened." When Terry stared at him mutely, he clarified his statement. "The hero deaths?"

"Oh yeah, right," Terry nodded.

"I came here to tell Soulfire he is next on the list." Oracle reached down and opened a compartment on his belt. From the compartment, he produced a dart. "The rumor is, this person has been viciously hunting down and murdering the heroes to fulfill some kind of mission. This person believes the Hero Factory has been compromised by forces who mean to do the city harm. Already there are doubts cast upon the Hero Program."

Terry folded his arms across his chest. "That's pretty hard to believe. How do you know all of this?"

Oracle cradled the dart in his hands and rubbed the tip along the edge of his index finger. He stroked it gently, as one would do with a pet. "I know this because the person hunting these people is me."

Terry's eyes widened. "What the f—"

Before Terry could finish the sentence, Oracle whipped the dart across the room, and it landed in Terry's neck with pinpoint accuracy. The tip penetrated the jugular and injected its poison into Terry's bloodstream. The venom inside the dart formerly belonged to a blue krait, a venomous snake native to Southeast Asia. Their venom is toxic, even more so than that of a cobra. Krait venom is neurotoxic and attacks the human nervous system, shutting it down. Death usually occurs twelve to twenty-four hours after a bite, if not treated. Terry Lincoln had just been injected directly into his jugular vein, which would carry the venom throughout his circulatory system quicker than a bite in a location such as a hand or foot. Even if krait anti-venom had been sitting on the shelf next to him, his chances for survival would have been 50/50. None of the three major hospitals in Crystal City carried krait anti-venom, which meant the only way to provide Terry with the antidote he required would be to fly some in from the nearest hospital. Currently, the closest hospital was over four hundred miles away. Terry Lincoln's chance of survival calculated at zero.

The venom began to take effect. Terry's muscles locked and he fell to the floor. He lost all ability to speak as the toxin attacked his diaphragm and worked its way to his heart. Oracle leaned over and watched Terry struggle to breathe. His eyes, filled with fear, soon turned glassy.

"You don't have much longer to live and you're probably wondering why I'm doing this." Oracle paused a moment to choose his next words carefully. "I'm not the bad guy here, Terry. I may appear to be at the moment; but, as time passes, people will look back on history and understand that what I'm doing was necessary. My actions, in time, will prove to be justified."

Terry ceased struggling and fell still. Oracle placed his hand across Terry's eyes and gently closed the lids.

"Unfortunately, you were at the wrong place at the wrong time," he lamented. As he straddled the corpse, he continued to address him. "But, as they say, in order to have peace you need to start a war. It's time to start a war, Terry."

* * *

Bryan exited the grocery store with a bag filled with a six-pack of Pepsi, a pound of boiled ham and a loaf of rye bread. The Hero Program paid all heroes a salary upon retirement, but since he had been removed involuntarily, they had agreed on half the normal amount, so he tried to stretch the little amount of money he had. When he left the house earlier, he decided it might be prudent to put something into his system that wasn't alcohol. So cheap, boiled ham it would be. By the time he reached his front door, he felt better, physically and emotionally. The brisk walk in the crisp morning air allowed his body to detox from all the hours spent inside the smoky confines of seedy taverns. He carried the groceries into the kitchen and laid them on the counter.

When he stepped from the kitchen, a shadow from the living room caught his attention. Bryan froze when he saw the shadow standing in the center of his living room. It seemed to be the tallest figure he had ever seen. The shadowy outline of the person's head stood only a foot below the ceiling fan, which, by Bryan's calculations, made the person roughly eight feet tall. Within the gloomy confines of the room,

Bryan's hand fumbled along the wall for the light switch. When his fingers located the switch, he flipped it on and formed a defensive posture. When the room lit up and revealed the figure, his eyes widened, his throat clenched and all strength seemed to ebb from him. When he regained control of his throat, he uttered a blood-curdling scream.

"*Noooooooo!*"

Terry hung from the ceiling fan with a bright yellow nylon cord wrapped tightly around his throat. Bryan rushed into the living room, grabbed his friend from around the waist and lifted him, easing the pressure around the neck. When he saw the color of Terry's face, Bryan knew he was too late. His face was discolored but not like someone who had been hung. Instead of a bluish hue, the skin tone was yellowed, almost orange. Bryan spotted a peculiar puncture wound in Terry's neck.

Bryan grabbed a butcher knife from the kitchen and cut him down. When his limp body fell to the ground, Bryan noticed a note pinned to his chest with a dart. Bryan put two and two together, assuming the dart was the cause of the puncture wound. He pulled the dart out and examined it. When he recognized it as Spidermancer's, he knew his friend had been poisoned. In a rage he threw it against the wall where the glass vial shattered. Bryan snatched the note and read it.

If it makes you feel any better, it was supposed to be you hanging here. For now, let's consider your friend collateral damage. You are probably asking yourself why. I have done cruel things up to this point and take no pleasure from what I have done. Sometimes in life, drastic measures are necessary. Implementing change in this city requires more than a scalpel. For change to happen in this city, it will require a sledgehammer. I am the sledgehammer, Soulfire. This city is not a cocoon from which a beautiful butterfly will emerge. It is a molten piece of metal which requires force and pressure before it becomes a magnificent blade. I will no longer bother looking for you, because I'm sure you will come for me. Just so you know, I will be waiting.

   -Oracle

Bryan read the name at the bottom of the note again. *And again.* He must have read it twenty times before the words sunk in. Not because he was a stupid man, but because he had a difficult time suspending his disbelief. He read the name one more time, grit his teeth and clenched his fist, crushing the paper underneath.

"Oracle," he hissed. He laid his hand upon his friend's forehead and ground his teeth until he feared they would fall out of his mouth.

"*ORACLE!*"

Bryan raised his head and howled the word like a werewolf would howl at the moon.

"*ORACLE!*" he howled again.

Soon, the paper began smoldering. His rage blanketed him, and he wrapped himself in its embrace. Everything around him turned red. When he shut his eyes, instead of blackness he saw dark red, the color of blood. Bryan stood in the hall, seething, as the color ebbed and flowed from his consciousness; and, when he opened his eyes, he was not surprised to see he was on fire. His clothes burned to ash and fell at his feet. The flames consumed his body and licked hungrily at the walls, seeking fuel for its rage. The flames snaked toward Terry's body as his rage grew, eventually consuming the corpse in its furor. Bryan no longer cared; Terry was gone, and he was the only thing connecting him to his former life. As the flames consumed his home, fury consumed Bryan Whittaker. When he stepped from his fully engulfed home, he was no longer Bryan Whittaker. Terry had died, and Bryan died along with him.

The foundation of his home burned, and his soul burned with it. Soulfire's thirst for vengeance would not be quenched until all who had been responsible for Terry's death paid for what they had done.

The Prisoner

The guard smiled at Tyler as he approached the processing desk. He returned the smile, knowing this would be the last day he walked these halls.

"Today's the day!" the guard exclaimed. He seemed to be more excited than Tyler.

Normally Tyler's smiles were forced, chewing back his hatred for this place as best he could. Today the smile was genuine. "Yes it is, Vince. God bless the criminal justice system as well as the parole board."

Vince shrugged. "I suppose so. What I do know is that you are one dedicated son of a bitch. To come visit him regularly for all those years; that, my friend, is loyalty."

"It was the least I could do. God gave me the strength, patience and determination to see Pete's punishment through to the end."

"Give me a minute to locate his personal property." The guard lifted himself out of the chair and entered the storage area behind the desk.

While the guard retrieved the property, Pete "Shorty" Williams exited the prison area escorted by another guard. Replacing the standard issue orange jumpsuit was a tweed sport jacket, T-shirt and jeans accompanied by a pair of beaten leather shoes. It was the first time Tyler had seen his uncle in something other than prison clothes. Tyler looked his uncle up and down before cocking an eyebrow and grinning mischievously.

"Don't judge me. There wasn't exactly a big choice in clothing around here," Pete scolded.

Tyler crossed the room and embraced him. "It's good to see you free."

Pete accepted the embraced and clapped him briskly on the back. "I had a lot of time to think in the joint." He held Tyler out at arm's length. "I had a lot of time to plan for this day and for the future."

"Here you go, Tyler." Vince slid a shoe box across the counter. He dropped a clipboard next to it and pointed at the bottom of the paper. "I just need you to sign here."

Inside the box sat two cigars, a matchbook, a wallet and a notepad. Pete removed everything carefully and turned them over in his hands, relishing each item. He placed each item in his pocket with the exception of cigars and matchbook.

"I had a lot of years to think about a lot of things. One of them was mortality." Pete thrust the items in Tyler's direction. "These things will kill you. Did you ever take up the habit?"

Tyler shook his head. "I never took up the habit."

Pete shrugged and placed them on the counter. "How about you, Vince?"

The guard shrugged. "Occasionally, when my wife lets me," he winked.

Pete chuckled and returned the wink. "They're yours."

Vince grabbed them and shoved them into his pocket. "Thanks, Pete. I wish you luck out there and I better not see you back in here, okay?"

Pete's eyes went dark but his smile remained. "I promise you I will not be back in this place." He turned to Tyler. "Let's get out of here."

Tyler led Pete toward a black Cadillac Escalade with tinted windows parked in one of the visitor spots. Tyler opened the rear passenger side door and motioned inside.

"Kids in the joint talked about these cars, but I haven't seen one personally." Pete ran his hand across the hood of the vehicle. "You did good, kid. I like your style." He smiled and hopped in.

Tyler closed the door and jumped into the driver seat. With a squeal of the tires, he guided the vehicle out of the prison parking area and onto the interstate.

Pete turned to the man seated next to him. "Vince's shift ends in four hours. That should give you enough time, correct?"

"More than enough," Oracle replied. "The incapacitating agent inside the cigars was released as soon as we pulled out of the parking lot."

"The guards won't be able to tell?" Pete rolled down the window and drew in a deep breath of fresh air. He closed the window and glanced at Oracle. "It won't explode or stink to high hell and fuck the entire plan up, right?"

Oracle shook his head. "No. It leaks too slowly from the cigar casing to be noticed, that's why it's important Vince sticks around inside the prison for a while. From what Tyler told me, he makes his rounds to and from the guard's break area pretty frequently. I will come back in four hours. At that time I will remove any guards not incapacitated by the chemical agent."

"And the Hero Factory?" Pete asked.

"Neutralized."

"What about the remaining heroes?" Pete pressed.

Oracle sighed. "I ran into a problem with Soulfire."

Pete tensed. "What kind of problem?"

"He wasn't home." Oracle turned to Pete and his face twisted sourly. "I had to leave a message."

Pete decided to not press the issue. The eerie look which had come over Oracle made him uncomfortable, and Pete hoped his trust in the man wasn't misplaced. Tyler assured him Oracle was on board with the mission, and Pete needed to trust his judgement.

"What about Brady? I would be disappointed if you had to eliminate him, but I'd understand, considering the circumstances.'

Oracle shook his head. "Well, you're in luck. I didn't have to eliminate him. He wasn't happy about the way things turned out, but he chose his life over resistance."

"Do you think he'll try any shenanigans?"

Oracle shook his head. "Don't worry, he'll play ball. I didn't leave him a choice."

"What about the staff?"

Oracle removed a folded piece of paper from his pocket and straightened it out. "This is the staff directory. Donald Runnels and the research team are on board. The security team is ours. The sourcing and projects team is mostly on board but I had to eliminate four of them." Pete pinched his face disapprovingly and Oracle shrugged. "Cost of doing business," he explained and tapped the paper. "Want to hear the rest?"

"Only if they will prove useful," Pete grumbled.

Oracle slid his finger down the paper as he browsed the names on the list. "Wendy Markus is missing. She is the lead scientist for the Hero Program and is extremely useful. I'm working on tracking her down. As for the others on this list, if they aren't on board they can easily be replaced." He folded the paper and shoved it into his pocket.

"What about the police?"

"Stamper proved to be more stubborn than originally thought. Even when shown the futility of his situation without the support of the Hero Factory, he still clung to his ideals."

"An idealist," Pete chuckled. "It's hard to find in today's age, but we have ways of dealing with those too. Where is he now?"

Oracle laughed. "Experiencing what it's like to be locked up in his own jail."

Pete removed the notepad from his jacket pocket. Tucked inside was a pen which he removed before he started writing. "There are ways to appeal to certain types of people without getting blood on your hands. Stamper sounds like a good man. We need good men." He finished writing and tore the page off, handing it to Oracle. "I wrote a number on that paper. Take that to him, and see if the number appeals to his ideals."

"You're going to bribe him?" Oracle asked incredulously.

Pete tucked the notepad inside his jacket. "Tell him we will buy him a newer, bigger, more modern police station. We will double his budget."

"Wait a minute, I thought we were taking the police out of the equation?"

"No. I plan on owning the police. If Stamper accepts my offer, he is in my debt." Pete recognized the doubtful look on Oracle's face and laid his hand upon his knee. "Oracle, an indebted man is more valuable than a dead one."

"I prefer our opposition eliminated, not coddled," Oracle grumbled.

"That is where you and I differ," Pete offered with a smile. "And this is how we counterbalance each other. I can turn to you when someone needs killing, and you can turn to me when we require a more diplomatic approach." He leaned in and lowered his voice. "Don't forget what we are working so hard to accomplish here. Always keep your eye on the prize."

Oracle nodded. "We're almost there. I just need to tie up a few loose ends."

"I assume you mean the others. From what Tyler said, it seems Soulfire may prove to be troublesome."

"It's nothing I can't handle," Oracle countered.

"The Hero Factory really messed up with that one," Tyler said as his reflection stared back at them from the rearview mirror. "I warned Donald not to mess with the serum. I nearly killed him when I discovered it."

"It's a good thing you didn't," Pete said. "We will need him if we are to complete the mission."

Oracle looked at his watch. "I'll return to the prison in four hours and clear out any stragglers." He turned to Tyler. "Make sure your men are ready. Some of the prisoners may not be receptive to our message so I may be forced to neutralize them."

"They'll be ready."

The car slowed as they approached the visitor's parking lot of the Hero Factory. Oracle checked the compartments on his belt. He frowned at how little remained of Spidermancer's darts.

"What's wrong?" Pete looked concerned.

"Nothing. It's just... it's just that I used up most of Spidermancer's arsenal."

Pete grabbed Oracle's arm and lifted the sleeve, revealing the hawk tattoo. He traced the tattoo with his index finger. "Soon you won't need them. It seems your powers are growing."

Oracle slid the sleeve down. "Brady is not aware of my real abilities."

Pete caressed Oracle's cheek. "This is what makes you special, Sam. If the Hero Factory knew who you were, you never would have been able to infiltrate their ranks. We can't do this without you." Pete saw the pain in his eyes and winced. "I'm sorry I had to give up on you all those years ago. It was for your own protection."

"You could have at least made an attempt to contact me. I could have kept them in the dark." Oracle looked down at the floor.

"It was for your own good. The world wasn't ready for you then. The city had their manufactured mutants, they weren't ready for a natural. If they knew what we knew, things would have turned out differently, just not for the best. They would have taken you, poked and prodded and perhaps even gone so far as to cut you open, just to find out what made you tick. I couldn't let that happen."

"Yeah, I guess," Oracle relented. "The mutagenic compound worked better than we ever imagined."

Pete smiled. "Yes it did."

The car stopped at the entrance to the Hero Factory. Tyler exited the vehicle and opened the rear door. Pete stepped out of the car and turned to Oracle.

"Always remember who you are. This city needs you now more than ever."

Tyler hopped in the driver seat and fastened his seat belt. He turned around and glanced at Oracle. "Ready when you are."

Pete moved to close the door but Oracle stopped him. He paused and fumbled for the right words to say. He had waited years to finally say what needed to be said, but he always struggled when it came to dealing with his emotions. After wrestling with his jumbled thoughts for a while, he just blurted it out.

"It's good to see you again, Dad."

Chase Stinson (The Illusionist)

Chase placed the plate of bacon and eggs on the table and sat to eat. He held a forkful of egg to his lips when a knock came from the door. Recent events had created tension in the city, and people became more cautious, locking their doors and peeping through windows at strangers when they passed. Not him, however, because he was too old to start worrying about impending doom now.

"Come in," he called out.

The door opened and a naked Bryan Whittaker entered. He shut the door and scanned the apartment sheepishly. When he felt Chase's eyes boring into him he blushed, and tried his best to cover up his more sensitive areas.

"I'm sorry. I didn't know where else to turn."

A wry grin formed on Chase's lips. "You're welcome to come in, but I have to warn you. Even though I've been single for years, I would much rather spend my free time in the company of a naked female."

Bryan, shivering from the cool weather outside, huddled in a corner. "You wouldn't happen to have some extra clothes lying around, would you?"

"Oh yeah." Chase eyeballed him before retreating to the bedroom and coming back with an old sweatshirt and a pair of faded jeans. "These were loose on me but should fit you."

Bryan dressed himself and took a seat at the kitchen table. He ran his fingers through his hair, trying to straighten it as best as he could.

"Sorry to barge in on you like this, but I had to go to someone." He took a deep breath and worked on regaining his composure. Just the mention of what had happened at his home brought tears to his eyes. "I came home to find my friend dead, along with a note. The note was from Oracle." Bryan looked down at the table and rubbed his hands together angrily. "He killed Terry and I'm looking to return the favor." His gaze moved from his fists to Chase's eyes. "Do you know where I can find him?"

Chase slid the plate of food aside and took a seat at the table. His eyes filled with sympathy when addressing Bryan. "I'm sorry to hear about your friend. Oracle seems to be responsible for a lot these days." Chase paused when he saw the expression on Bryan's face. "Judging by the lack of surprise on your face, you already know this."

"I know he's responsible for the deaths of the other heroes."

Chase nodded slowly. "Yeah, but that's not all."

When Bryan narrowed his eyes and cocked his head with concern, Chase tightened his lips and shook his head slowly.

"You don't know, do you?"

Bryan cocked his head inquisitively. "Know what?"

For a minute Chase said nothing, instead choosing to remain silent while studying Bryan, who squirmed under the stare. After a moment passed, Chase ceased staring daggers into Bryan's soul and turned his attention to the hall.

"You can come out now," Chase said. "I think our friend is telling us the truth. Either that or he is equipping the best poker face in the world."

Two women emerged from the room. One was Wendy Markus. The other was a red-headed, slimly built middle-aged woman with her hair tied back and a baseball cap pulled low over her forehead. Despite her attempts to conceal her appearance, Bryan recognized her immediately.

"Hex?"

"Hello, Soulfire. It's been a long time," she replied

"I thought you were dead!" Bryan exclaimed.

"She would have been, had she showed up to her scheduled meeting," Chase grumbled.

Bryan turned his attention to Wendy. Her long black hair draped haphazardly across her shoulders. She wore yoga pants with a spaghetti strap shirt and looked as if she had just woken up.

"Hello, Wendy. It's good to see you again."

Wendy smiled. Despite her unkempt appearance, she was still attractive and her smile improved on her beauty. She took a seat at the table, next to Chase.

"It's good to see you too. I'm glad to see the rumors weren't true."

"Rumors?" asked Bryan.

Wendy shifted uncomfortably in the chair. "Rumors had spread you were somehow involved in the murder of the others."

Bryan looked down, diverting his gaze so he didn't have to look her in the eyes when he said what needed to be said. "Honestly, I don't care about rumors. I didn't give a shit what happened with the Hero Factory, any of its heroes or this city. When I was kicked out of the Hero Program, I crawled down the bottom of a liquor bottle and called it home."

Wendy reached across the table and placed her hand on his wrist. "I overheard from the hall what you said earlier about revenge against Oracle. It's much bigger than him now. The Hero Factory has been compromised. Oracle is in the process of rallying former gang leaders to his cause. He infiltrated both the ranks of the Hero Factory, as well as the police force. With each new addition to his forces, his strength grows every day."

Bryan's eyes widened. "Why would he do that? What's his end game?"

Wendy shook her head. "I don't know. I took off as soon as I saw what was happening. Most of the staff sided with Oracle either because they believed in his cause or out of fear for their safety. If I didn't leave when I did, I would be dead. Just like the mayor."

"We know you want revenge against Oracle," added Hex. "You are one of the most powerful heroes to emerge from the Hero Program.

Illusionist convinced us we should help you stop Oracle and prevent this city from descending into madness."

Bryan frowned and shook his head. "I'm no hero. I'm not looking to save a city; I'm looking for vengeance."

"Then why are you here?" asked Chase.

"I told you; I need your help finding Oracle."

"Let us help you then," Wendy interrupted. "Once Oracle is defeated, we can take back the Hero Factory and stop this war before it begins."

"But you are heroes," Bryan argued. "I'm no hero. I'm just an old, washed up drunk looking out for his own self-interests."

Wendy removed her hand and glared at him. "Oh, really?" She touched her finger to her index finger, counting as she spoke. "Three months into your service a woman was beaten, raped and nearly dead. The only reason she survived is because you stopped her attacker and performed CPR until paramedics arrived. One month later, seven hostages were rescued, unharmed, from a hostage standoff during a bank robbery. There is more I could list from your term, but I think I prove my point."

"That man is gone," Bryan grumbled, trying to avoid her gaze but failing miserably.

Wendy and Chase exchanged glances. Chase nodded slowly and she ran her hands over her face with a sigh and let her breath run slowly between her clenched teeth. Hex frowned and shrugged with resignation. Wendy turned slowly to the kitchen window and stared outside. Without looking at Bryan, she continued.

"Once upon a time, long ago, I heard a story. It must have been about four years ago when I heard it, but I'm not quite sure because sometimes I have a hard time remembering what I did the previous day as age catches up to me," she coughed, cleared her throat and continued. "The story was about a man who rushed into a burning building and rescued a woman along with her two infant children, despite warnings that the building was found to be unstable and ready to collapse at any moment. If I remember all the details correctly, I believe this guy even saved the family dog." She turned and stared icily at Bryan. "Can you believe that? A guy ran into a burning building, despite the danger to himself, and saved a family *plus* the family pet. Can you believe the stupidity of this guy? I mean, what the hell was he thinking?" She turned and focused once again on the landscape beyond the window. "Oh wait, now I remember! The guy was a fireman, so technically he was being paid to run into burning buildings, but I guess that's not really important. A job is a job, right?"

Wendy lifted an index finger into the air, as if an amazing idea just sprung on her. "Ah, yes! Now that I remember the details, this guy's commander even chewed his ass out when he exited the building." She turned once again to face Bryan, with a mock look of surprise on her face. "What kind of man would defy his own boss to do something so stupid? So *heroic*?"

"I'm beginning to pick up your sarcasm," Bryan muttered.

"Good, because I'm really laying it on kind of thick," replied Wendy. She snapped her fingers, as if another idea had just been revealed. "This guy could be categorized as a hero. Heroes do these kinds of things!"

"What's your point?" Bryan grumbled.

"My point is this: that fireman didn't undergo any type of radical gene mutation to *become* a hero. He didn't come with abilities like super strength, x-ray vision or the ability to fly. He wasn't bulletproof or fireproof. Fire could actually kill this person. This poor man was just your average Joe, risking his life to do what he loved." Wendy's eyes narrowed angrily, and she approached Bryan and poked him in the chest, right above the heart "This man did what he felt was right. That is who *you* are. You were a hero before you ever stepped foot inside the Hero Factory. Don't sit there and tell me some bullshit story about how that man is gone. He's sitting right here and I know he will do what's right."

Bryan drew a deep breath and looked down, this time ashamed to meet her gaze. He knew she was right. Darker times forced him to seek the shelter of booze, tucked away in shadowy corners of smoke-filled taverns. He knew, even then, that no matter how much liquor he poured down his throat, he would never wash away what he truly was, nor would it ever erase the pain that threatened to consume him.

"Nice speech," he looked down at the table. "My wife used to nag me like that. Anytime I'd come home from a really bad call, she'd be there to pick me up and tell me how bullheaded I was for going with my gut instead of logic."

"Does that mean you're with us?" Wendy asked.

"I'm not against you, which I suppose is a good start."

"I guess we'll have to take it," Chase said.

"So what's your plan?" Bryan asked.

"We're outnumbered," Hex admitted. "Oracle is amassing an army. The first thing we need to do is gather those who are against him."

"Leave that to me," Chase replied and glanced at Wendy. "Do you think you can get inside the Hero Factory?"

Wendy rubbed her chin thoughtfully. "I can sneak in during the off hours when staff is minimal. With that said, I'm sure Oracle will have a fully armed security detail posted twenty-four hours a day."

"I'll go with her and take some of the heat off," Hex volunteered.

"I'll go too," Bryan added.

Chase stopped him. "Wait. I could use your assistance elsewhere."

"I want Oracle," Bryan argued. "His ass is mine and I won't rest until I'm standing over his corpse."

Chase frowned. "Oracle won't be at the Hero Factory; his focus will be elsewhere." He moved to the kitchen and removed a small note-book from a drawer. "I've been keeping tabs on several people since my retirement, but one in particular is a person by the name of Tyler McDermott. That name won't mean anything to you guys, but I had my reasons for keeping a close eye on him. Since my retirement, I've been keeping tabs on the family members of Pete "Shorty" Williams, the mastermind behind the unification of the gangs back in the seventies. I was the one responsible for apprehending him and his eventual incarceration. Call it a hunch, but I had this nagging suspicion that someone in his family would attempt to pick up where he had left off."

"So who's this dude and what does he have to do with anything?" Bryan asked.

"Tyler is Pete's cousin. For years he has been making regularly scheduled stops at the prison to visit his cousin."

"That's not out of the ordinary," Hex countered.

Chase smiled. "No, it's not. What's out of the ordinary is where Tyler would go after these visits. Like clockwork, he would visit an abandoned warehouse on the corner of Gillette and Fifth. One day I tailed him inside."

"And what did you find?" Wendy asked.

"An army," he replied grimly. "At least a hundred, well-armed gang members to be exact."

"You can't be serious!" Hex gasped.

"Jesus Christ," Bryan uttered softly. "All this time, they were right under our noses, gathering numbers, while waiting for the right time to strike."

"And now Oracle controls the Hero Factory as well as the city government, which means his army will continue to grow, unchallenged."

"Except by us," Hex offered with a weak smile. "Three heroes, along with one scientist, will save the world. Hopefully God will be looking out for us."

Bryan frowned and turned his gaze to the floor. He slowly clasped his hands together in front of his body. For a long time he sat, head bowed, staring mutely at the table. After several minutes had passed, Wendy broke the silence.

"Bryan, what's wrong?"

Bryan lifted his head and the pained look in his eyes made her wince. "I was thinking of my wife and child along with all the people who had died at City Hall and..." he trailed off.

"What is it?" Hex pressed.

Bryan rubbed his temple. "I guess your mention of God got me thinking. For a long time I have been wallowing in a quagmire of depression and self-loathing. Sometimes I lay awake at night questioning if there even is a God. What kind of God would allow my wife and child to die like they did? What kind of God would allow the horrors which occurred each and every day across the globe? Some nights I lay awake and ask him why. Why do the guilty survive while the innocent are murdered in the streets?"

Bryan slammed his fist upon the table and stood abruptly, startling the others. "Where is His justice? Where is His judgement upon those who wish to do evil to the world?"

Bryan stood next to Wendy and looked out the window. Beyond Chase's property were children playing hockey in the street, while across the way a neighbor washed his car. A young woman pushed a baby stroller along the sidewalk, waving at the neighbor before proceeding along her way. Bryan pursed his lips as if he had bit into a lemon.

"After I discovered the body of my best friend, a revelation revealed itself." He turned and looked sideways at everyone. "Perhaps God has already answered my question. Maybe His answer to the world is this: *Here is your justice. Here, in me.*"

Bryan studied their faces. They looked at him with a blend of concern and wonder. He assumed their concern was for his mental wellbeing. Perhaps they thought he was about to dive, feet first, into the pit of insanity. As he watched them, though, it appeared they were absorbing what he said, marinating on the words like a fresh steak.

After several moments Chase finally spoke. "Those are some strong feelings, Bryan. I have to admit I am not much of a religious man, but your words are thought-provoking to say the least."

Bryan shrugged, avoiding any further discussion on the matter. "So are we going to do this or what? Where do you need me?"

Chase smirked. "Well, son, you have the most important job of us all."

Bryan narrowed his eyes. "Oh yeah?"

"I'm going to need you to head to the warehouse," Chase said, running his fingers through his hair. "I have a feeling that is where you will find the answers to your questions."

"You may be right," Bryan replied, rubbing his chin thoughtfully. "What about you?"

"I think I will visit the prison," Chase replied sourly. "Let me see what I can dig up over there."

Hex and Wendy leaned back in their chairs with resigned looks in their faces. They knew the score. Currently over three hundred and seventy-five prisoners were incarcerated there. If Pete Williams was indeed planning some grandiose scheme, adding those prisoners to an already sizable army would be extremely difficult, almost impossible, for the city to overcome.

Bryan laughed and Wendy turned and glared at him. "Is there something about this that you find funny?"

"No, I was just thinking of a quote I read back in high school. For some reason it popped into my head and seemed applicable to our current predicament."

"Well, I'm all ears," Wendy said, placing her hand on her hips.

Bryan stopped laughing and his smile faded. His expression suddenly went cold, which caused Wendy's irritation to melt away. The look sent a chill up her spine when he repeated the quote to her.

"The two most important days in your life are the day you were born and the day you find out why."

Under New Management

Brady sat at his desk, fists clenched, as traitors gathered around him. Betrayal was a bitter pill to swallow, but when he saw who had betrayed him, it was as if the pill had been washed down with a cup of vinegar. The sour look on his face reflected his thoughts as his anger threatened to consume him. His legacy slipped through his fingers, and he wanted to do nothing more than lash out at the people responsible. The gesture would have been foolish and amount to nothing more than suicide, and he realized it.

"Don't look so glum, Brady. Nothing lasts forever, you know. Even someone as intelligent and as innovative as yourself must understand that."

Pete Williams took a seat across from Brady and propped his feet on the desk. He sipped a glass of brandy taken from Brady's private bar, which only served to infuriate Brady even further. Behind him stood Donald Runnels, James Stout and three of his security team, equipped with automatic weapons and tactical gear.

"What the hell are we waiting for?" growled Brady. He swept his hand across the room. "Congratulations, you have everything. What more do you want from me?"

Pete placed the glass on the desk and frowned. "Brady, don't be like that. I would like us to work together. Our goals are not that much different. We both wish for a peaceful, unified Crystal City."

"You're full of shit. What you want to do is turn this city into your personal playground." He pointed at him and narrowed his eyes angrily. "The citizens of this city have enjoyed decades of protection provided by the Hero Factory. You have taken that from them, but they will never accept going back to the way it was. *NEVER!*"

Brady's outburst caused the armed guards to tense and grip their assault rifles a bit more tightly. Pete held his hand up, calming them.

"I think you misunderstand me. I'm not trying to turn this city into what it was." He stood and placed his palm against his chest. "I'm a businessman. The old way was bad for business, there was too much competition. I'm offering this city real peace, one where they can walk the streets safely at night without fear, no matter which section of the city they live in. Whether they live in the Palisades or the projects in Ironbound, they will be able to sleep at night knowing their safety is guaranteed."

"How can you guarantee their safety?" Brady scoffed. "You're insane!"

"You cannot fight crime, because it will always fight back," Pete replied. "The Hero Factory, while perfectly acceptable in concept, was flawed in design. You need to control crime, make it work to your advantage."

"Surely you can't be serious!" Brady shouted.

"I'm dead serious. People view the concept of a criminal as something evil, something bad that should be defeated and locked away forever. I look at it in a different light." He picked up the glass of brandy and held it in front of him. "This glass of alcohol can be construed as something bad. Alcohol is bad, it impairs you, destroys your liver and rots you from top to bottom, if abused. However, if used in moderation, it tastes good, relaxes a person and relieves a person's stress." Pete set the glass down. "Crime is not unlike alcohol. If abused, if you have too much, you can rot a city from top to bottom. You can destroy the fragile infrastructure which pumps the lifeblood through the city. If used in moderation, however, you can control a city in a way that works for the people, protects them and keeps them happy. Keeps them *relaxed.*"

"The people aren't interested in your voodoo, nor will they fall for your lies. They are interested in the truth, and they will seek the truth no matter where they find it," Brady argued.

Pete shrugged with a wry smile on his face. "Maybe a long time ago, when you and I were young. Now they are more interested in celebrity divorces and cat videos on the internet. Times have changed, Brady. The issues we face today are too complicated for them to understand. These issues take too much focus away from updating their statuses on social networking sites or flipping through the thousands of channels on TV. It's up to people like me to make sure society does not succumb, where they will eventually descend into anarchy."

"I guess I have more faith in the citizens of this city."

Pete laughed. "Who's the crazy one now? You and I both know Joe Q Public can't take care of himself. That's why people like you and I exist."

Brady turned away from him and focused his attention toward the window. As he stared out the window, he wrestled with his emotions. Gently rubbing his temples, he thought about the heroes who died on his watch. He worried about the current state of the city and found himself wondering if Pete's words were laced with truth. There would be no point arguing his point, however, because Brady truly believed Pete was incorrect in his assessment. Brady was old enough to remember what the city was like when the criminals ran things, and he refused to accept the fact the city would be better off reverting to the way it was. He turned toward Pete who smugly sipped his drink.

Brady would rather die than let it happen again.

* * *

The shadow of dusk draped over the city. Beyond the Aqueducts, the Metrodome, the Galileo Theatre and Columbus Park loomed the Hero Factory. Once it had been a home to her but was now nothing more than a virus, one which needed to be purged in order to save those whom Wendy cared about the most.

"What do you think?" Hex whispered.

They were huddled behind the cover of bushes just out of reach of the cobra head lighting spanning the length of the parking lot. Wendy stared intently at the building in quiet contemplation. Out of the dozens of windows, only two were lit up inside. Judging by the few cars parked in the lot, it appeared most of the employees had left for the day.

"We may be okay. It seems most of the employees have left." Wendy pointed toward the side of the building. "Just beyond those trees is a service entrance for truck drivers and contractors. That entrance will be our best way inside because security rarely keeps it locked. They don't bother since it's so close to the security office."

"That's like stepping from a lion's den into the mouth of the lion," Hex grumbled.

"It may not be as bad as you think. Security rarely stays in the office," Wendy said, inching her way closer to get a better look. "If they stick to routine, they should be making their rounds on the upper levels right about now. Let's go!"

Wendy bolted from the brush and raced across the parking and Hex followed. Breathing heavily, she leaned back against the wall next to the door, and Hex fell in line next to her.

"I didn't realize I was so out of shape," Wendy wheezed.

Hex peered around her, studying the digital screen embedded in the wall next to the door. It was a security system designed to accept an employee's thumbprint to gain access. Wendy would normally have access to the facility, but if the Hero Factory had been compromised, it was highly likely the codes changed.

"Even if they didn't remove my access, there is no way I would swipe myself in," Wendy said, as if reading Hex's thoughts. "That would just be announcing our presence to everyone."

"So what now?" Hex asked.

"God, what I wouldn't do to have Volt here right now to short circuit the whole damn system." Wendy slid around Hex and examined the panel. From her pocket she removed a tiny flashlight and a pocket knife. "I guess we will have to settle for this."

Using the pocket knife, she removed the four flat head screws holding the panel in place. Several wires fell from the bottom of the screen like discarded spaghetti. Gently she slid the panel aside and removed the top of the flashlight. Instead of a battery compartment, there were two small, metal prongs. Wendy placed the prongs inside the system and pushed the button. A sizzling sound pierced the quiet solitude of the parking lot as sparks flew from the device. The panel quickly died.

"What the hell was that?" Hex asked with an astonished expression.

"A mini Taser," Wendy replied. "I picked it up at a gun show a few weeks ago. They sell them for personal defense. I just defended myself against an uncooperative digital panel." She smiled and returned the knife and flashlight to her pocket.

Wendy's hand fell on the door handle when a booming voice shouted behind them. "FREEZE!"

Slowly they turned in unison to see one of the Hero Factory's security personnel pointing a 9MM in their direction. Slowly, their hands raised into the air.

"What are you doing?" he demanded.

The hands of Hex flickered with a pale, reddish yellow light, like candles in a gentle breeze. As she raised her hands in the air, the light's intensity increased, morphing from candlelight to a light as bright as the sun.

"What are you—" the guard cried but stopped in midsentence.

His eyes widened with fear, and he uttered small, choking gasps. Dropping the gun, he grabbed his throat with both hands. He continued to claw at his throat while his face turned a deep shade of red. As his face went from red to an ugly purple, the color of an angry bruise, he fell to the ground and curled into the fetal position. He weakly clawed at his throat while Hex approached him confidently. She leaned over and cupped his head in her hands, whispering in his ear.

"I could continue until all oxygen is sucked away, leaving you with nothing left to inhale but death. Fortunately for you, we are short on time, and I don't want your death on my conscience."

The light surrounding her fists exploded around the guard's head. The light was so intense Wendy had to divert her eyes. As the sun spots faded from her vision, she feared Hex blew the man's head off. As the light cleared, however, she noticed the man's head was still firmly attached to his shoulder but he was no longer writhing on the ground in agony.

"Is he dead?" Wendy asked.

Hex shook her head. "He's unconscious and will remain that way until we're long gone."

They entered the building and proceeded cautiously down the hall. At the end, on the right hand side, was the security office. Wendy breathed a sigh of relief when she saw the door to the office was closed. They treaded carefully as they made their way past the office.

"How far is your office?" Hex whispered.

Wendy pointed to a set of stairs ahead. "Just up those stairs and to the left is the research lab. At this hour, it should be empty," she replied.

Even though they ascended the stairs slowly, every little creak of protest the stairs made sounded like a gunshot in the silent confines of the stairwell. When they reached the top without resistance, Wendy counted her blessings. Ahead, the offices were empty, and the only light drifting into the hall was coming from the emergency after-hours lights overhead. Wendy never locked the doors to the lab since a security team had been put into place, so she wasn't at all surprised when she came upon them unlocked. They entered the lab and were quickly enveloped by gloom. The only light filtering into the office came from an area between the window and the drawn shades. She removed her stun gun/flashlight and switched it on.

"That sure is a handy little gadget," Hex remarked.

"Indeed," Wendy replied and slithered toward her desk in the corner. She flipped on the computer and, while she waited for it to boot up, removed a flash drive from her pocket. "Inside this flash drive is a virus

I will download into the system." She paused, her hand cradling the USB drive. "All of our years of research will be destroyed. Everything we have built will be destroyed."

Hex winced when she noticed the regret in Wendy's eyes. "I know it sucks, but we can't take the chance they might use this technology against the city."

Wendy sighed, knowing Hex spoke the truth. With the Hero Factory under their control, Oracle could essentially create a mutant army capable of taking over the city and beyond. With an army of superheroes, no one would be able to stop the carnage that would ensue. As much as she loathed destroying her life's work, she understood the consequences of inaction. The computer booted up and she slid the flash drive into the USB port. Hex leaned over her shoulder, watching the computer screen with solemn anticipation. Wendy typed away on the keyboard, working to access the drive in which the Hero Program data was stored. Just as she was about to access the virus program, Hex groaned, which caused Wendy to pause.

Hex fell to the ground, a dart protruding at an angle from her neck. Panicked, Wendy swung around to see Pete Williams surrounded by a group of armed guards. The lead guard lowered a dart gun while the others pointed semi-automatic weapons at her. As she studied them she calculated her odds of executing the program before they shot her dead. While she wrestled with the pros and cons of such an action, she bit her bottom lip with frustration. When she raised her hand toward the keyboard, Pete pointed his index finger at her.

"I wouldn't do that if I were you."

The guards stiffened and their fingers tensed on the triggers of their weapons. Wendy muttered silent curses and lowered her hand to her side, knowing she would never be able to execute the program in time. The resigned look on her face elicited a smile from Pete.

"That's good, I knew you were smart." Pete strolled over and lifted her chin with his index finger.

"Are you going to kill me?" she asked solemnly.

Pete widened his eyes and returned her stare with feigned indignation. "I'm not a monster, Dr. Markus. On the contrary, I plan on keeping you with me; because I believe you will prove to be a formidable ally, and your value to this business cannot be understated." He looked down at Hex's unconscious form. "You may make an excellent insurance policy as well."

"What do you mean?"

"I'm no fool, Dr. Markus. I know Soulfire and Illusionist are out there somewhere. I believe they would be hesitant to attack us directly if they knew you two were inside with us."

"I won't help you," she vowed.

Pete produced a glass vial filled with a murky green liquid. Along the side was stenciled a letter.

X.

As soon as she saw it her heart sank. She fell to the floor where she remained firmly planted on her butt, staring at the vial through wild eyes. At that moment she wished she had super powers so she could shrink to the size of an ant and scurry from the room.

"You made *more*," Wendy gasped.

Pete grinned. "Yes, we did."

Her eyes moved from the vial to Pete. "How? I am the only one who knows the formula."

Pete looked down at the vial and turned it over in his hands. "You'd be amazed how much of your research had been monitored and recorded. You encrypted most of your files, but it was a wasted effort. Some people can be so nosy sometimes."

"Donald!" she blurted.

Pete didn't respond. He didn't need to. Instead, he turned to one of the guards and flicked a thumb over his shoulder.

"Take her to Brady's office for now, until I can figure out a more comfortable place to stash her."

Two of the guards grabbed her and pulled her up by her arms, forcing her to stand. The two guards escorted her toward the door while the remaining guards trained their weapons on her.

"They'll come for me, you know," Wendy spat angrily into Pete's face as the guards escorted her through the door.

Pete's smile never wavered, despite tiny beads of spittle making their way down his cheeks. He removed a handkerchief from his back pocket and dabbed at them gently. When he finished, he returned the cloth to his pocket and cleared his throat.

"My dear, I'm counting on it."

The Prison

The chair behind the registration desk sat empty, which was the first sign something was wrong. The second sign was the unlocked and open door leading into the bowels of the prison. Illusionist pulled the collar of his jacket up, suddenly feeling a cold chill course through him despite the dry, warm air circulating within the building. He stood by the open door and cocked his head, listening for the slightest sound. During his hero career, he carried no weapons except his staff. He preferred deception, magic and illusion so he could confuse and disorient his enemies. For this mission, he wouldn't be against having a machine gun by his side. The hairs on his neck stood at attention, and deep down he had a feeling that Oracle was still inside the prison. Perhaps he would be better off with a tank by his side. Oracle was a powerful foe, and Illusionist would not make the mistake of underestimating him.

Illusionist crept carefully toward the open door and inched it open. When he stepped into the hall, he noticed most of the cells sat empty. The cells in this wing housed the less violent offenders. All of the cell doors stood open, and as he walked past each empty cell his heart sank a little further into his stomach. A double door with a single pane of glass across the top was located at the end of the hall which led to an area known as the dome. Illusionist had only entered the dome once, long ago, during a tour of the facility. The dome housed some of the most violent offenders in Crystal City history. Repeat offenders.

Child rapists. Serial killers. It was like a housing development for the criminally insane.

The main hall branched off into smaller halls forming an X. In the center of the X, down one level, sat four desks surrounded by video monitors. On a normal day, the desks would be manned by prison guards. Today they were empty. Bodies of two guards were crumpled on the floor close to the desks. Illusionist approached the closest one and placed two fingers along the man's neck. His breathing came slow but steady. He was still alive.

They must have been knocked out by something, but he didn't see any signs of a struggle or any type of physical trauma. He looked away from the body and surveyed the area. Several unconscious guards were scattered along the halls. Most of the doors to the cells stood open and vacant. Illusionist ran his fingers through his hair and shuddered. If Oracle released all of these violent offenders, the destruction would be catastrophic. He was about to leave the area when a metallic grating sound came from the far end of the dome. As he turned to it and listened, it fluctuated in intensity.

Creeeeeeeeak.

The sound reminded him of a rusty hinge fastened to a door straight out of a horror movie. It was slow and methodical, as if the person opening it was taking his time and relishing every second. When he heard Oracle's voice coming from the area, he knew it must have been him opening a cell door.

Carefully he made his way along the north hall, toward the source of the sounds. As he navigated his way along the corridor, he came across another body. This one belonged to a prisoner, not a guard. Startled, he crouched down and pressed his fingers to the man's neck, slightly beneath the tattoo of a dragon. When he felt no pulse, he knew the man was dead.

"What the hell?" Illusionist muttered to himself.

Illusionist could see no visible wounds on the man's body, and when he turned the man's head, it swiveled too easily. Hidden next to the tattoo was an angry purple mark which led toward the back of the neck. A broken neck had been this man's cause of demise.

One of the voices elevated to the point of agitation. Illusionist stood and made his way further down the hall. When he reached the last cell, he saw a man's back. The voices were clear now and he recognized Oracle's voice instantly.

"What the fuck you want with me, man?" a man shouted with a thick Hispanic accent from within the cell. "Are you letting me out of here or not?"

Illusionist crept forward until his ear was merely inches from the door. He dared to go no further, because the last thing he needed was Oracle becoming aware of his presence. The best chance he had in defeating Oracle was taking him by surprise. If Illusionist was correct in his assumptions, Oracle was much more powerful than he had been led to believe.

"I'm afraid I can't do that," Oracle responded to the prisoner.

"Why the fuck not?"

"The reason I'm here is to recruit people who I feel would best serve our cause with fierce loyalty and unquestionable honor."

The convict bellowed with laughter. "Man, you're in the wrong place."

"You see," Oracle continued, unabated. "The problem with you is you're a child rapist. A pedophile. The lowest form of scum known to man. I wouldn't hire you to clean shithouses."

"What the hell did you say to me?" the prisoner roared. "Dude, I should break your neck right now. Who the fuck do you think you are? Why did you even open the—" the man's sentence abruptly ended with a choked gasp.

Oracle disappeared inside the cell and a gurgling sound followed. Illusionist backed up and ducked inside the next cell as soon as Oracle moved forward. Cautiously, he peered around the corner to see what Oracle's next move would be. He didn't wait long before Oracle emerged from the cell, dragging the prisoner by one leg. The man wore the standard orange prison jumpsuit and was covered in tattoos on every inch of bare skin. The unfortunate man's head had been twisted 180 degrees. While the dead prisoner stared at his own back, Oracle dragged him to the steel railing separating the hall from the main level below. The man must have weighed about two hundred and fifty pounds, but Oracle lifted him over his head like he was a sack of cotton balls. With a fierce growl, he threw the man with such fury that the impact of the body split one of the desks in half, shattering the monitor into nothing more than scrap in the process.

Oracle stared over the railing at the carnage where he remained still for several minutes, silent and brooding. He clenched the railing, and Illusionist noticed every muscle in his hands tightening. Eventually he let go of the railing, drew a deep breath and looked toward the ceiling.

"Some folks say we are doomed to repeat the mistakes of the past," Oracle said. "I prefer to believe the past makes a great learning tool to prevent mistakes in the future."

Illusionist thought there was another person in the prison Oracle was addressing, but as he surveyed the area he could see no one. The prison had been emptied with the exception of the two men who stood several feet apart from one another. Oracle's rampage had made short work of the place. Whatever prisoners he didn't murder, he freed. A single person managed to overwhelm an entire prison. *How badly did we underestimate his powers and abilities?*

Oracle turned and tossed Illusionist a sideways glance. "I had a feeling it would be you who would come. I suppose it was inevitable." He waved his hands in the air for dramatic effect. "The hero from the past comes to save the day and put an end to the villainous tyranny perpetrated upon this fine city by a rogue hero of the present!" He dropped his hands and closed his eyes, as if relishing the moment. "Damn, this would have made a great movie."

"What are you doing, Oracle?" Illusionist stepped from the shadows. "Why are you here murdering prisoners?" He hoped making small talk would distract his adversary and allow him to catch Oracle off-guard.

Oracle leaned against the railing and smiled. "I've done cruel things. I take no pleasure from any of it but in life sometimes drastic measures are necessary. In order for us to implement real change, a sledgehammer was required, not a scalpel." He pointed his index finger at himself. "You're looking at the sledgehammer."

"You're not making sense," Illusionist argued. "There was nothing wrong with this city. You are probably too young to remember its past, but I'm not. This city was nothing more than a cesspool, a haven for criminals, before the Hero Program." He placed his hands into his pockets, in an effort to convince Oracle he was not a threat. "The Hero Factory brought stability and structure to this city. People can walk the streets without the fear of a boogeyman springing from the shadows to hurt them."

Oracle leaned his head back and bellowed laughter. After a minute passed, he composed himself and wiped a tear from the corner of his eye. "Oh my, I haven't laughed like that in forever. You make this city sound like some exotic cocoon from which a beautiful butterfly will emerge." He shook his head slowly and stepped away from the railing. "No, my old friend, this city is no cocoon. It is more like a festering sore which needs to be cut out before it infects the rest of the world. Your blind faith in the Hero Program is your undoing. My mission will continue and I will not be stopped."

Oracle lifted his hands in the air quickly and pointed them towards Illusionist. The action was so quick, it was impossible to respond in time. Several bolts of electricity flew from his fingertips and engulfed Illusionist's body. Smoke poured from his body until an entire cloud of it engulfed him in a dense fog, minimizing visibility.

"That was too easy."

Oracle strolled confidently toward the cloud as it dissipated. When the cloud vanished, there was nothing but mere wisps which quickly evaporated into the air. Illusionist's body was gone.

"Did you really think it would be that easy?" a voice called from behind.

Oracle spun around to face the source, but the hall was empty. He smirked. "I'm glad to see I was incorrect. It would have been such a letdown to kill you that easily."

"Kill me?" Illusionist laughed. "I don't think that's gonna happen today."

Oracle's hand fell to the holster by his side. He unsnapped the buckle and removed his 9MM. Movement from the corner of his eye caused him to swivel north, toward the end of the hall. Illusionist stood in the doorway of the cell where he killed the pedophile.

"I'm not like those you have killed," Illusionist said. "I think you and I both know that."

Oracle pointed the gun and fired. The bullet went through Illusionist's body and embedded itself in the wall behind him.

"Now you're just being silly."

Oracle spun toward the voice to see Illusionist standing at the far end of the hall. He fired and once again the bullet passed through the illusion.

"COME OUT AND FACE ME, DAMMIT!" Oracle roared.

"Nah, I don't think so."

The voice came from the level below, where the body of the rapist now rested. Oracle rushed across the hall and peered over the railing. Illusionist sat in one of the chairs with his feet propped up on the remaining desk.

Oracle holstered the weapon and smiled. "It is things like this that make you one of the best superheroes in Crystal City history. You probably drove your adversaries to the point of insanity with your hijinks."

Illusionist shrugged. "Occasionally."

Oracle closed his eyes and concentrated, summoning the power he had absorbed from Spectre. He phased through the floor and fell into the cell beneath him. The cell had been one of the rare empty ones within the confines of the prison. The cell door was closed, but Oracle could see Illusionist through the bars. His smile grew when he noticed Illusionist's eyes widen with surprise.

"You see, Illusionist, I can conjure up a few tricks of my own."

Oracle phased through the cell door and approached Illusionist carefully. Despite catching the old man off guard, he was never one to underestimate his adversary. He may be projecting a whole bunch of bravado at this point in their fight, but deep down he knew Illusionist was tougher than the others. He rolled up his sleeve, revealing the hawk tattoo.

"So it's true," Illusionist muttered. "Mnemonic abilities are indeed possible. The ability to alter the mutagenic compound to successfully produce one had been nothing but pure science fiction until now."

"Oh... you ain't seen nothing yet."

The hawk tore from Oracle's arm with lightning speed. It dove at Illusionist, scratching the side of his face and leaving an angry red line on his left cheek which quickly welled with blood. Oracle followed up with a blast of electricity from his fingertips, catching Illusionist in the chest and sending him sprawling backwards over the desk.

Illusionist coughed as pain ricocheted through his body. He felt like he had just licked a 400–ton, nine-volt battery. A numb, tingling sensation shot through every pore in his body.

Oracle, filled with confidence, strolled toward the desk. Illusionist, sprawled out sideways, coughed again and struggled to stand. The blast of electricity felt like being hit by a Taser on steroids. Oracle removed the 9MM and shoved the desk aside. Illusionist swiveled his head slowly and glanced up at him with a defeat in his eyes. Oracle lifted the weapon and pointed it at Illusionist's head. Illusionist resigned himself to his fate; there would be no last minute trick to get him out of this.

"FREEZE!" a voice cried from the front of the prison.

Oracle spun around to see Chief Tommy Stamper pointing an AR-15 rifle at him. The police chief had his legs spread in a combat stance and held the rifle up so he could look through the scope. A tiny red dot marked Oracle's chest.

"If you move one inch, I'm going to empty this clip into you, you son of a bitch," the Chief growled.

A wry smile formed on Oracle's lips. He whipped the gun toward the chief and fired. His reflexes were so fast the cop had no chance to respond. The bullet entered his left shoulder with such impact that the cop dropped the gun and fell backwards over the unconscious body of a prison guard.

With a cry of pain, Chief Stamper clutched his shoulder and crawled backwards as Oracle approached. Oracle descended upon him with a demonic smile. Stamper crawled backwards with one arm as best he could, leaving snail trails of blood along the floor in the process. His efforts were in vain, however, because Oracle easily caught up with him.

Straddling the prone form of the Chief, Oracle lifted the gun slowly. "You should have stayed out of this one, buddy." He pulled the trigger. *Click.*

The gun was empty. Oracle turned it over in his hand and laughed, as if it was not a gun at all but an entertaining toy placed there for his amusement. "Well, I'll be damned." The hawk returned to him and perched itself on his shoulder. "I guess I will have to take care of you the old fashioned way."

Oracle reached down and grabbed the Chief and pulled him to his feet, causing him to cry out in pain. Oracle flipped the Chief around and wrapped his arm around his throat.

"Don't worry, this will be over quickly."

Before Oracle could twist and break the man's neck, a snorting, shuffling sound behind him caught his attention. He dropped the Chief and turned around. Standing before him was a ten foot tall humanoid with the body of a man and the head of a cow. Each horn jutting from the top of the head had to be at least two feet long. Oracle recognized the beast from his days in school studying ancient Greek mythology.

A Minotaur.

"That's a neat trick, Illusionist," Oracle chuckled. "Will you pull a rabbit out of a hat next?"

The Minotaur raised his head and roared. The shout echoed throughout the halls of the prison and froze Oracle's blood, despite his bravado. The Minotaur lowered his head and charged, striking Oracle squarely in the chest and knocking him into the far wall. The impact of the charge knocked him unconscious. As soon as Oracle's body hit the floor, the illusion vanished.

Chief Stamper's eyelids felt heavy, but before he lost consciousness he glanced at Illusionist as he crouched over him.

"Come on, Chief, let's get out of here." Illusionist stumbled as he tried to pull the Chief to his feet which sent a fresh wave of pain rocketing through his body.

Stamper succumbed to the darkness before he reached the exit.

The Warehouse

Soulfire sat on the roof for hours, watching the warehouse across the street and hoping for any sign of gang activity. He had expected more activity than what had transpired to this point. Within the last hour, only two people entered with one person leaving. It was not exactly what one could call a high traffic location. He found himself wondering if Illusionist had been incorrect in his assessment of Oracle's strength. When the sun settled behind the building and shadow blanketed the area, he decided to depart from his vantage point and risk approaching for a closer look.

Soulfire descended the stairs and made his way to the first floor. Once there, he left via the back door and made his way around to the front of the building. He stopped when he spotted a car pulling up to the front of the warehouse. In the fading light of dusk, it was difficult to make out the details of the vehicle but it appeared to be a dark colored SUV. The vehicle stopped in front of the loading dock. The driver exited, walked around to the passenger side and opened the rear door. A man stepped from the rear of the vehicle, talking into a cell phone while smoking a cigarette.

Soulfire cursed the shadowy gloom created by fading sunlight. From this distance, he was not able to see their faces or whether the men were armed. He pressed himself tightly against the wall and peered around the corner to avoid being spotted. In order to confirm Illusionist's suspicions, he needed to get closer to the warehouse, and the last thing he needed was the men spotting him and raising an alarm. Nobody walked these streets, especially at this time at night, unless they were into something suspicious. The desolation surrounding the area would allow him to approach the warehouse with little chance of being spotted.

Carefully he crept closer to the warehouse, making sure to remain under the cover of shadows. The two men were heavily involved in their conversation, so Soulfire was able to approach without being noticed. As soon as he got close enough to hear what they were saying, he stopped. He wasn't going to risk going any further until he was sure something ominous was going on inside.

"What the hell is taking him so long?" the smoking man asked.

The driver shrugged. "He keeps his own schedule. You know better than anybody that nobody can keep track of him."

The smoking man took a final drag on the cigarette before flicking it aside. "We got shit to do. I'm not gonna wait for him any longer, I got places to be. You stay here and make sure no one gets curious around here. The last thing we need is some lookie-loo getting nosy."

"Sure thing, Buzzsaw," the driver responded and leaned back against the vehicle as the smoking man stepped inside the building.

Buzzsaw? The name was familiar to Soulfire. He closed his eyes and tried to remember where he heard the name. In a flash, he remembered something he had learned in his high school history class, when the teacher covered the gang wars of the 1970s. This man's name came up as the leader of the Raging 86's. According to the textbook, the man was a sociopath and earned his nickname the hard way; he killed for it.

Soulfire clenched his fists in anger as flashbacks of his wife and child's murder flashed before his eyes. *Gangs.* It appeared Illusionist wasn't wrong after all. If a high ranking member like Brian "Buzzsaw" Kelly was here, perhaps there had been merit to his story. Soulfire pushed the anger aside and focused on the task on hand. Before he could get inside, he would need to take out the driver. He couldn't take the risk of the driver alerting whoever lurked inside the building.

The man removed a cigarette pack from his pocket, slid one out and lit it. He took a long drag and leaned his head back, staring at the stars. A movement from the corner of his eye caused him to look toward the alley alongside the warehouse. Very little light drifted into the alley, so he needed to squint to make out anything in the gloom. After a minute passed, he shrugged it off as a figment of his imagination. He leaned his head back again and took another drag of the cigarette, letting the smoke drift slowly between his teeth and spilling tiny wisps of smoke into the night air.

Clang!

The sound echoed from the alley, like an empty soup can striking the pavement. He tossed the cigarette aside, and his hand fell to the revolver tucked inside his jacket.

"Hello?" he called out.

Silence.

"Listen, if someone is over there, your ass better come out before I put one right between your eyes!" He peered into the darkness trying to identify shapes from the gloom.

Silence.

The man took one step toward the alley. He assumed a stray cat knocked some garbage around inside the dumpster, but he needed to make sure no curious onlooker was loitering around the warehouse. Before he was able to take another step, a light flickered inside the alley. At first it was barely visible but increased in luminescence over time, as if someone had lit a candle and approached him with it.

"Who's there?" He removed the .38 from the holster and pointed it toward the alley. "You got three seconds to identify yourself before I start blasting away."

The light continued to get brighter until a dog stepped from the alley. The driver's jaw dropped when it revealed itself. The animal was bigger than a St. Bernard but, to the man's surprise, it was on fire. As it approached, he noticed it wasn't a dog at all. It was a wolf. *An enormous, flaming wolf.*

"What the—?"

The man was cut off when he felt an intense burning in the hand holding the gun. When he looked down, his eyes widened in horror. The gun barrel started *melting*. With a cry of alarm, he tossed the deformed chunk of metal aside. Panicked, the man jumped behind the vehicle. When he peered around the side of the SUV, he noticed the wolf had stopped advancing. It continued to eye him hungrily. He turned and ran toward the warehouse, but before he could make it, a strong arm wrapped around his throat, immediately cutting off his air supply.

"Peekaboo," Soulfire whispered into the man's ear.

The man tried to claw at Soulfire's arm, but the effort was futile. As Soulfire squeezed, the man's strength ebbed until he lost consciousness and slumped forward. He let go, and the man fell, smacking his face on the pavement. The wolf cocked its head, looking upon his master eagerly.

Soulfire held out his hand and the wolf came forward. Just as the animal's muzzle touched his outstretched fingers, it vanished in a wisp of smoke. Before the smoke evaporated, his hand became engulfed in flame. Soulfire closed his hand into a fist and approached the door where Buzzsaw entered earlier. He opened the door slowly, wincing because he expected the hinges to have rusted over. Fortunately for him, the door opened without a sound. The well-oiled hinges further proved Illusionist had been correct. No one oiled hinges to doors on abandoned warehouses unless they planned on using them.

Soulfire stepped into the hallway. Four linear fluorescent light fixtures had been installed overhead; however, only one worked, giving off a pale yellowish light, barely lighting the hall. Fifty feet ahead stood the door leading to the receiving dock. The door was open so he approached it carefully, peering slowly around the corner. As he scanned the docks, he could see the area was empty, with the exception of several long metal racks which had rusted over long ago.

The back of the receiving area fed into a large staging area. Long aisles of shelves once held a vast amount of inventory but now lay bare, filled with cobwebs instead. Off to the right, a door led toward the sales and administrative offices. Two thick planks of wood were nailed in an X across the door where years of dust and cobwebs had accumulated. No one had passed through those doors in a long time.

Soulfire moved through the warehousing area. The west side of the warehouse opened into the manufacturing area. As he approached, he heard several voices echoing throughout the area. When he reached the back of the warehouse, he peered around the corner. The actual manufacturing area was located one level below the receiving dock. A long row of steel stairs led down into the area, but he approached them cautiously. The last thing he needed was to bump into a thug who strayed too far from the crowd. He took each stair slowly, careful to not attract any unwanted attention. When he reached the bottom, he froze.

Two hundred yards from the bottom of the stairs, a crowd gathered around Brian "Buzzsaw" Kelly. Standing next to him was a large, bald, black man wearing an expensive, tailor-made suit with his arms folded across his chest, eyeballing the crowd silently. Soulfire counted thirty people altogether, all armed with weapons ranging from pistols to semi-automatic rifles. Luckily his position by the stairs kept him out of range from prying eyes. He took cover behind a large milling machine and approached the crowd carefully until he got within earshot. Instead of a bunch of jumbled noise, Soulfire could now hear what they were saying.

"You people know why we brought you here. It's time to finish what we started, boys." He pointed to the man standing next to him. "Tyler will brief you on the details."

"The future is now, gentlemen," Tyler said. "When I think about what lies ahead for us, I like to turn to one of my favorite passages in the bible."

Scattered groans emanated from the crowd, some gang members looked down at the ground and shook their heads. None of that seemed to have bothered Tyler. He continued with his message despite the rumbles of dissent.

"Philippians 4:13," Tyler continued. "I can do all things through Christ that strengthens me." With a fierce gaze, he swept his arm across the room. "Make no mistake, folks, God is on our side. He knows this city needs to be cleansed, and through us He will continue to do His work. We will not be stopped!"

Cheers replaced groans when the crowd erupted. With weapons raised high, they shouted and cheered with excitement. Soulfire noticed most of them wore blue-gray bandannas tied around their biceps and recognized them immediately. Those colors were the same worn around the head of the gangbanger who murdered his family. A fit of rage overcame him. For a moment, he could see nothing but red, the seething, burning color of fury. His family's killer had died, but he saw his face in every person standing in the room. Finally, Soulfire's unsated thirst for vengeance would soon be quenched.

No longer caring about stealth, he stepped from behind the machine. Soulfire succumbed to his rage which, in turn, blinded him by hate. The poorly lit, gloomy confines of the manufacturing area flared with light as if someone had unleashed the sun. Flames consumed his body while fury consumed his soul. All heads turned toward him, followed by many gun barrels.

Buzzsaw's jaw dropped. "How the hell are you even here? I thought Oracle took care of all you heroes?"

"Yeah, well, sorry to disappoint you," Soulfire hissed through clenched teeth. "Maybe he isn't as good as you think he is. Maybe you should think about attaching yourself to another teat."

"Why you son of a bitch," Buzzsaw roared. "SHOOT THAT DUM-BASS!"

Before anyone could fire their weapon, Soulfire hurled two basketball-sized orbs of fire toward them. They crashed on the floor in the middle of the group and split into hundreds of flaming spiders. The flaming insects skittered across the floor, branching out to cover the entire floor. Several managed to find their way onto the legs of gang members, causing their clothes to smolder and ignite in places. In a panic, the gangsters dropped their weapons and swiped at the flames. Soulfire was relentless. He advanced upon them without hesitation or mercy, following up his spider attack by blasting a group of ten with spirals of flame. They were the unfortunate first victims to feel his wrath. The flames engulfed them, and their blood curdling screams echoed from the rooftops. Three of the ten survived the initial blast but suffered severe burns. They were the unfortunate ones, because they were alive long enough to feel themselves fry like bacon on a hot stove.

Soulfire held no sympathy in his heart and fed off their pain. His only regret was he could not inject into them the emotional trauma he had suffered. The loss of his family had cut him like a hot knife through frozen butter, and he was more than willing to return the favor tenfold.

Fire raged through the warehouse, burning man and equipment alike. The surviving gangsters scattered like ants as Soulfire cut through them like a chainsaw. His flames overwhelmed the fleeing criminals like a tidal wave of fire. By the time he finished his attack all of them either lay dead or dying, with the exception of Tyler and Buzzsaw. Buzzsaw's weapon lay beside him, the heat warping it to nothing more than useless knot of metal. Tyler, however, pointed a functioning shotgun in Soulfire's direction. His face twisted with fury as he pulled the trigger.

BOOM.

The shot missed but caught Soulfire off balance as he jumped sideways to avoid it. He fell to the floor and cracked his skull on the corner of an industrial sized pipe cutting machine. The sharp corner opened a deep gash in his right temple, causing blood to flow like river across his face. Pain radiated throughout his skull as the blood seeped into his eyes, obstructing his vision. Through streaks of red, he observed Tyler pumping the shotgun and advancing, intent on finishing him off.

Tyler positioned himself over Soulfire and leveled the weapon toward him. "Matthew 26:52 says 'put up again thy sword into his place, for all they that take the sword shall perish by the sword.' It is time for you to perish by the sword."

Out of instinct, Soulfire raised his hand. Tyler grinned, incorrectly assuming the maneuver was one of surrender.

"You first, asshole," Soulfire growled.

Thick strands of flame leapt from Soulfire's fingertips like bright orange ribbons, wrapping themselves around Tyler. He screamed, dropped the shotgun and swatted at the flames, but it was too late. The flames crawled over him like maggots on a carcass, and they accepted his flesh eagerly. The flames took no longer than a minute to consume him. His screams penetrated the roar of the flames for a brief moment before fading into silence.

Buzzsaw, his eyes as wide as dinner plates, eyed his fallen comrade with horror. "Look what you did!"

As soon as he said it, Buzzsaw realized the folly in his statement as he surveyed the carnage around him. Instead of mourning his fallen comrades, he sprang for Tyler's discarded shotgun. Before Soulfire was able to react, Buzzsaw fired.

A sharp pain, followed by a burning sensation, radiated from his shoulder as if a swarm of bees had been let loose upon the affected area. Because of the distance between them, the buckshot did no serious damage. Soulfire looked down at the blood flowing from several small wounds and winced at the shredded flesh. Luckily, it looked worse than it felt.

"You shouldn't have done that!" Soulfire growled and let loose a torrent of flame from his fingertips.

The weapon melted in Buzzsaw hands. His jaw dropped and he stared at it, dumbfounded. Soulfire advanced on him, and Buzzsaw did the only thing he could at that moment. He hurled the mangled weapon at him. Soulfire quickly sidestepped it and continued his advance.

"I think it's time you and I had a little chat," Soulfire said.

Buzzsaw scurried backwards until he hit the wall. Like a desperate animal trapped with no way out, he lashed out at his enemy, swinging his fist at Soulfire who easily ducked the punch.

"Before I deep fry your ass like a Thanksgiving turkey, I have some questions," Soulfire snarled.

Buzzsaw responded by throwing another punch. "Go fuck yourself!"

Soulfire easily swatted it aside like a troublesome fly. "You're not paying attention."

"Then go fuck yourself again!" Buzzsaw grabbed a discarded board lying nearby and swung viciously.

Soulfire ducked, knocked the board out of his hand and pinned him up against the wall. He locked onto Buzzsaw's throat, wrapping his hand tightly around it and squeezing. His other hand remained ablaze and he lifted it to the side of the man's face. The scream which erupted from the man was drowned out with the sizzling sound of frying flesh. Soulfire removed his hand, leaving behind a charred, blistered patch of skin along his cheekbone.

"I only have one question for you, then I will release you from your pain. Where can I find Oracle?" Soulfire raised his burning hand once again and waved it near Buzzsaw's face menacingly.

Sweat streamed down the man's face and he struggled to catch his breath. "No," Buzzsaw rasped. "No more. I'll tell you whatever you want to know."

"I only want to know where he is."

Buzzsaw's lips formed a tight white line of pain. He flinched as Soulfire's hand drifted closer. "He was supposed to meet us here after he was done at the prison. I swear to God he's late!"

Soulfire narrowed his eyes. "You wouldn't be lying to me now, would you?" His hand drifted closer to the man's face and watched as he squirmed helplessly. "Why would he come here?"

"If I tell you, he'll kill me," Buzzsaw croaked.

"Right now, Oracle is the least of your worries," Soulfire replied. The flaming fist drifted closer to emphasize the point.

Buzzsaw paled, watching the fist drift closer. For a moment, Soulfire believed the man would not give up his secret; but as the flames licked the air mere inches from his cheek, he finally acquiesced.

"*ALRIGHT!* Get that thing away from me!" he shouted.

Soulfire dropped his hand to his side. "Tell me."

Buzzsaw's eyes darted back and forth, scanning the room, as if a ghost would jump from one of the shadows and eat his soul.

"Oracle wants to take over the city," he blurted. "Shorty is just a pawn in his game. Oracle needs his help, but once it's done he plans on taking him out."

Soulfire's mood darkened. "That's bullshit!" He squeezed Buzzsaw's neck, forcing a choked gasp to escape from his lips. "This Shorty guy wants the same thing. What you're telling me doesn't make any damn sense!"

Buzzsaw shook his head violently, forcing Soulfire to loosen his grip to allow the man to breathe. "No, you idiot. Shorty wants to use the Hero Factory to create more superheroes under his control. He plans on using that serum crap on his closest advisors." He sucked in a breath as he regained some color in his face. "Oracle wants the exact opposite. He wants to destroy the Hero Factory and all the heroes, making him the only one with the power to control the entire city."

"So no honor among thieves, huh?" Soulfire let go of Buzzsaw, who rubbed his neck and pouted. "So I assume you people were gathered in here waiting for the right time to strike."

Buzzsaw looked down and rubbed his neck, like a kid caught with his hand in the cookie jar. "Not everyone was in on the plan."

"What do you mean?"

Buzzsaw looked at the charred corpse of Tyler. "He was Shorty's nephew. No matter what happened, he would have remained loyal to his uncle." He let out a long, drawn out sigh. "You did us a favor. We would have had to take him out sooner or later."

Pondering the pain and suffering he wrought upon the room, Soulfire scanned the area and winced. Charred bodies were scattered everywhere, looking like charcoal briquettes tossed around the place. The unlucky ones had survived. They scraped and clawed on the ground, trying to crawl away as they lay dying. Soulfire felt a pang of remorse as he looked upon the destruction he had caused. This was not who he was, and deep down he knew his family would not approve. Despite the icy blackness which had filled the void in his heart at their passing, he still clung to the sliver of humanity left deep down within his soul

While Soulfire was preoccupied with the destruction he had caused, a cold, sharp pain filled his belly. He looked down at his abdomen to see Buzzsaw's hand holding the handle of a switchblade with the blade embedded in Soulfire's gut. He looked into Buzzsaw's eyes as they sparkled with malicious glee.

"How's that feel, asshole?" Buzzsaw purred.

Soulfire smiled, and Buzzsaw's melted away. Flames danced in the dark recesses of Soulfire's eyes, but that may have just been Buzzsaw's imagination playing tricks on him.

"Not as bad as this will."

Soulfire ignited both hands, lifted them towards the man's head. As soon as they were parallel from one another, he slammed them together. As both hands closed against the sides of Buzzsaw's head, the skin on his face sizzled and the scent of burning hair filled Soulfire's nostrils. The man screamed and mustered all his strength in an attempt to wriggle out of his grip. Despite the stab wound he had suffered, Soulfire's grip remained strong. The sensation of melting skin against his palms made his stomach lurch, but he kept his hands in place.

Buzzsaw continued his bone chilling screams until the damage to his voice box was too great. His eyeballs popped from their sockets like popcorn; mercifully, he was dead by then.

Soulfire let go, and the corpse fell to the floor with a wet, sucking sound. His hand fell to the wound in his abdomen and came back wet with blood. Between the gunshot wound to the shoulder and the stab wound, he realized he would soon become weak from the blood loss. Hurrying through the warehouse, he ran to Buzzsaw's vehicle in an effort to seek medical attention before he passed out. His plans were sidetracked as soon as he burst out the exit door.

Next to the bay doors, Oracle crouched over the unconscious body of Buzzsaw's driver, examining him. When he heard the door open, he stopped and turned around. His eyes fell on Soulfire and they widened with a mixture of surprise and irritation.

"You seem surprised to see me," Soulfire growled through clenched teeth. Despite being weakened from blood loss, the sight of Oracle renewed his strength.

"Surprised?" Oracle blurted in disbelief and shook his head. "Shitting a unicorn, that would be a surprise. No, you standing here right now is a goddamn catastrophe."

"You and I have unfinished business," Soulfire snarled, feeling the familiar burn coursing through his veins.

Oracle rubbed his face wearily and sighed. "Buddy, you ain't kidding."

Burn

Illusionist always felt Baptist Memorial Hospital was a cold place. The temperature was fine, mind you, it was more like the feeling he got from doctors, nurses and other staff members. It was as if their job had been the result of a community service punishment handed down from some bitter, vindictive judge. Even the décor of the place was cold. The halls, painted drab gray, reminded him of a morgue. The color clashed quite nicely with the sickly green color of the rooms. Most of the time he had to resist the urge to vomit whenever he stepped into one. He had flashbacks of the scene from the movie Exorcist when the little girl blew chunks all over the bed. Whoever chose the paint color should have been shot before they could commit the horrendous crime of design fail.

The sole reason he chose this hospital over Mercy General was due to the residency of Dr. Jane Valentine, a personal friend. As soon as he phoned her about the Chief's condition, she urged him to come in immediately. When he pulled up to the emergency room entrance, she stood waiting with her arms crossed and a look of impatience.

"How bad is he?" she asked, looking through the window.

Chief Stamper remained unconscious in the back seat. Illusionist had to borrow the Chief's police cruiser, but since he was trying to save his life, he didn't think the Chief would mind. Taking the cruiser allowed Illusionist the ability to speed through the streets with lights and sirens, providing a clear and unimpeded path to the hospital.

"He took a good one to the shoulder," Illusionist replied, watching as she pressed a stethoscope to the Chief's chest. "What do you think?"

Jane's lips tightened and her brow furrowed. She brushed her long, black hair out of her face and sighed. "His breathing is staggered. The wound looks nasty, but I can't tell the severity of it with all the blood. I won't know more until I get him inside and hook him up to the monitors."

A nurse burst through the emergency room doors pushing a gurney. Jane turned and waved her toward the car.

"Gunshot wound. Breathing is strained and there is too much blood to be able to tell the severity of the wound. We need to get him to ICU. I need BP and HR readings."

The nurse nodded, and the two of them carefully lifted the Chief from the back seat and laid him gently on top of the gurney. The nurse pushed him through the door. Jane stopped and turned toward Illusionist.

"We'll take it from here. I can hold off the pencil pushers for a bit, but we'll eventually need some forms filled out." She looked at him and her gaze softened. "We have to report all gunshot wounds."

"That will have to wait. There are bigger issues needing to be addressed," he replied.

Jane offered him a smile and nodded slowly. "You heroes," she clucked and shook her head. "You're always trying to save the world."

"Not the world, just the city. Baby steps, Jane." He offered her a wry smile and laid his hand gently on her cheek. "I owe you for this."

Jane laid her hand across his. "Maybe you will take me on that date you have been promising me." She let go of his hand, turned and entered the hospital.

"If I live that long," Illusionist muttered to himself before hopping into the cruiser.

Illusionist wrestled between the decision to go to the warehouse to back up Soulfire or head to the Hero Factory and assist Wendy. In the end he decided Wendy and Hex would be able to handle the infiltration of the Hero Factory. Soulfire, on the other hand, would be outnumbered.

Illusionist drove off toward the warehouse. On the way, he dialed Wendy's cell phone, but the call went straight to voicemail. He pressed "end call" and stared at the phone, wondering if he made the correct decision in choosing the warehouse over the Hero Factory. He shoved the phone in his pocket and stared, glassy-eyed, at the road ahead. There was no point second guessing himself at this point.

A block away from the warehouse, Illusionist killed the headlights. It would be best to sneak up on the warehouse just in case shit had hit the fan. When he arrived at the warehouse, his abdomen felt as if someone had shoved a bag of broken glass straight into his stomach. A man crouched over a body on the ground, and Illusionist couldn't help but think the worst. It was too dark to identify either the man or the body, but he continued to remain cautious. He parked the cruiser behind a set of dumpsters a hundred yards away, out of view.

Illusionist stepped from the cruiser and closed the door softly, minimizing the sound. He did not want to alert the man until he could determine if he was friend or foe. Being careful to stay away from streetlights, he approached the warehouse, blanketed by shadow. When he got close enough to see the man more clearly, a person stepped from the warehouse.

Soulfire.

Illusionist approached slowly, the shadows making him nearly invisible against the dark walls of the nearby alley. When he got within earshot, he caught the final words of the conversation.

"You and I have unfinished business," Soulfire said.

"Brother, you ain't kidding," the man responded.

Illusionist recognized the voice immediately. Before he had a chance to react, Oracle blasted Soulfire with bolts of lightning, hurling him backwards into the warehouse. Illusionist hurried to the door, hoping to catch Oracle off-guard, but he stepped into the warehouse before the hero could reach him.

"You're starting to become a nuisance," Oracle said. "From what I understand, it's only you and the old man now." He accentuated the statement by pumping more volts of electricity Soulfire's way.

Soulfire rolled out of the way, causing the bolts to miss him by inches. Soulfire crouched on one knee and hurled a bowling ball-sized fireball at Oracle. He ducked out of the way quickly, and the fireball struck the door and set the wood door frame ablaze. The flames forced Illusionist to leap back the way he came to avoid being fried.

Illusionist heard sounds of combat, but the flames surrounding the door made it impossible for him to enter. He muttered silent curses and looked around for something that could put the flames out before it overwhelmed the entire entrance.

"Damn it," Illusionist grumbled when he couldn't

Illusionist threw open the back door to the SUV. He came face-to-face with the body of a young blond girl in a short, leather skirt, tank top and high heels. The light from inside the vehicle reflected off a substance covering her ruby-red lips which he mistook for blood initially. Upon closer inspection he determined it was lipstick. On the front of her dark green tank top were traces of a white powdery substance. He placed his fingers on her neck and found a pulse.

"Great, this is the last thing I need," Illusionist grumbled.

The girl, who appeared to be about twenty-five years old, was in a drug-induced unconscious state. When he looked down at her skirt, he saw the outline of her thong underwear protruding from underneath. Gently he reached over and pulled down her skirt, covering as much of her leg as the skirt would allow. If there hadn't been a fight to the death occurring inside the warehouse, he would take the girl to a hospital and scold her on the consequences of drug abuse. At that moment, however, he needed to attend to more pressing matters. She would be safer inside the vehicle anyway.

Inside a cup holder near her leg sat a water bottle, but it wouldn't make much of an impact on the fire. Based on the volume of flames currently blocking the front entrance, it would have been more effective to just piss on the fire.

Illusionist turned and scowled as the flames moved past the door frame and licked at the walls. Luckily, despite the age of the warehouse, the building had been constructed to stringent fire standards. The door was metal so it wouldn't burn easily. Underneath the sheetrock walls stood metal beams and flame retardant insulation. If he could find something quickly, he could combat the fire effectively enough to make his way inside and join the battle before it was too late.

Illusionist ran to the back of the vehicle and threw open the rear cargo door. Several assault rifles along with a large, sealed cardboard box lay inside. He tore open the box, only to find boxes of ammunition. Muttering a few more curses, he flung the box inside and was ready to give up until he spotted a large canvas bag shoved to the rear of the vehicle. Sliding it forward, he unzipped it and shuffled through the contents.

Road flares, a blanket and a first aid kit were the first things he came across. As he continued to rifle through the contents, his fingers ran across something metal. He shoved the blanket aside and pulled the item out. His eyes lit up when he saw what it was.

A portable fire extinguisher.

Illusionist grabbed the canister and ran to the entrance. He drained the extinguisher, which was effective in putting out the flames around the doorway, which would allow him to access the inside. He tossed the empty extinguisher away and ran inside.

Oracle, bare-chested, stood over Soulfire. His jacket and shirt lay smoldering in the corner of the room next to the ruined remains of Oracle's handgun. The side of Oracle's face as well as the top portion of his chest was an angry shade of scarlet, like a serious case of sunburn. Oracle clutched one of Spidermancer's darts in his hand in a stabbing position, as if he were about to plunge it into Soulfire's neck.

Oracle heard the rustling behind him when Illusionist entered the room. He turned toward his newest threat, still clutching the dart menacingly. "How nice to see you, Illusionist. I'll be right with you." Oracle tossed him a demonic smile and lifted the dart.

Soulfire used the distraction to his advantage. He willed his entire body into an explosion of flame, causing a startled Oracle to retreat backwards from the heat. The fire aura surrounding Soulfire's body increased in intensity until the room became a giant sauna. Oracle shielded his face and backed away, inching slowly toward Illusionist and the exit.

Soulfire turned his attention to Illusionist. Despite the inferno surrounding his entire head, Illusionist observed a coldness deep within his eyes. It was an icy stare that no amount of flame would melt away. Illusionist's eyes widened, realizing what Soulfire was about to do.

"Make sure you finish this!" Soulfire shouted above the roar of the crackling flames. "*RUN!*"

Illusionist's eyes widened, and he raced through the door, welcoming the cool night breeze as it entered his lungs. Once he reached the police cruiser, he turned his attention to the warehouse.

A few seconds later, the warehouse was consumed in a blaze nearly as bright as the sun itself. As the building burned, neither Oracle nor Soulfire exited the building. Illusionist took a few steps toward the building but realized the futility of any action. What could he do? No fire extinguisher on the planet would put out this blaze. He ran both hands through his hair and watched helplessly as the building burned, sending enormous embers of flame and ash into the night sky. It took only a few moments for the intense heat to cause the building to collapse. Sirens screamed in the distance, but it would be too late to save the building or the occupants trapped inside.

Illusionist's eyes darted back and forth, scanning the inferno for any signs of life, knowing the chances of survival were minimal. Anger and sorrow raged within him, and he slammed his fist onto the cruiser's hood.

"NO!" he howled.

Once the rage slowly ebbed from Illusionist, he hopped into the cruiser and released the remaining rage by punching the steering wheel several times. Exhaustion eventually took over and he laid his forehead upon it. Oracle's demise was the only bit of good news he could embrace from the entire situation. There was still work to be done. He still needed to take out the army within the Hero Factory and stop the corruption before it could devour the city. With Soulfire gone, however, the task just became exponentially more difficult.

Illusionist shifted the car into drive and headed toward the Hero Factory.

Risen from the Ashes

Soulfire stepped naked from the burning warehouse after Illusionist sped off. Despite the intense heat radiating from the burning wreckage, he felt a chill course through his body, where it settled in his heart. He watched the flames ebb and flow, continuing to search for more combustible material to feed on. Looking at the collapsed warehouse, he knew Oracle was dead, but the fact did not comfort him nor remove the icy cocoon from his heart. Death and destruction followed him wherever he went, as if he had been cursed to forever serve as the angel of death.

A rustling sound caught Soulfire's attention and he turned to see Brian Kelly's driver struggling to stand. He sized up the man and determined he was a similar size and build. The guy's khaki pants and polo shirt was not his preferred choice of fashion but it was better than running around in his birthday suit.

The man reached into his pants pocket, retrieved a cell phone and dialed. "Yeah it's me. We may have a problem."

Soulfire grabbed the man by the back of the head and smashed his face into the hood of the car. His skull impacted with a sickening crunch, and he fell to the ground in a motionless heap, blood flowing from his nose and upper lip. A cracked tooth fell from the man's mouth and landed next to his body. Soulfire kicked the discarded incisor aside and retrieved the phone, placing it against his ear.

"*Hello? Mike, are you still there?*" the voice on the other end asked.

"Mike had to head out," Soulfire responded.

"*Who is this?*"

"This is the tooth fairy, who's this?"

The voice went silent for a minute. Soulfire knew the man was still on the line because he heard heavy breathing on the other end. After a few more grunts and breaths the man finally spoke again.

"*This must be Soulfire,*" the man sneered. "*I knew you would be the one to hit the warehouse. Illusionist would have had no choice but to send you because you're all he has left.*" The man clucked his tongue. "*I guess it is safe to assume Buzzsaw didn't make it?*"

"He had a barbecue to attend," Soulfire replied. "Your buddy Oracle is dead too."

The man fell silent, including the heavy breathing. Soulfire strained to listen and wondered if the man hung up.

"No response, huh?" Soulfire taunted. "Now that all of your puppets are dead, it is time to come for the puppet master. I'll see you real soon."

The man on the other end chuckled. It started as a giggle but eventually ramped up into roaring laughter. The man brayed like a donkey, angering Soulfire to the point he almost snapped the cell phone in half. Eventually the laughter died down and the man regained his composure.

"*That is an awesome story, Soulfire. I guess the only thing I can say is, good luck.*"

The line went dead and Soulfire smashed the cell phone on the ground and kicked at the remains. He stripped the clothes off of the unconscious driver and dressed himself. The keys sat in the ignition of the vehicle. Once he was done dressing himself, he climbed into the driver seat and turned the key to start the engine. Before he could take off, a soft moaning sound came from the back seat.

Soulfire turned and saw the unconscious girl in the back seat. Her eyelids fluttered and she mewled pathetically before falling silent. Her head lolled to the side and made a soft thump against the door.

"You've got to be kidding me!" Soulfire muttered.

He exhaled violently and gripped the steering wheel. He watched the taillights of the cruiser fade in the distance and muttered a few more silent curses before putting the SUV into drive.

"Well, baby, it looks like you are going to get the ride of your life, just not in the way you intended."

Soulfire was halfway to City Hall when exhaustion finally washed over him. His eyelids became heavy and he barely focused on the road ahead. After trying several times to wipe the cobwebs from his vision, he pulled the vehicle to the side of the road.

"I'm not going to get anything done like this," he grumbled.

Further down the road, six hundred yards ahead, a motel sign illuminated the side of the road. Soulfire pulled the vehicle into the parking lot and stared at the front of the building. He had no money. All of his possessions went up in flames along with his clothes. The front pocket of his stolen clothes contained nothing more than a pack of matches and a pack of cigarettes, but the back pocket contained the man's wallet. He pulled it out and rifled through it.

A debit card, credit card, a gym membership card and thirty-five dollars was everything he found inside. He doubted he would get a room for thirty-five in cash so he had to chance using the man's credit card, and hoped he didn't regain consciousness and report it stolen.

Inside the motel, a surly looking fellow sat behind the counter, growling at his computer screen. Soulfire wandered over to the counter and rapped his fingers upon the countertop. The man continued to grumble at the computer screen, ignoring Soulfire's incessant tapping. He slammed his hands on the countertop and cleared his throat forcefully. Startled, the man looked up but the scowl remained plastered to his face.

"Yes?" he rumbled.

"I can see you're really busy looking ugly, but if it wouldn't be too much trouble, I could use a room for the night," Soulfire replied coolly.

The clerk flashed him a toothy smile but there was no humor in it. "Let me see what we have available."

After pounding on the keyboard for a few minutes the clerk looked up from the screen. "I have a room with two double beds. Cost is 69.99 a night."

Soulfire pulled an American Express card from the wallet. "Do you take Amex? I never leave home without it."

The man nodded, took the card and swiped it through the credit card machine. He tapped his finger on the desk impatiently as he waited for the routing to go through. As the bank details were being verified, the man narrowed his eyes and studied Soulfire. The card seemed to take an eternity to be approved, and Soulfire worried he would be forced to sleep in the car with a passed out girl in the back. Before he could explode with irritation, the card was approved. The manager retrieved a card key and handed it to Soulfire.

"Check out is eleven. Breakfast is served between 6:00 and 9:30." He motioned toward a back room filled with tables, chairs and a coffee machine on the counter. "Coffee is available now. I make it myself because I wouldn't make it through this shift without my caffeine rush."

Soulfire grabbed the card and nodded. "Thanks."

His room was located on the second floor, which concerned him. He wanted to bring the girl inside and at least make her comfortable on a couch or bed, but it would look a tad suspicious dragging an unconscious hooker up to the second floor. He was too exhausted to look for another place to stay, so he left her in the car and promised to check on her once he got some sleep. His body ached, and he yearned for a hot shower. As soon as he got to the room he fell on the bed and fell asleep. All hopes of a shower faded in a cacophony of snores. For the first time in weeks, he slept nightmare free.

* * *

Soulfire didn't wake until 9:30. When he looked at the clock on the nightstand the first thing that came to mind was his disappointment at missing a free breakfast, but then he thought of the girl in the car. He hopped out of bed and headed to the vehicle.

When he opened the door of the vehicle and saw she was gone, he harbored mixed feelings. He was relieved he wouldn't have to babysit but concerned for her safety. At this point the only thing he could do was hope for the best, for he had more important matters to attend to.

Soulfire hurried to his room, flipped on the TV, and went into the bathroom to splash some water on his face and make himself look presentable. When he caught a glimpse of himself in the mirror, he was surprised how vibrant and refreshed he looked. All those months of drinking and wallowing in despair seemed to have been washed away by a good night's sleep. The dark circles under his eyes faded, and he seemed to be getting color back in his face. All of his time had been recently spent living in the dark, whether in his home or some dumpy tavern nestled in the heart of the inner city. His pale skin reflected that, making him look like some B-movie vampire. Prior to his downward spiral, he prided himself on his physique and skin tone, always making sure to split time evenly between the gym and the beach as best he could.

"Jesus Christ, Bryan, you are going to need a vacation when this is all over," he muttered, splashing some more cold water across his face.

When he stepped out of the bathroom, he froze. On the TV, Brady Simmonelli stood behind a podium with scores of microphones, preparing to address a crowd of reporters. Stress seemed to take its toll on Brady. Deep lines carved their way from his eyes to his cheekbones, and the dark circles under his eyes revealed he hadn't been sleeping well recently. A large blue tapestry, adorned with the emblem of the Hero Factory, hung on the wall behind him. Soulfire turned up the volume on the TV.

"I assure you the people of Crystal City are safe. I have, and always will, place the safety of the citizens of the city as the highest priority. Due to the loss of several of our heroes, the Hero Factory was required to make some personnel changes. Dr. Wendy Markus is no longer in charge of the Hero Program. That responsibility will now fall to our head of research, Donald Runnels. Along with this change, I am here to inform you that I will be turning in my resignation and stepping down as CEO effective

midnight tonight. We have captured the rogue hero responsible for the murders of our heroes, and I would like to assure you that the streets of our city will be safe tonight."

Cameras flashed and a frenzied roar erupted from the crowd. Every reporter, eager to ask questions, spoke up at once. Brady waved his hand in an attempt to settle down the raucous crowd.

"Hold on, we will take questions in a moment. First I would like to introduce the new CEO of the Hero Factory, Mr. Pete Williams."

Brady gestured off screen and the camera panned left, revealing Pete Williams standing next to Head of Security, James Stout. Pete flashed his pearly white teeth and waved to the crowd. Soulfire felt as if someone had dropped an anvil on his chest.

"Mr. Williams will not be taking any questions at this time, but I will try to answer any questions you may have," Brady continued.

The reporters started machine gunning questions at Brady, but Soulfire focused his attention elsewhere. He couldn't help but focus on what Brady had said. *Captured the rogue hero responsible.* Oracle was buried beneath a pile of smoldering rubble, so who did they capture?

Soulfire looked toward the hotel phone on top of the nightstand and picked up the receiver. He dialed Wendy's number and it went straight to voicemail. Dialing the number again achieved the same result.

"Fuck!" he shouted and slammed the receiver down.

They must have gotten Wendy and Hex. *Damn!* Soulfire paced back and forth in front of the TV, trying to decide what to do next. He cursed himself for not following Illusionist when he had the chance. Once again, he found himself alone; but what scared him the most was the feeling didn't even bother him anymore. Loneliness seemed to be his most reliable colleague. Soulfire ceased pacing when Pete Williams took the podium. He returned his attention to the TV.

Standing there, smiling behind all those microphones, only served to anger Soulfire further. The camera panned the area, revealing the actual size of the crowd. Half of the city must have been in attendance. There were four rows of folding chairs, twenty in each row, where the reporters sat. Behind the roped off press area stood hundreds of citizens, not counting the police who served as the security detail and the emergency crews who were off to the side as a precaution. Soulfire spotted Mac, his old Fire Chief, standing off to the side conversing with the fire marshal, and his anger faded at the sight of his former boss. The camera returned to Pete Williams, who unfolded a piece of paper and laid it out before him.

"*Fellow citizens, although I will not be taking questions at this time, I felt a duty and an obligation to explain to you the plans I have for the future success of the Hero Factory. We understand you may feel a bit apprehensive at the protection we would be able to provide after losing many of our own. However, despite your apprehension, I would like to read for you something I have prepared.*" He cleared his throat and straightened the paper out.

First off, I would like to apologize. I'm sorry the Hero Factory has let you down, made you feel as if you were not safe walking the streets alone at night. I want to ensure you I will not become some sort of dictator ordering you around, telling you when you can leave your homes or where you should go. No, that's not my business. It shouldn't matter what time of day it is nor where you are. Whether it is the Ironbound section or the Palisades, you should feel safe to go about your business. Sometimes when greed poisons men's souls, they tend to barricade the world with hate, misery and bloodshed. The person responsible for these tragic events was poisoned by greed. However, as the CEO of the Hero Factory, I will make sure these tragic events will never be repeated. I will work to regain the confidence this city once had in this fine program. I will remove the greed and corruption which poisoned City Hall and reared its ugly head within the ranks of the Hero Program. I will restore dignity to this program and regain your trust and confidence. This is my agenda and my personal mission statement. Thank you."

With a wave of his hand, Pete Williams walked off stage, and the camera panned to a reporter who covered the day's events. Soulfire turned off the TV and waved his middle finger at it.

"Restore dignity, my ass," he grumbled.

Soulfire grabbed the car keys off the bathroom counter and stormed from the room. He jumped into the SUV and sped off, leaving a trail of skid marks in the parking lot. In his zeal to get to the Hero Factory, he blew through a stop sign and ran a red light. His knuckles cracked on the steering wheel, gripping it harder each time he ran Pete Williams' speech through his head. The longer he thought about it, the more the puzzle pieces slid into place. Winning the Hero Factory would not be enough, Pete had to win the hearts and minds of the people. His speech was the first step in achieving the goal.

He blew through another red light, leaving a driver in the middle of the intersection honking and shaking his fist angrily. Soulfire didn't care; he would run people over if he had to in order to reach his destination.

"Slow down, Speed Racer," a voice from the back seat begged.

Soulfire slammed on the brakes and yanked the wheel, guiding it toward the side of the road, taking out a street sign in the process. He whirled around so fast, he nearly gave himself whiplash.

"What the—?"

Soulfire's jaw snapped closed when he recognized the man in his back seat. Illusionist tossed him a wry grin.

"I'd say between the broken traffic laws and the damage to the street sign, you are accumulating quite a plethora of traffic citations," Illusionist quipped.

"How the hell did you find me?" Soulfire asked.

"I have my way of finding people. Sometimes it's even intentional," he joked. When he noticed Soulfire's sour expression, he shrugged. "Oh well, I see you aren't in a joking mood."

"This isn't a joking matter," Soulfire replied curtly.

"There are four things you should never lose. Never lose your sense of humor, your perspective, your mind or your car keys." Illusionist tapped the tip of each finger as he listed them. When he noticed Soulfire's sour expression, he sighed. "I came across the girl."

Soulfire did not need to ask who Illusionist referred to. He felt better knowing she wasn't dragged from the vehicle and murdered in an alley.

"Is she okay?"

Illusionist smiled. "First she told me where to find the vehicle which, in turn, led me to you. Next, I scolded her and explained to her the error of her ways, and she promised to check herself into rehab. It was the best I could do on short notice," he said with a shrug.

"I assume you didn't hear Pete Williams' speech?" Soulfire asked.

"I heard it on the radio," Illusionist replied matter-of-factly.

Illusionist's nonchalance toward the situation irritated Soulfire. He buried his face in his hands and laid his forehead on the steering wheel. "Now you can see why the last thing I cared about was traffic laws."

Illusionist clucked disapprovingly from the back seat. "So what were you planning to do, drive this car through the gates of the Hero Factory, jump out and burn the place to the ground? How many citizens were you planning on killing? How many innocent bystanders would have been left writhing in pain, permanently maimed or disfigured in your roaring rampage of revenge?"

"I guess I didn't quite think it through," Soulfire admitted.

Illusionist placed his finger against his temple and tapped. "That's been your problem, reacting instead of proactively thinking through problems to achieve the desired result."

"Thanks, Socrates," Soulfire grumbled.

Illusionist sighed and pointed at the damaged street sign. "We better get out of here before you attract unwanted attention."

Illusionist was right. There was a strong probability Williams had compromised the police force, and the last thing they needed was a responding officer to recognize them. He backed the vehicle away from the sign and drove off.

"I can't reach Wendy on her cellphone," Soulfire said. "If she wasn't able to download the virus, you realize we're screwed right?"

Illusionist rubbed his chin, distracted. "Perhaps this was inevitable," he mumbled.

"I'm sorry I couldn't hear you, what was that?" Soulfire asked. He blew through another red light which elicited a reprimanding frown from Illusionist.

"I was just contemplating something. Perhaps this scenario was inevitable. The road to hell is paved with good intentions."

"What are you rambling about?" Soulfire asked as he blew through another stop sign, leaving a startled old lady in the crosswalk.

"I'm in the unique position of being the first hero to walk the streets of Crystal City," explained Illusionist. "I've seen the horrors of what plagued this city before the program's inception. Heroes were the tools necessary to combat the criminals and draw out the corruption which shook the very foundation of the city. But it was a flawed design from the start. The program required people. Sure, there were stringent background checks required to weed out the good people from the bad. But the design was flawed because the very component required to make it work was flawed in itself: People. The overwhelming desire for power can consume even the noblest person."

Soulfire nodded. "I guess you're right. If history taught us anything, we should have probably seen this coming."

"The question is, can the program be salvaged from this?" Illusionist asked. "As of right now, the people don't know what we know. If we can get in, eliminate Williams, then get out, we just may be able to save this thing. By getting rid of Oracle, you have already completed the hard part."

Soulfire didn't care about the Hero Factory nor did he care whether the Hero Program was restored. The whole place could burn to the ground and he wouldn't shed a single tear. His primary objective was to eliminate Pete Williams and destroy his gang network. His secondary objective was to rescue Wendy. She didn't deserve to be in the middle of all of this.

The Hero Factory loomed in the distance. Illusionist tapped Soulfire on the shoulder and motioned to a bank on the corner.

"Pull into the parking lot over there."

Soulfire eyeballed him via the rear view mirror. "You have a withdrawal to make or something?"

Illusionist sighed and shook his head with exasperation. "We need to come up with a plan."

Soulfire pulled the vehicle into the parking lot and tossed Illusionist a sour expression. "I guess driving this SUV through the front door is out of the question?"

Illusionist ignored the jab. "It's the middle of the day, so security will be tight. We also have to think of collateral damage. There will be bystanders like visitors and reporters still lingering. Even some of the staff remain innocently unaware of William' intentions." He rubbed his temples, deep in thought. "Just give me a minute, let me think of something."

Soulfire leaned his head back and closed his eyes. Illusionist was right. He almost charged into a situation, filled with bloodlust, without thinking of the consequences. The situation brought memories flooding back to what caused him to get booted from the Hero Program in the first place. The more he thought about their current dilemma, the more he felt the walls closing in around him. For the first time in a long time he felt unsure how to proceed. Illusionist was smarter than he was, he would never deny that, but even he struggled to come up with a plan. Suddenly an idea occurred to him, and he could almost feel the lightbulb lingering on top of his head.

Soulfire threw open the door of the vehicle and ran to the curb. Cars drove past, oblivious to the wild-eyed man on the side of the road looking around frantically as if he had lost his child. He turned his attention east, toward the main entrance leading to the Hero Factory. His right hand formed a fist and he slammed it into the palm of his left hand. Illusionist exited the vehicle and rushed to his side.

"What is it? What's wrong?"

Soulfire turned to him with a grin. "I have an idea!"

Reshaping Visions

As expected, security inside the Hero Factory had increased. What Illusionist didn't expect was the military gear and heavy assault weapons the security personnel now carried. They have been armed for war under premise the Hero Factory would soon become a battle zone.

"Shit," Soulfire grumbled.

Their plan to assault the Hero Factory from the front flew out the window. They overestimated their opponent's confidence level. Pete Williams sent Oracle to kill Soulfire, and they assumed his confidence would be high and security light. Somehow, Williams believed a threat remained outside these walls and Soulfire's outburst had perfectly conveyed Illusionist's feeling on the matter.

"I can take out the two at the door quietly enough, but with the tinted glass covering the front entrance, it's hard to tell how many are inside," Illusionist said. "The last thing we need is for someone inside to raise the alarm."

Soulfire nodded his head in agreement. "This has to go down quietly. We have no idea where they are holding Hex and Wendy. If security is alerted, those two may end up paying the price for our mistake."

Soulfire studied the two men surrounding the door, one tall and one short, like two lopsided bookends. There would be no Option B, so discretion was of utmost importance. He didn't recognize the guards at the door, so he tapped Illusionist on the shoulder and pointed at them.

"Do you recognize them?"

Illusionist studied them for a moment. He cocked his head to one side like a puppy waiting for his master to feed him a treat. He squinted and studied them for a minute.

"No, as a matter of fact I don't," Illusionist replied. "Why do you ask?"

Soulfire grinned. "I think I have an idea. I'll bet an ice cold six-pack, Pete hired more people to the security team. The Hero Factory didn't have enough personnel to guard the place like a fortress."

"So?" Illusionist replied.

"So that would mean there is a chance some of these guards don't know each other. Perhaps we can use that to our advantage." He grinned mischievously.

Realization dawned on Illusionist. "So a couple new guards wandering around wouldn't be out of the ordinary."

"Exactly! Do you think you can be convincing enough to make these two leave their posts?"

Illusionist turned to Soulfire and stabbed him in the chest with his index finger. "Son, I have been running black ops sleight of hand trickery since you were nothing more than a gleam in your momma's eye."

Soulfire eyeballed him sourly. "Okay, it's your turn then, grandpa."

"Already done," Illusionist replied.

Soulfire swung around to see two well-armed men in tactical swat gear approaching the two guards. The guards' assault weapons were draped across their shoulders, and they slid their hands toward the belts. Instead of removing them, they approached the advancing illusions and engaged in conversation.

"I am Lieutenant Marcus of Crystal City Police Department, and this is Danny Trevoya, contractor from Security Plus."

Soulfire heard the words as if he stood next to them. The words were spoken by Illusionist, but came from the illusions. *Illusionist the ventriloquist*, he thought with an amused grin.

The two guards eyed the illusions warily. They spoke to the illusions, but Soulfire could not hear what they were saying. Panicking, he turned and looked at Illusionist. Fortunately he heard the guard, because he quickly responded to their inquiry.

"We are here to relieve you," Illusionist replied. "James wants to keep the shifts fresh so the boys stay sharp. I'm the ranking officer here, so he tasked me with keeping the shifts rotating evenly. If you have a problem with that then take it up with him."

The guards glanced at one another and exchanged a few words. A moment later they shrugged and departed the area. The illusions took their place at guarding the entrance, one on each side of the main door.

"I bought us some time," Illusionist said, turning to Soulfire. "I won't be able to hold these illusions for long. When I get inside, as I move further from them, they will eventually vanish."

"How long do we have?" Soulfire asked.

"Fifteen...twenty minutes tops," Illusionist replied. "If we don't find Wendy and Hex by that time, then we won't need to worry about discretion."

"What do we do once we get inside?" asked Soulfire. "You do realize the goal isn't to just get through the front door, right?"

Before Illusionist responded, his features twisted and changed, morphing into Pete Williams. Startled, Soulfire took a step back. It would take three lifetimes before he would ever get used to Illusionist's tricks.

"I know what the goal is," Illusionist said. "Let's just hope we don't run into Pete."

"What about me?"

"Unfortunately, I cannot project illusions onto others," Illusionist replied. He rubbed his hands together briskly while staring curiously at the illusions by the front door. "Otherwise I would have turned you into a frog a long time ago."

A sour look crossed Soulfire's face. "So there is some bad news here, I can see it on your face."

Illusionist sighed. "I won't be able to maintain this illusion for long." He gestured toward the guards. "Especially since I need to keep those two up for as long as possible. I won't be able to get inside, find

Wendy and Hex and get out without the illusion fading. There just isn't enough time."

"So what do you suggest?"

"I was initially going to bring you inside as a prisoner under the pretext of escort, but I'm afraid I will need to go in alone," Illusionist explained.

Soulfire shook his head vigorously. "There has to be another way."

Illusionist looked at him somberly. "Time is not on our side. I will need to be quick and stealthy, only falling back on this illusion if absolutely necessary."

"I can't let you go in there alone," Soulfire argued, but as soon as he saw the look of determination on his face, he resigned himself to the task at hand and sighed deeply. "I can recognize your determination even if you are wearing another person's face. You aren't going to listen to me, are you?"

"You can't stop me from going in, unless you plan on frying me right here." His steely gaze locked onto Soulfire. "You don't plan on doing that I hope?"

"No," Soulfire responded dejectedly. "You're probably the only friend I have left."

Illusionist smiled and laid his hand upon Soulfire's back. "Try not to worry too much. I know my way around in there. From what I recall there is only two places they could keep Wendy and Hex. They have to be locked up on the 2nd floor either in the conference room or hoteling room. All other rooms would contain either a computer or data line from which either one of them could hack into the computer systems. Williams is too cunning to take a chance like that."

"So what do you want me to do out here? Send up a smoke signal if I spot trouble?" Soulfire asked bitterly.

Illusionist pointed toward a window on the second floor. "That room is the 2nd floor logistics office. It has remained empty ever since the Logistics Manager retired. If I find them, I will signal from that room. I will need you to create a distraction and draw the guards outside so we can make our escape."

"And if you don't find them?"

Illusionist continued to look at the second floor window, purposefully avoiding Soulfire's gaze. "If I don't then the only option left is to pray for them and go to Plan B."

"Plan B?" Soulfire parroted.

"Destroy the Hero Factory," Illusionist said softly.

Soulfire's eyes widened. "Destroy it? Are you crazy? You will still be inside and so will they!"

Illusionist turned a fierce gaze upon Soulfire. "Don't you think I know that? It's a small price we will need to pay. If we let the Hero Program technology fall into the wrong hands, much worse will happen. I abhor death as much as you do, but we will need to consider it collateral damage."

Soulfire rubbed his face wearily. His refusal to allow any more innocents to die was ironclad. He wanted to grab Illusionist by the shoulders, shake him and argue until he was blue in the face, but he knew it would be pointless. In the end, he was right. They would be powerless to stop Pete Williams if he succeeded.

"I need to go before the illusions fade," Illusionist said. "You know what to do."

Illusionist, concealed by the Pete Williams guise approached the Hero Factory and entered the building. It wasn't until the doors closed behind him when Soulfire realized he had been holding his breath. He let it out in one big gush of air and watched the second floor window.

Several moments passed. Soulfire estimated, barring any obstacles in his way, it would take Illusionist roughly five minutes to get to the second floor offices, assuming he had taken the stairs. Waiting for the elevator would have only added time to the trip and every second was precious. Illusionist estimated he would lose his disguise by the time he reached the hoteling room. So Soulfire did the only thing he could do, he waited. Two minutes passed.

Three.

Five.

At the six minute mark, Soulfire began sweating. At the eight minute mark he paced. At ten minutes, he panicked.

"Where the hell are you?" he muttered to himself.

At the ten minute mark, the illusions at the front door vanished. At the eleven minute mark, Soulfire thought his heart would burst forth from his chest and run screaming down the street. Soulfire was about to enter the Hero Factory when the window on the second floor flew open. Illusionist poked his head out and waved. Soulfire returned the wave, but his chest tightened when he noticed the grim expression on his face. Wendy poked her head out the window with a look of defeat. Something was wrong.

Soulfire held up three fingers, a silent question asking current status on Hex. When Illusionist slowly shook his head in response, all the wind had been knocked out of him like a punch to the gut. Soulfire held up his hands in a "what now" gesture.

Illusionist turned away from the window and disappeared into the room. Wendy turned to look back into the room, tossing Soulfire a frantic look before following Illusionist's lead.

"What the hell?" Soulfire muttered.

A minute later Illusionist returned to the window with a harried look on his face. Soulfire swallowed hard and his mouth felt like he just chewed sandpaper. Illusionist ran his finger across his throat several times before turning away, as if his attention was diverted toward something happening inside the room. Soulfire imagined the worst when he heard Wendy's scream burst from the open window. Illusionist turned his attention out the window, cupped his hands on each side of his mouth and shouted.

"BURN IT DOWN, SOULFIRE! *NOW!*"

Before he could do anything else, several hands grabbed Illusionist around the throat and pulled him inside.

"Fuck!" Soulfire cursed. He closed his eyes and concentrated, feeling a familiar burn rising from within.

"I wouldn't do that," a voice called out.

Soulfire opened his eyes to see Pete Williams approaching with five armed security personnel. Williams was unarmed but his security people had their assault weapons trained on him. Five laser dots fanned out before coming together on the middle of his chest.

Soulfire was not ablaze, but it would only take a few more seconds of concentration to engulf himself in flame. Already, the burning sensation coursed through his veins, and he silently calculated the odds. He wondered if he had enough time to gather all of his strength and take them out before they shot him down.

"It's over, Soulfire. There's no need for further bloodshed," Pete commanded. "I can see what you are trying to do, and that would not be the wisest course of action."

The men crept closer, keeping their aim locked onto him. They stood fifteen yards away, close enough for him to burn them to a crisp, yet uncomfortably close enough for them to turn him into a slab of Swiss cheese. He debated sacrificing himself and deep frying them where they stood, until James Stout and two armed guards exited the building, escorting Illusionist and Wendy. His heart sank when he recognized the guards from the front entrance. They must have been onto them from the very beginning.

"DO IT!" Illusionist shouted.

One of the guards cuffed him on the back of the head with the butt of his weapon, sending Illusionist to his knees. He looked up, his eyes pleading with Soulfire to unleash hell. Illusionist was prepared to sacrifice them all to prevent the Hero Factory from falling into the wrong hands. Soulfire hesitated, causing Illusionist to look toward the ground in resignation. The guards lifted him up and pushed the two of them toward Soulfire. Wendy stumbled but Soulfire caught her before she fell.

"Ow!" she yelped and pulled back quickly. Angry red handprints formed on her arms where he grabbed her.

Soulfire had been distracted by the events playing out before him and completely forgot his body temperature had been slowly increasing. Illusionist noticed as well and when the two locked eyes, he offered Soulfire a slow nod of approval.

Soulfire knew what had to be done. It only took a few more seconds to become fully engulfed by flame. The explosion of flame startled the guards and they stepped away. The distraction bought him the few precious seconds he needed to unleash his attack.

His attack never came.

Shots rang out. Blood sprayed across Illusionist's face as the guard closest to him dropped to the ground. Perfectly centered in the back of the man's head was a bullet hole so deep the pavement could be seen underneath. Before he had time to react, the other guards dropped in conjunction as holes appeared in their foreheads with perfect precision. The blood pooling underneath the corpses trickled toward the startled onlookers.

Pete Williams, unarmed and defenseless, spun around, searching the area frantically in an effort to locate the assassin. A shadowy outline exited the Hero Factory, carrying a high precision .308 sniper rifle.

"It can't be," Illusionist muttered to himself.

The gun-toting assassin was Oracle, bare-chested and bleeding from several small cuts. Several angry red patches of skin spread across the top of his abdomen and lower part of his chest, burned but very much alive.

"What the hell are you doing?" Pete demanded.

Soulfire was stunned. There could have been no way he survived the battle at the warehouse, yet here he stood. His appearance defied logic and Soulfire found himself wondering if the man was immortal.

"What I am doing is what needs to be done!" Oracle answered and leveled the rifle at him "You want the Hero Factory as your own personal playground, creating heroes you can use as pawns to turn this city into the cesspool it was before. I have a better idea, Dad."

"Dad?" Soulfire, Illusionist and Wendy blurted in unison.

Oracle turned his attention toward them. "Yeah, that's right. More proof of the Hero Factory's ineptitude. I was adopted at a young age because apparently being a crime lord doesn't allow a lot of time for raising a child. Of course, I didn't believe him at first. When he told me the news, I admit the first thought I had initially was to beat him into nothing more than a pile of bloody sausage. But then he showed me a copy of the adoption papers he had kept all these years. He was great at keeping records."

"Sam, you have it all wrong—" Pete argued.

Oracle's face burned red with rage. "That's not my fucking name anymore! Sam Fowler is dead!"

Oracle lifted the rifle and fired, blowing half of Pete's head off. When Oracle pointed the rifle at Wendy, Soulfire found himself unable to move. It was as if his mind and his body had disconnected from one another. His mind busied itself with processing the events at a million miles an hour but his body seemed a million miles away.

"How are you still alive?" Soulfire blurted. "I dropped the entire goddamn building on top of you."

Oracle paused and lowered the weapon. "Being a Class 5 has its perks."

"Is immortality one of them?" Illusionist spat. The mask of disgust on his face couldn't be more obvious.

Oracle chuckled. "No, nothing like that. It's all about mnemonics. It is like a computer code designed to remember something and recreate it perfectly. As a kid, I used to read full-length novels in an hour and recall every single detail contained within. I received straight A's without even batting an eye. I was considered a savant by my teachers and a nerd by my peers. I agreed, until one day a circus came to town. I remember watching a high wire artist perform death-defying stunts. Later that day, I tied a rope between my parent's house and the neighbor's house and performed the same stunts with pinpoint accuracy."

Wendy snapped from her silence as if she had been slapped. "That explains it!"

"That explains what?" Illusionist asked.

"As a research assistant, I studied mnemonic abilities in autistic savants," she explained. "The root cause of autism is still up for debate but ten percent of people who ranked high on the autism spectrum disorder exhibited abilities similar to what Oracle described. Anything from discovering how many cards were in a deck by dropping them on the floor to reenacting elaborate stunts after watching were signs of these mnemonic abilities."

"That's right, kiddos. I'm a savant, ain't life grand," boasted Oracle. "The mutagenic compound used in the Hero Program boosted my abilities, allowing me to copy any of your hero abilities simply by watching."

"His ability must have somehow fooled the measurement system as well," Wendy surmised.

Illusionist muttered a curse under his breath. "He must have phased through the floor before the building crashed down. I have seen his trick before."

Oracle pointed the rifle barrel at him. "Exactly! You had the nerve to bring a building down on me. I simply phased through the floor into the storeroom below, allowing me to escape through an emergency exit."

"What do you hope to gain from this?" Illusionist growled, his face twisting angrily.

"What I will gain is this city. I'm the most powerful hero to emerge from the Hero Program." He pointed the gun barrel at Pete's body. "As you can see, I have eliminated my competition and I now have the keys to this city. I also control the Hero Factory, which was the only thing that could have stopped me."

"I can stop you," Soulfire growled. Flames formed around his balled fists and he took a step toward Oracle.

Oracle pointed the rifle at Wendy. "Hold on a minute there, Sparky. You might be able to fry me to a crisp from where you are standing, but the pressure I have on this trigger would cause this rifle to go off. We wouldn't want to see this pretty little lady's face laying on the pavement now would we?"

Soulfire kept his hands tightly by his sides, realizing Oracle was right. Illusionist leaned in closer, his mouth only inches from Soulfire's ear.

"Do it," he whispered. "We can't let him get away with this."

Soulfire glanced at Wendy. He recognized the desperate fear hidden within her pale, blue eyes. Her upper lip trembled slightly, knowing any wrong move would cause her death. Never before had Soulfire realized how beautiful she really was. Her curvy figure, perfectly manicured nails and full lips were better suited on an actress or model, not a research scientist. He couldn't do it. He couldn't take the chance she might be killed from his actions.

Soulfire's flames extinguished, which prompted a broad grin from Oracle and a dejected sigh from Illusionist.

"I see you're a man of reason," Oracle said. "Unfortunately, you represent a powerful threat to my mission."

Oracle turned the weapon on Soulfire and fired. The shot was like a wrecking ball slamming into his chest. Soulfire was tossed backwards against the perimeter fence. He struggled to breathe and panicked when he noticed the ragged wound weeping blood in the center of his chest. Wendy screamed while Illusionist ran to his side, cradling Soulfire's head in his arms.

Soulfire looked up, staring deep into Illusionist's eyes while the coppery taste of blood filled his mouth. He turned his head to the side to allow the mouthful of blood to escape along the side of his cheek where it pooled on the ground. Wendy flanked Illusionist and placed her hand on Soulfire's arm. She didn't say anything, only studied the wound oddly, as if she expected an alien to spring forth from the hole.

"Damn fool," Illusionist grumbled. He stared icily at Oracle, who lowered the rifle and shrugged.

Soulfire looked at Oracle, but the sun caught his gaze, forcing him to shut his eyes and allow the spots to pass from his vision. When he opened them again, Oracle no longer held a weapon. It was nowhere to be found, as if it simply vanished from this plane of existence. The sun passed behind a cloud, allowing Soulfire to see Oracle with the Hero Factory in the background. The building became fuzzy, like a picture shifting out of focus. Soulfire blamed the blurry vision on the fact he was dying, but then Oracle did something so strange, it caused him to rethink his current situation. He apologized.

"I'm sorry," Oracle said with a shrug. "You and I both know most of the time it ends just like this."

As Soulfire watched Oracle, the man began to shift out of focus just like the Hero Factory. When his gaze returned to the building, pieces of it started falling upwards. It was like someone took apart a jigsaw puzzle and turned on a giant vacuum in the sky. As he watched pieces of the Hero Factory fall away, he felt an icy tentacle caress his body, causing his extremities to go numb.

"I'm dying," Soulfire rasped. It was the only explanation capable of explaining the scene before him.

The building completely fell away, leaving a backdrop of blue behind Oracle, as if the sky fell and became one with the ground.

"No need to apologize, Oracle. You made your choice based on what you felt was the most logical course," Illusionist replied. There was no anger or reproach in Illusionist's voice. It was as if a parent were explaining to a child the facts of life.

"Looks....like you're the...last hero." Soulfire choked out the words between mouthfuls of blood.

Illusionist and Wendy exchanged looks. To Soulfire's surprise they both smiled, and Wendy slipped an arm underneath his head and cradled it. Illusionist stood and stepped away from them.

"No, Bryan. You are."

"What..." Soulfire's statement was cut off when he saw Illusionist had vanished, just like the Oracle's weapon. Confused, he looked toward Oracle, but he had vanished as well. He spat out another bloody wad of phlegm and turned to Wendy as blackness descended upon him. "What? I...don't...understand," he rasped.

Wendy placed her hand on Soulfire's forehead, and her lips pulled back in a wide smile, revealing perfectly white teeth. Wendy was unable to explain everything to him before he died, but her smile was the last thing he saw, and the last words she spoke were a comfort to him.

"You will."

You Will

The Bible describes death as a journey. Your soul will either journey to heaven or hell, depending on your point of view. Some believe ascension into heaven is a birthright of the saved, as if a cosmic train will pick up one's soul and transport it to the pearly gates. Some ancient religions believe a skeletal figure will ferry their soul across the river Styx, guiding it into the afterlife. Others believe the only way into heaven is to die in glorious battle. Any of those things would have ranked high on the coolness factor, but for Bryan Whittaker, he ended up sorely disappointed. Death wasn't a journey but a stopping point. Nothing but infinite blackness surrounded him. There was no light at the end of the tunnel. To his dismay, there wasn't even a tunnel. No robed figure prepared to ferry him to the other side. Even though he died in what some would perceive as glorious battle, there would be no Valhalla for him, no Valkyrie to whisk him away to the afterlife.

Nothingness. The big empty. The basin of blackness.

In church he had been told death was a gateway to everlasting life. Bryan knew it was a whole crock of crap now. Death was dead, nothing more than a gateway to eternal claustrophobia and blindness.

"Heart... blood pressure... vitals."

The words floated toward him from somewhere deep within the void. The dark stretched for infinity, so he had no idea where the words originated from. They were fragmented at first, eventually merging together to form complete sentences. The words became clearer, and the blackness surrounding him seemed to cascade, going from pitch black to charcoal gray, ebbing like a tide. The words increased. The voices were familiar.

"It always seems to end the same. Why is that?"

A man's voice.

"We don't have time for that, give me vitals!"

A woman's voice.

"The program has been terminated, correct?"

A different man's voice, one which Bryan recognized as Brady Simmonelli.

Bryan placed names with voices as the charcoal gray of eternity ebbed and flowed, swirling onto itself before changing color again. Not unlike a kaleidoscope, it merged into a lighter shade of gray, the color of freshly poured concrete. As colors began to form and spiraled around him, the voices seemed to get louder. He distinguished shapes in the distance, shadowy outlines of heads moving frantically in a circular motion around him. When they came into focus, he started matching voices to heads.

"Blood pressure is 100 over 70 and climbing."

This voice belonged to Donald Runnels.

"The adrenalin shot worked."

A voice belonging to Wendy Markus.

Bryan felt slight pressure on the sides of his head. His head ached, and a vast array of colors swirled around him, as if someone used a rainbow to jump rope on his skull. The shadowy outlines blurred, like a camera out of focus. His eyes cleared and he was able to match names with faces as they gathered around him. Donald Runnels, Wendy Markus and Brady Simmonelli circled around him, surrounded by diagnostic equipment. He was back in the research lab of the Hero Factory, strapped to a gurney with his wrists bound by his sides.

Panicking, he struggled against the bonds. Wendy laid a hand on his shoulder. "Bryan, calm down. Everything's okay!"

Bryan's head swiveled frantically, examining his surroundings. Several leads, connected by wires, had been attached to his bare chest and temples. A blood pressure cuff had been strapped to his right bicep. An I.V. had been hooked up to his left arm. When he looked down at his chest, his eyes widened, a mixture of confusion and fear. His chest was unmarked. There was no gaping wound nor even a scar. It was as if he hadn't been shot at all.

"What the hell is going on?" Bryan shouted. "Where is Illusionist? Where is Oracle?"

"*I am right here,*" a voice called out.

The voice seemed to originate from the ceiling. Bryan looked up and winced against the bright fluorescent lighting. As his eyes adjusted to the glare, he noticed speakers mounted in the ceiling.

"Where?" Bryan asked.

"*I am not quite sure how to clarify my answer. I am here.*"

Bryan turned to Wendy. "The voice… it belongs to Oracle." He struggled against his restraints. "Where is he? We have to stop him!"

Brady moved beside Wendy and smiled. "Relax Bryan, it is over."

"Over?" Bryan asked, confused.

Wendy offered him a warm smile, rubbed his shoulder gently and glanced at the heart monitor mounted on top of a rolling cabinet parked next to the gurney. "Vitals look good." She turned her attention to Bryan. "The voice you hear does belong to Oracle, just not in the way you think."

"What do you mean?" Bryan asked.

Wendy turned to Brady and Donald. "Test is a success. We can issue a formal statement now."

Donald nodded and left the room. Brady smiled and patted Bryan on his calf. "Well done, son. Welcome aboard," he said before following Donald out of the room.

"What the hell is going on? Where is Illusionist?" Bryan asked, pulling against his restraints.

"The information will be a lot to process, but let me try to sum up as best as I can," Wendy explained. "First, Oracle is not a person but a computer program, designed by the Hero Factory. It stands for Organized Rational Aptitude Computerized Logic Examiner." Bryan cocked an eyebrow and Wendy shrugged. "We're not paid to come up with acronyms. I guess we are better research scientists than wordsmiths." She looked up toward the speakers. "Say 'hello,' Oracle."

"*Hello, Oracle*," the speaker repeated.

Wendy sighed. "Oracle has a tendency toward the literal sense." She pointed at a mainframe computer located in the corner of the room. "It's a simulation program, developed in conjunction with Brady Simmonelli and Illusionist to measure an applicant's ability in various fields of mental as well as physical strength. I don't need to really explain the test to you since you've just been through it, right?" Wendy unbuckled the restraints.

Bryan shook his head and rubbed his eyes wearily. "Are you trying to tell me that all the shit I have just been through was nothing more than a test?"

"Precisely. From the moment you entered this lab, you were being tested. I'm not sure if you're aware, Mr. Whittaker, but we take our Hero Program seriously." Wendy removed the leads from Bryan's head and chest.

Freed from the restraints, Bryan struggled to sit up. Wendy placed her arm behind his back and helped him rise to a sitting position.

"City Hall?" Bryan asked.

Wendy grinned. "Still standing."

Bryan's eyes widened. "Terry?"

Wendy's smile turned warm and comforting. "Still alive."

Bryan rubbed his temples as a dull throb assaulted the back of his skull. "Jesus Christ, it all seemed so real."

"That's the point." Wendy's smile faded when she noticed Bryan's discomfort. "We weren't able to work out all the side effects of the serum. Unfortunately, a migraine is one of the more common."

"I'll take it over death, I suppose," Bryan muttered. When he hopped off the gurney the room spun, and he had to grab hold of a cabinet to steady himself. "Whoa, stop the world I want to get off."

Wendy brought him a bottle of water. "Here, drink this."

Bryan lifted the bottle to his lips and allowed the cool water to flow down his throat. As the refreshing fluid ran down his throat, he realized how thirsty he was and guzzled the rest.

With a satisfied grunt, he placed the bottle on the cabinet and turned to Wendy. "Can you answer a question?"

Wendy cocked her head inquisitively and smiled. "I guess it depends on the question."

Bryan rubbed his hands together briskly and flexed his fingers. Being tied to a gurney slowed the blood flow to his extremities. He flexed faster, working out the pins and needles assaulting his fingers.

"Am I Soulfire?"

Wendy's pale eyes sparkled. "No."

Bryan frowned and tossed the empty water bottle into a garbage can. Wendy's hand fell on his arm gently. He turned to her but couldn't hide the disappointment on his face.

"Who the hell am I, then?" he asked.

Wendy pointed across the lab toward a door. A sign above the door read PROCESSING and Bryan recognized it as the door he had entered when testing first began.

"Let's find out who you are, shall we?" Wendy replied.

"Wait a minute," Bryan said. "I failed the test, didn't I?"

Wendy looked at him mutely and she pinched her face in confusion. "I'm sorry, what do you mean?"

"I failed to save the city," Bryan explained. "I let a lot of people die and eventually got myself killed. Oracle won."

Wendy's features softened. "Bryan, life is not a fairytale. Not everyone gets a happy ending. The purpose of the test is to gauge your actions, not your ability to win. In the end, no one gets out of life alive." She curled her lip in a wry grin.

"That's a bit morbid," Bryan grumbled. "Are you trying to tell me being a hero is a no win situation?"

Wendy didn't answer the question. Maybe she didn't have an answer, or perhaps she simply chose to keep the answer to herself. She took Bryan's hand gently and led him carefully to the door, making

sure he didn't suffer any more ill effects of vertigo and end up trip-
ping over something in the lab. The last thing he needed was to fall
into the cabinet and spill a vial of acetic acid all over himself. They
reached the door and she punched in her security code. The doors slid
open, revealing a team of scientists dressed in white milling about,
fretting over various machines.

Wendy turned to Bryan, her eyes reflecting the room's fluorescent
lighting in the process. Behind her, Bryan recognized one of the machines, the one which tested his powers. She stabbed an index finger
in the air, toward the machine.

"Just so you know, heroes are not made in here," she explained.

"They're not?" he asked.

Wendy shook her head and turned her finger toward Bryan's chest,
right above where the heart is located. "No, they are made in here."

Bryan looked away and his eyes fell on the machine. He stared at it
for what seemed like eons, remembering what it was like to experience
the power which coursed through his body. Remembering his time as
Soulfire, he recalled his experiences in the virtual world both positive
and negative. They had seemed so real to him, and he vowed silently
to learn from his mistakes. Although his adventures as a hero were
virtual, the pain of loss which still lingered deep within his heart was
not. He owed it to wife and son to be a better man. He owed it to this
city to be a better hero.

"Are you ready?" asked Wendy

Bryan placed his hand over his heart and breathed in deeply. To
say he felt a sense of déjà vu would be an understatement. This time,
though, it would be for real. He took a step toward the machine and
looked at Wendy. For the first time since the death of his family, he
felt confidence with making a decision.

"I am ready."

Dear reader,

We hope you enjoyed reading *The Last Hero*. Please take a moment to leave a review, even if it's a short one. Your opinion is important to us.

Discover more books by Craig Gaydas at https://www.nextchapter.pub/authors/craig-gaydas

Want to know when one of our books is free or discounted? Join the newsletter at http://eepurl.com/bqqB3H

Best regards,
Craig Gaydas and the Next Chapter Team

You could also like:

The Cartographer by Craig Gaydas

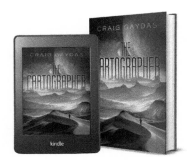

To read the first chapter for free, please head to:
https://www.nextchapter.pub/books/science-fiction-adventure-the-
cartographer

The Last Hero
ISBN: 978-4-86752-817-4

Published by
Next Chapter
1-60-20 Minami-Otsuka
170-0005 Toshima-Ku, Tokyo
+818035793528
10th August 2021